TIME TO S

Former journalist S.D. Robertson quit his role as a local newspaper editor to pursue a lifelong ambition of becoming a novelist.

An English graduate from the University of Manchester, he's also worked as a holiday rep, door-to-door salesman, train cleaner, kitchen porter and mobile phone network engineer.

Over the years Stuart has spent time in France, Holland and Australia, but home these days is back in the UK. He lives in a village near Manchester with his wife and daughter. There's also his cat, Bernard, who likes to distract him from writing – usually by breaking things.

S.D. ROBERTSON

TIME TO SAY GOODBYE

AVON

This novel is entirely a work of fiction.
The names, characters and incidents portrayed in it are
the work of the author's imagination. Any resemblance to
actual persons, living or dead, events or localities is
entirely coincidental.

AVON

A division of HarperCollins*Publishers*
The News Building
1 London Bridge Street
London SE1 9GF

www.harpercollins.co.uk

A Paperback Original 2016

1

A catalogue record for this book is
available from the British Library

ISBN-13: 978-0-00-810067-4

Set in Sabon by Born Group using Atomik ePublisher from Easypress

Printed and bound in Great Britain by
Clays Ltd, St Ives plc

MIX
Paper from
responsible sources
FSC
www.fsc.org   FSC™ C007454

Acknowledgements

Various people have played a role in bringing this book to life. It's been a long road to publication and I wouldn't have made it without their help.

Thank you first and foremost to my family for believing in me without question. Thanks for reading the earliest of drafts, being there for all my queries and anxieties, and allowing me the freedom to achieve my dream. Claudia, Kirsten, Mum, Dad and Lindsay, you're all amazing.

Next I must thank my literary agent, Pat Lomax. You've been brilliant at guiding me through this process from start to finish. You believed in the book right away. You saw what others didn't and have been fighting my corner ever since. All your hard work and support is greatly appreciated.

Thank you to the wonderful team at Avon/HarperCollins – particularly Lydia Vassar-Smith, Katy Loftus, Eleanor Dryden and Kate Ellis – who made the editing process a pleasure. I doubt there's a friendlier place to learn the ropes of being a published author.

Before I had an agent or publisher, a few friends were kind enough to read and give feedback on early drafts of this novel. I'm grateful Mervyn Kay, Tim Smith and Nick Coligan. You're all stars.

I must also mention Maurice Cohen, Rosie Kaye and Hillary Shaw. Your help was invaluable.

And lastly, thanks to you, the reader. You're the reason I write.

For Claudia and Kirsten

CHAPTER 1

2.36 P.M., THURSDAY 29 SEPTEMBER 2016

Dying wasn't on the to-do list I'd drafted earlier that afternoon. No doubt the 4x4 driver hadn't planned on killing a cyclist either. But that's what happened. Her giant black car swerved into my path. It hit me head on. There was no time to react. Just an awful screeching sound, a brief sensation of flying and a sudden agonizing pain. Then I blacked out.

Next thing I knew, I was standing on the pavement watching two paramedics fight to revive my battered, bloody body. I desperately willed them to succeed, even moving closer in the hope I could jump back into my skin at the right moment, but it was futile. I was pronounced dead minutes later.

But I'm still here, I told myself. What does that make me? And then my thoughts turned to Ella. What would happen to her if I was dead? She'd be all alone, abandoned

1

by both of her parents: the very thing I'd sworn she'd never face.

'Wait! Don't give up,' I shouted at the paramedics. 'Don't stop! I'm still here. You've got to keep trying. You don't know what you're doing. Don't fucking give up on me! I'm not dead.'

I screamed my lungs out, begging and pleading with them to try to revive me again, but they couldn't hear me. I was invisible to them and, ironically, to the onlookers gathered at the police cordon – several waving camera phones – keen to catch a glimpse of the dead guy.

In desperation, I tried to grab one of the paramedics. But as my hand touched his right shoulder, I was hurled backwards by an invisible force. It left me sprawling on the tarmac. I was stunned but, oddly, not in any physical pain. I picked myself up and tried again with the man's colleague, only to find myself thrown to the floor again. What the hell was going on?

Then I saw the driver who'd killed me. She was chain-smoking menthol cigarettes under the watchful eye of a young bobby. 'It was an accident,' she told him in between drags. 'The sat nav. It fell on to the floor. By my feet. I was just trying to pick it up when – oh God, I can still see his face hitting my windscreen. What have I done? Is he going to be okay? Tell me he's going to make it.'

'Do I look okay?' I ask, standing in front of her, staring her in the face and willing her to see me. 'Does it seem like I'm going to make it? You've killed me. I'm dead. All because of a bloody sat nav. Look at me, for God's sake. I'm right here.'

She'd have looked glamorous without the vomit on her high-heeled shoes and in the ends of her straightened hair. She was deathly pale and shaking so much that I didn't have the heart to continue. She knew what she'd done.

'Why am I still here?' I yelled at the sky.

'Have you got the time?' one police officer asked another.

'Three o'clock.'

Shit. Home time. Ella's primary school was a good fifteen-minute walk away; instinct kicked in and I started to run.

The last few stragglers were leaving the school gates by the time I arrived. The knock-on effect of my accident was already evident in the snake of cars – squashed noses and curious eyes at their rear windows – that filled one side of the suburban street. I rushed to the back of the building, where Ella would be waiting, and saw her standing there alone, a forlorn look on her face. 'Over here, darling!' I shouted, waving as I ran across the empty yard. 'It's okay. I'm here now.'

I don't know what I was thinking. Why would she see me when no one else had? Watching my six-year-old daughter stare straight through me was quite the reality check.

'Ella, Daddy's here,' I said for the umpteenth time, kneeling in front of her so we were face to face, but not daring to touch her after what had happened with the paramedics. Her lips were chapped and her right hand, which was clenching her Hello Kitty lunchbox, was covered in red felt-tip ink. I gasped as I realized I wouldn't be able

3

to remind her to use her lip balm or to help her 'scrub those mucky paws'. Oblivious to my presence, she stared expectantly towards the far end of the playground.

Mrs Afzal emerged from the open door behind Ella. 'Is he still not here, love? You'd better get inside now.'

'He'll be here in a minute,' Ella told her teacher. 'His watch might need a new battery again.'

'Come on. We'll get the office to give him a call.'

Panic knifed through me as I pictured my mobile ringing in the back of the ambulance while they drove away my dead body. I imagined one of the paramedics, my blood still splattered across his green shirt, rooting through my pockets to find it. How long before Ella discovered what had happened?

I was about to follow them inside when I felt a tap on my shoulder. Startled, I spun around.

'Hello, William. Sorry to sneak up on you like that. I, um, I'm Lizzie.'

A stumpy woman in a dowdy grey skirt suit and beige mac was standing before me, one arm outstretched for a handshake. Gingerly, fearing another run-in with the tarmac, I reached out towards her podgy hand. It felt cool despite the unseasonal late September sunshine.

'How do you know my name?' I asked. 'And how come I can touch you?'

'I was sent to meet you when you died. You've probably got a few questions.'

'What are you: some kind of angel? Pull the other one.'

Lizzie, who appeared to be in her late twenties, ran a hand through her wavy black hair, which was tied in a

4

loose ponytail. Her nose twitched in a way that reminded me of a rabbit.

'Um, no. I'm not an angel. We're on the same team, but they're higher up the pecking order. Think of me as a guide. This can be a confusing time. I'm here to make your transition from life to death as smooth as possible. How are you doing so far?'

'Well, I'm dead. Apart from you, no one can see me. Not even my little girl, who's about to learn she's an orphan. How do you think I'm doing?'

'Right. Sorry. Is there anything I can do to help?'

'How about bringing me back to life and taking that bloody lunatic driver instead? It's her fault I'm here.'

She shook her head. 'That's not possible, I'm afraid. Anything else?'

'What about helping me to communicate with Ella? If I'm really a ghost, doesn't that mean people can see me in certain circumstances? I need her to know that I'm still here; that I haven't abandoned her.'

'We don't tend to use the G-word. It has too many negative connotations. We prefer the term "spirit".'

'Whatever. You're splitting hairs. Can I talk to Ella or not?'

'She can't see you. You said so yourself. That's not the way this works. The reason I'm here is to guide you across to the other side and show you the ropes.'

'What if I don't want to come?'

'There's nothing left for you here.'

'What about my little girl? She needs me.'

'She's not your responsibility any more, William. It's out of your control. You're a spirit now; what's waiting

5

for you on the other side is incredible beyond words.'

'You didn't answer my question. What if I don't want to come? Will you drag me kicking and screaming?'

'I won't take you anywhere you don't want to go.'

'So I can stay?'

She shrugged her shoulders. 'It's your choice.'

'And if I do go with you? Can I change my mind and come back?'

'No. It's a one-way ticket.'

'How about the other way round? If I don't come with you now, can I come later?'

Lizzie hesitated for a moment before nodding her head. 'There's a grace period.'

'Now we're getting somewhere. How long?'

'That depends.' She looked up to the sky. 'It's a top-level decision. I'd have to get back to you.'

'Right. I'll get back to you too, then. How do I get hold of you?'

As the words left my mouth, I was distracted by the sound of two chattering teachers walking towards us. I turned for the briefest of moments to look at them and when I turned back Lizzie had vanished.

I looked from left to right in confusion. 'Hello? Are you there? Can you still hear me? You didn't answer my question. And why can't I touch anyone – except you?'

I paused, expecting her to reappear, but she didn't. 'Great,' I said. 'I guess I'm on my own.'

I'd abandoned my only daughter. I'd broken the promise I'd made to her countless times, usually as she was lying in bed at night, asking about her mother, eyes intense and probing.

'Daddy, you'll never leave me, will you?'

'No, of course not, darling. I'm not going anywhere. I'll never leave you.'

'Promise?'

'Promise. From the bottom of my heart.'

Back inside the school it was obvious that they'd found something out. Ella was moved from the corridor outside the office back to her classroom, where Mrs Afzal kept her occupied doing some drawing. Her teacher was smiling the whole time, but I could see pity in her eyes. She told Ella there was a slight problem and she'd have to wait at school a little longer.

'When will my daddy get here?'

'I'm not sure how long you'll have to wait, Ella. But I'll stay with you until someone comes to pick you up.'

'He's never been this late before. Last time his watch battery broke he was only a bit late. I wasn't even the last one waiting.'

Mrs Afzal knelt down next to Ella. 'What's that you're drawing?'

'An ice cream. Look, that's the chocolate stick and I'm going to add some red sauce. Daddy said I could have one after tea today because it's summer in India.'

It was my mother who eventually arrived to pick Ella up. She put on a show of normality for her granddaughter's sake, but I could see the anguish in her eyes. She knew. Usually she'd have had a chinwag with Mrs Afzal about her own days as a primary school teacher. Not today.

'Nana!' Ella said, running over to give her a big hug. 'I didn't know you were coming to pick me up. Daddy's really late.'

I saw Mum's face crumple as she held Ella tightly against her own short, slender frame. But she fought to hide her pain again when they parted.

'Hi, Mum,' I whispered, from as close as I could get to her without touching. 'I messed up. I'm so sorry. I'm going to need you to look after her for me.'

Mum drove Ella home and sat her down in the lounge. I couldn't believe what was about to happen. I watched as tears started to fall down her cheeks. It terrified me, but it was the only thing to do. Ella needed to know the truth.

'What's the matter, Nana? Why are you crying? What's happened? Is Daddy okay?'

'No, darling. I have to tell you some terrible news.'

'What is it? What's wrong? Has he hurt himself? Is he in hospital?'

Tears were flooding down Mum's face. I could hardly bear to watch. 'There was a terrible accident, my love. Daddy was really badly hurt and … I'm so sorry … he died.'

Ella was silent for a moment before asking: 'What do you mean? What kind of accident?'

'Daddy was riding his bicycle. He was, um. He was in a crash.'

'A crash? How? What hurted him?'

'It was a car.'

'Where is he now? Has he gone to the hospital?'

'No, darling. He died. He's not here any more. He's in Heaven. He's with your mummy.'

Ella stood up. 'He can't be. He's taking me to get an ice cream later. He's just a bit late. It's naughty to tell lies, Nana. Do you want to see my new hairband? I'll go and get it. It's in my bedroom.'

She ran out of the room and up the stairs, leaving Mum distraught.

'Go after her!' I cried.

But at that moment Mum's mobile phone started ringing. 'Hello? Oh, Tom, it's you. Thank goodness. Are you still with the police?'

I left Mum talking to Dad and went upstairs to Ella's bedroom, which she'd persuaded me to paint bright pink about a year ago. I couldn't see where she was at first; then I heard a rustling sound coming from inside the princess castle I'd given her the birthday before last. We had talked about taking the pink play tent down, as she hadn't used it for a while, but when I peered through the mesh window, there she was. She was hugging Kitten, her favourite soft toy, and staring at the floor.

I knelt down right by the window. 'I wish you could hear me, Ella. You're my world, my everything. I'm here for you and I'm not going anywhere.'

'I know you're not dead, Daddy,' she said, startling me.

'Ella?' I replied, reaching my arm into the tent to touch her – to make contact – only to find myself flying backwards through the air and slamming against the wall on the far side of the room. No pain again, but it was clear I wasn't able to touch anyone.

9

'Please come home soon, so Nana can see that she's wrong,' she continued, oblivious to what had just happened. 'You promised you'd never leave me and I know you meant it. Please come home, Daddy. I miss you.'

CHAPTER 2

SEVEN HOURS DEAD

Mum and Dad decided to stay at our house for the night, to keep things as normal as possible for Ella. They took the poky third bedroom, which was only slightly bigger than the double bed it contained. I'd have rather they used my room, but they felt it wasn't appropriate – and it wasn't like they could hear my protests.

I was finding it increasingly frustrating that no one could hear or see anything I said or did. The only external confirmation of my existence came in the form of my parents' dog, Sam, who'd arrived with Dad. A usually placid King Charles spaniel, he barked incessantly and ran around in circles whenever we were in the same room. It excited me at first, as I wondered whether I might be able to use him to make contact with my family. But it soon became clear that there was little chance of any Lassie-type behaviour. He wasn't the brightest of pets. Plus he'd never liked me much when I was alive and apparently death hadn't changed that. Trying to talk to him only served to increase the volume of his barking, so I soon abandoned that possibility.

There was another moment of excitement when, to my surprise, I realized I could see my reflection in the mirror. My mother was brushing her teeth in the bathroom. I must have passed mirrors before that, but this was the first time it had registered.

'Hey,' I shouted, jumping up and down; waving like a lunatic. 'Look, Mum. Here I am.'

But she couldn't see my reflection any more than she could hear what I was saying.

I waited for Dad to follow her and tried again. I stood beside him as he too brushed his teeth and washed his face. There I was, clear as day, right next to him, asking him to look at me. But apparently I was the only one who could see it.

At least I looked to be in one piece. I was relieved not to see any sign of the injuries I'd suffered in the crash.

'None of this feels real,' Mum said to Dad after the two of them got into bed. 'I keep thinking – hoping – I'll wake up and it'll all have been a bad dream.'

Dad took her hand and let out a sigh.

'I just feel numb,' she continued. 'After the initial shock of it all – after telling Ella what happened – it's like … I don't know. As if it's happening to someone else. Not me. Why aren't I crying now? I feel I'm not reacting as I should be.'

'There is no right way to react,' Dad replied. 'Parents aren't meant to outlive their children.'

'But how do you feel, Tom?'

He sighed again. 'I'm putting one foot in front of the other. We have to be strong for Ella.'

I couldn't listen to any more of their conversation. It felt too much like eavesdropping, so I walked to Ella's room instead. Sitting down on the floor next to her bed, I was consumed by a rush of fears and anxieties.

How on earth would this fragile little girl manage without me? Would I ever get through to her and, if not, how could I survive here alone?

Oh my God, I'm dead, I thought, the terrible truth starting to sink in. I'm actually dead. My life's over. I'll never hug Ella again. I'll never wash her hair, brush her teeth or read her a story again. All those little things I used to take for granted. Gone. Forever.

Then I thought back to the accident. Why the hell did I go out on my bike in the first place?

Ella coughed in her sleep. I looked over at her flushed face and her blond curls, matted and unruly across the pillow, and it was enough to jolt me out of my spiral of self-pity. 'Stop it,' I said. 'Stop feeling sorry for yourself. She's the only thing that matters now.'

I hadn't got a clue whether or not ghosts – or spirits, as Lizzie put it – were able to sleep. I didn't feel particularly tired. But I lay down on the floor next to the bed and tried to clear my mind, if only to be able to do my best to get through to Ella in the morning. It took a while, but eventually I drifted off.

I woke up the next morning alone in Ella's bedroom. Apparently she'd already got up. To my dismay, I noticed the door was shut. My experience so far as a spirit had been that I couldn't interact with anything around me. This meant I was trapped. However, I remembered a scene in the film *Ghost* in which Patrick Swayze's character had to learn to pass through a closed door. It was a flimsy information source, but what else did I have to go on?

I walked up to it, held my hands out in front of me and tried to push them into the wood. Nothing. I didn't get thrown backwards as I had after touching Ella or the paramedics. I just couldn't move past it. Next I tried to turn the handle, although that was no use either. My hand stopped upon reaching it, but I couldn't feel or exert any pressure on it.

I went back to trying to pass through the door. I imagined myself doing so, pushing through like it was made of liquid. I even tried running at it, shouting and screaming, hoping my anger might unlock some hidden ability. But nothing worked. I really was trapped until Ella came in to get a jumper from her wardrobe a short while later and I was able to exit the traditional way.

The death knock came just after lunch. I'd been expecting it. I'd been out on plenty of them myself early in my career; little had I imagined that a few years later I'd be the subject of one. Considering my family circumstances and the way in which I'd died, it was inevitable that a local newspaper reporter would call at the house soon.

'Can you get that, Tom?' Mum shouted from upstairs, where she was plaiting Ella's hair.

'Right,' Dad shouted, stubbing out the cigarette he'd been smoking at the back door and trudging through the hall. He was a big man, although he was one of the lucky few who carried it well. Thanks partly to his strong jawline and broad shoulders, he'd managed to stay handsome in spite of the extra weight. He enjoyed his food and drink and rarely rushed anywhere; today he was even slower than usual. He opened the door to an attractive girl in her mid-twenties.

'Hello there,' she said, wearing her best sympathetic smile. 'I'm awfully sorry to bother you. I'm Kate Andrews, from the *Evening Journal*. We heard about the horrific accident yesterday involving William Curtis. I just wondered if a family member was available for a quick chat. We're very interested in running a tribute article.'

I smiled to myself. 'Tribute' was the term I used to use on death knocks. I'd always found it an effective way of getting the family onside.

Dad, whose years as a solicitor had fostered a distrust of the press that I'd never been able to shift, demanded proof of ID. After he'd given her pass the once-over, he left her on the doorstep while he went to confer with Mum.

'Come on, old man,' I said, the journalist in me realizing it would be hypocritical not to allow her an interview. 'Give the girl a break.'

'What do you think?' he asked Mum. 'I'm not convinced it's a good idea.'

'Why not?'

'Do you really want our private business splashed all over the news?'

15

'I'm sure it's what Will would have wanted. He was a journalist, after all. It's only right there's a tribute to him in the local paper.'

'Really? And what if they get it all wrong?'

'Surely that's more likely if we don't talk to them, isn't it? There'll be a story one way or another, Tom. They won't just ignore it. Better we have some input.'

'Well I'm not getting involved. You speak to her, if you must. But don't let her put words into your mouth and steer clear of talking about the accident – particularly who might have been to blame. I'll take Ella out for a walk. I don't want her involved either.'

I decided to stay to hear the interview.

'Thanks for agreeing to speak to me,' Kate said, sipping on the cup of tea Mum had made for her before they sat down in the lounge. Mum was dressed casually, in a navy cardigan and jeans; I noticed she'd applied some lipstick and combed her short dark hair before coming downstairs. I could see she was trying her best to put a brave face on it.

'That's okay. It only seems right, what with Will being a journalist too.'

'Really? I had no idea. Who did he work for?'

'He used to be a staff reporter on *The Times*. He was based in London at that point but moved back up north about six years ago and went freelance. He still mainly writes – sorry, wrote – for *The Times*, but he also did work for other national papers and some magazines. I'm surprised you've not heard of him.'

Kate didn't get another word in edgeways until she'd been subjected to a gushing, cringeworthy history of my entire career, from my days on a local weekly up to the present. She eventually got the chance to ask a question about my family life. I saw her eyes light up when Mum explained I'd been a single parent; that Ella's mother was also dead.

'Ah, now we've got your interest,' I said, peering over her shoulder at her shorthand notes. 'Yes, it'll make a decent news story. Nothing like a good tragedy to shift a few papers. You never know, it might even make front page.'

'How's Ella dealing with it?' Kate asked. 'I can't begin to imagine how she must be feeling.'

I was furious. 'Don't give me that fake sympathy shit!' I shouted. 'Leave her out of it. She's just a little girl.'

Mum shuffled on the couch. 'I, er, don't really want to go into that.'

'Of course,' Kate replied. 'I understand. What about you and your husband, then? It must have been such an awful shock.'

Calm down, I told myself, shocked by how easily I'd flown off the handle. It's okay. Mum can deal with this. The girl's doing her job, that's all; I'd have asked exactly the same things.

'Yes,' Mum whispered. She took several deep breaths before adding: 'It hasn't sunk in yet. We're both still in shock. No one expects to outlive their children. It's like we're on autopilot, holding things together for Ella.'

Once Kate had gleaned all the information she needed to write her story, she asked Mum if there was a picture of me she could borrow to run alongside it. Well, she actually asked for a photo of me with Ella, but Mum had the good sense to say no. She rooted around in her handbag and pulled out a small leather wallet containing snaps of her nearest and dearest. There was an old one of me that I'd never much liked. She stared at it for a moment and I feared she was about to start crying. But after fanning herself and taking some more gasps of air, she held her composure.

'How about this? It's not that recent, but it's a nice picture of him. It shows off his lovely blue eyes.'

'Yes, that'll be ideal.'

'He'd not changed much, apart from a few more grey hairs. They started to come in his twenties. Probably caused by stress. He was handsome, don't you think?'

I cringed as Kate was forced to agree.

'You will look after it, won't you?' Mum asked her. 'It's precious. I need it returned in one piece.'

'Of course. I'll drop it back in a couple of days, if that's okay. Thanks ever so much for chatting to me. And sorry again for your loss. I hope everything goes all right with the funeral.'

'Thanks, love. You will make it a nice piece, won't you? The last thing we need is any more upset.'

Kate flashed that sympathetic smile of hers again. 'Of course. The article will be in tomorrow's paper. It should be on the website too.'

It was only a few minutes later that Mum and I heard Dad and Ella return from their walk. Ella was in tears.

'What on earth happened?' Mum asked as we both rushed to the front door.

Dad had Ella over his left shoulder and, from the way he was out of breath and sweating, he must have carried her some way. His right arm was straining against the pull of Sam on his lead, barking as usual.

Mum took her granddaughter and lifted her into a hug. She may have been much shorter and thinner than Dad – Little and Large, I often called them – but she'd always been strong and fit. She had apparently been a smoker once, like him, but not for as long as I could remember. She was the healthy one: a pocket dynamo who enjoyed exercise and watched what she ate. Their relationship was definitely a case of opposites attract.

'There, there. Come to Nana. What's wrong, darling? What's the matter?'

'She had a bit of a fright, Ann. That's all. She'll be fine in a few minutes.'

'What do you mean she had a fright, Tom? Tell me what happened, for goodness' sake.'

'It's no big deal. We had a nice walk for the most part. We went down by the old railway line so Sam could have a run off his lead. Then we walked back along the main road. Unfortunately, we witnessed a bit of a prang. One car caught the side of another as it was pulling out from a parking space. No one was hurt, but it was all rather noisy and, well, it clearly reminded Ella of—'

'Yes, yes. I'm not stupid, thank you. What were you thinking, taking her along the main road? Come on, Ella. Let's go and have a nice sit-down in the lounge. Grandad will get you a drink. Would you like some juice?'

Ella nodded through her tears.

'Did you hear that, Grandad? And can you please put Sam in the back garden. I don't know why he's barking

19

so much. He's been like this ever since we brought him here.'

'That'll be my fault,' I said as I watched Mum try to comfort Ella. 'It's all my fault. Please don't cry, Ella. It's okay. Daddy's here.' But she couldn't hear me; I was still hidden from her. I wanted so badly to take her into my arms and wipe away her tears. This was torture. It was breaking my heart. I determined that when she was next on her own, I would do my utmost to try to get through to her.

My opportunity didn't come until she was in bed that night. After she'd had a bath and a book, Mum tucked her in and gave her a kiss goodnight.

'Do you feel like you want to talk about anything before you go to sleep?' Mum asked.

'No. I'm okay.'

'Well, any time you want to talk – especially about your daddy – I'm right here for you. Grandad is too. You know that, don't you?'

'Yes.'

'Goodnight, my love. Sleep tight. Don't let the bedbugs bite.'

Ella shook her head, a sad look on her face. That was what I always used to say to her at bedtime. I guess I learned it from hearing it myself as a boy.

As Mum got up to leave, Ella jerked upright. 'Is my nightlight on, Nana?'

'Yes, dear. We put it on together before I read you a story. You'll see it when I turn the main light off.'

'And the landing light? You won't switch it off, will you? Daddy always lets me have it on. I don't like the dark.'

'Don't worry. We'll leave it on for you.'

'All night?'

'All night.'

Once Mum was downstairs, I knelt at the side of the bed. 'Ella?' I whispered into her ear. 'Can you hear me? It's Daddy. I'm still here. I promised I'd never leave you and I haven't. Can't you sense me at all?'

Nothing. No sign that she had any clue I was there. Her saucer-like eyes, the same beautiful pale green as her mother's, were wide open but staring blankly at the ceiling. Letting out a frustrated sigh, I stood up and started pacing around the room. What could I do to get through to her? If the dog could sense me, surely there was a chance that Ella could too, no matter what Lizzie had told me. What about all the claims of ghost sightings over the years? There had to be something in it. And didn't they say that children were more open to that kind of thing than adults?

Ironically, before I died I'd been a complete non-believer when it came to the supernatural. As a journalist, I'd built a wall of scepticism around myself that only hard facts could penetrate. I remembered laughing with colleagues about people who'd phoned in with stories of hauntings, dubbing them 'crackpots'. Now here I was with a whole different perspective.

Other than the little I'd gleaned from Lizzie, my only knowledge of what it meant to be a ghost – sorry, a spirit – was based on fiction. But what I was experiencing, which I'd only started to analyse once the initial shock of being dead had eased, wasn't anything like the books I'd read or films I'd seen. Try as I might, I still wasn't able to do

21

a Patrick Swayze and pass through solid objects. I could walk about and sit or lie down, but that was pretty much it. Taking care not to get trapped behind closed doors had already become second nature. My sense of touch had vanished. I was as numb as if I'd been anaesthetized. It was like I had no mass and was enveloped in a thick bubble that kept me apart from the world around me. And yet, conversely, when I wasn't trying to interact with that world, I still felt as real and solid as I had before my death.

Then there was the whole thing about not being able to touch people. I'd tried it several times now; on each occasion I'd been repelled with the same violent force, which didn't hurt me but knocked me for six and always went completely unnoticed by the person involved. Smell and taste had abandoned me too, along with the need or desire for food or drink. My sight and hearing were all I had left. And yet that hadn't been the case when I'd met Lizzie. I could definitely recall feeling her tap me on the shoulder and that cool handshake of hers in contrast to the sunny weather. What does that matter? I thought. She's not here any more. I sent her away.

So how could I break through to my daughter? I couldn't get the lights to flicker; I couldn't move inanimate objects or make my presence known at all. 'Come on, Ella,' I said. 'Give me something. Give me some sign that you can sense me. You must be able to. I'm right here, darling.'

Without warning, she got out of bed, forcing me to dive out of her way. She knelt where I'd been a moment earlier. I wondered what she was doing until she started talking in a quiet voice. 'God? Are you there? My name's

22

Ella. The vicar at school says we can talk to you like this if we're sad. Is my daddy with you? Nana says he is. She says he's in Heaven. I really miss him, you see. I was thinking that maybe you could let him come back soon. He said he'd get me an ice cream. Nana and Grandad are looking after me, but I'd still really like him to come home. I hate feeling sad all the time. Amen.'

Her words were like a needle pushing through my soul. They spurred me on to talk to her some more, desperate for that breakthrough I craved, but whatever I said and however I said it, it made no difference. She still couldn't hear me. All the same, I stayed at her bedside and whispered tales of gruffaloes, captured princesses, a dancing dog, and a cat called Mog: stories committed to memory after countless nights of reading them to her. I carried on long after she fell asleep, hoping beyond hope that some part of her might hear me and feel comforted.

'Goodnight, my beautiful girl,' I said eventually, my repertoire complete. I leaned over the bed, where she lay in a deep sleep, and blew a kiss goodnight as close as I dared to the soft skin of her forehead.

'Night night, Daddy,' she muttered.

CHAPTER 3

ONE DAY DEAD

I couldn't believe it. She'd replied. I'd said 'goodnight' and she'd heard my voice; she'd said 'night night' back to me. My instinct was to shout and scream, hoping she'd wake up and see me. But I couldn't bring myself to do it. Part of me was afraid it wouldn't work, but mainly I didn't want to interrupt her sleep. She looked so peaceful and I knew how much she needed her rest. Be patient, I told myself. Now's not the right time, but it will come.

I was buzzing. I felt hope. If I could get through to her when she was asleep, then surely there was a chance to do the same when she was awake.

I decided it was time to try to contact Lizzie. She'd given me the impression that it would be impossible for Ella to see or hear me, but now, after what I'd just witnessed, I was sure she was wrong. I needed to get some proper answers.

I walked down the stairs, tiptoeing past the closed door of the kitchen, where Sam was sleeping, to enter the lounge. The landing light barely stretched this far, so the room was shrouded in darkness. I knew my way around, though, and manoeuvred myself into my favourite leather recliner, remembering how comfy it used to feel. Now it didn't feel like anything. Comfort and discomfort were indistinguishable in my current state. And I could no more push the seat back into the reclined position than I could turn on the TV or pick up the paperback I'd left on the coffee table a couple of nights ago, blissfully unaware that I'd die before finishing it.

'Hello?' I said. 'Are you there, Lizzie? Can you hear me? I need a word.'

'William,' a voice replied from across the dark room. 'I thought you'd never call.'

There was a clicking sound and all the lights turned on. Lizzie was perched on the couch, looking exactly the same as when we'd last met: skirt suit, mac, ponytail.

She smiled. 'Hello, stranger. Like the dark, do you?'

'Not especially, but I don't seem to be able to do simple things like switching on a light any more. Unlike you. How does that work? Is it something I can learn or am I stuck like this? I kind of assumed I'd be less … useless.'

'You should never assume anything. Assume makes an ass of you and me. You've heard that saying, right?'

I waited for her to continue – to answer some of my questions – yet nothing else came. I bore the silence for as long as I could, throwing her my most pathetic, help-less look in a desperate bid to penetrate her defences. But it was futile: she just stared right back at me.

'Come on,' I wailed. 'Give me something. At least tell me why I get hurled against the nearest hard surface whenever I get too close to someone. What's that all about?'

Lizzie grimaced. 'Yes. That can be unpleasant. It's best avoided. There's nothing you can do, I'm afraid. You simply can't share the same space as a living person.'

'Great. Anything else?'

She shook her head. 'Your stay here as a spirit is supposed to be temporary. Of course if you agree to come with me – to move on – you'll get all the answers you need. But remember, the clock's ticking on that option.'

'How long?'

'That's not yet been decided. I'll let you know as soon as I hear. Do I sense a change of heart? You must be getting lonely on your own.'

'I'm not on my own. I'm with Ella and my parents.'

'They can't see you.'

'That's actually what I wanted to talk to you about.'

'Oh?'

I shifted forward in my chair. 'I've had a breakthrough.'

Lizzie raised an eyebrow. 'How so?'

'I was telling Ella some of her favourite stories after she went to bed tonight. I didn't think she could hear me, but I did it anyway. It felt right, so I carried on for ages. Then I stopped and said goodnight – and she said it back to me.'

'She said goodnight to you? I thought she was asleep.'

'She was. It was like she was talking in her sleep.'

'It was probably a coincidence. Perhaps she was having a dream in which you said goodnight to her. It's likely she'll dream about you as her mind processes what's happened.'

26

'At exactly the same moment? Really? I don't think so. I'm convinced she could hear me, at least subconsciously. If I can tap into that, why can't I get through to her when she's awake? Look at the dog: he knows I'm still here.'

'The dog?'

'Sam, my parents' King Charles. He can't stop barking at me. Lizzie, I'm not going to be fobbed off. Tell me the truth. Please. I'm begging you.'

Lizzie sat up and fixed her chocolate-brown eyes on me. Her nose gave that odd rabbit twitch again, which I guessed was a tic. There was a long pause before she said: 'It's complicated.'

'What does that mean?'

'There are certain things I'm not permitted to talk to you about. My job is to help you move on.'

'But if Sam can see me, why can't she?'

'She's not a dog.'

'I'm glad you cleared that up. Come on, Lizzie, don't be obstructive. You know what I'm asking.'

'I'm stating facts. These things work differently for animals from how they do for humans.'

'You can't do this to me. You're all I've got. Please, tell me. Don't you have a heart? This is my six-year-old daughter we're talking about. Ella used to make me promise that I'd never leave her – that she'd never be alone – and now, as far as she's concerned, I have. She thinks I've broken my promise, abandoning her without even saying goodbye. What will that do to her as she grows up?'

'I'm sorry, but I can't help you. At least Ella has her grandparents to look after her. They obviously love her very much.'

'Yes, but they're my parents, not hers. I'm her father. Please, Lizzie. Imagine if you were Ella. Wouldn't you want to see me again? Wouldn't you want to know the truth? You must have had a father once.'

Lizzie stared at her hands. I was getting somewhere. 'Come on,' I said. 'Give me something, anything. I'm right, aren't I? It is possible that I might be able to communicate with Ella. Give me that.'

'There's nothing I can do.'

The lights flicked off again.

'Lizzie?' I said. 'Are you there?' But I already knew the answer. It made me want to scream with frustration.

'Some guide you are,' I said to the empty lounge. Then I remembered those three magical words again: 'Night night, Daddy.' They fuelled my passion and kept me positive. I'd given Lizzie plenty of opportunity to deny the possibility of me communicating with my daughter, but she hadn't. I could cling to that.

CHAPTER 4

SIX DAYS DEAD

There were no more breakthroughs over the next few days. I tried again and again but got nowhere. It made me wonder whether I should have taken the opportunity when I had it and tried to wake her up. I even feared that perhaps Lizzie was doing something to hinder my progress. But I persevered. I stayed glued to Ella's side day and night, talking to her the whole time like she could hear me.

I was so occupied by this that I paid little attention to my 'tribute' when it appeared in the paper, other than noting it was the lead story on page five and Mum seemed happy with the wording. In the grand scheme of things, the article was of little concern. Of far more importance was the fact that Ella wasn't herself. She had major mood swings. One minute she'd seem happy, playing with her dolls or running around the garden with Sam. Next she'd be in tears about some minor thing that had upset her or, worse, she'd fall silent, withdrawing into herself.

She wet her bed one night, which she hadn't done in ages, and was really upset when she woke up and realized. It was heart-breaking to watch her frantically trying to change the sheets herself at 3 a.m. Luckily, Mum heard her and came to the rescue. 'What are you doing, silly sausage? You don't need to do that yourself. That's what I'm here for. Why didn't you come and get me?'

Ella, cheeks bright red, ran to hide in her princess castle.

'Don't worry, darling. These things happen. It's only normal.'

'It wasn't me. It must have been Kitten.'

Meanwhile, Mum and Dad had their work cut out juggling the police, who were pursuing a charge of death by dangerous driving against the 4x4 driver; the coroner, who had opened an inquest into my death; and the funeral director, who was busy arranging my send-off. There was also legal guardianship of Ella and my estate to sort out. Just as well I'd heeded Dad's advice to write a will, which kept things clear cut.

My parents were doing their best to stay positive and to hold things together for Ella, but I could see how hard it was for them. Dad was drinking and smoking more than ever and Mum, usually a picture of health, looked like she'd not slept in weeks. They were still staying at our place, although they were missing their own home comforts and had discussed moving Ella soon after the funeral. Their house was only a twenty-minute drive away, so the plan was for her to stay in the same school for the time being.

They kept her out of classes for a few days, but then she asked to go back. I decided to accompany her, to make

30

sure she was okay, but I didn't stay long. I felt like I was intruding. That was her space – her private time away from home – and she'd always been protective of it. Ever since her early days in reception, we'd got into a daily routine of me asking what she'd done at school and her replying that she couldn't remember. I'd found it strange at first, but a lot of parents said their children were the same.

Anyway, I stayed for about forty-five minutes on that first day. She was very quiet to start with and she had a little cry on the way to the classroom after assembly. But things improved after her best friend, Jada, gave her a hug and said she'd look after her. I headed home, only to find that Mum and Dad had gone out and I had no way of getting inside.

'Fantastic,' I said, slumping on to the doorstep and sitting there with my head in my hands, feeling sorry for myself. It started to rain. I should have been cold and wet out there, wearing just the frayed jeans and T-shirt I'd been stuck in since I died, but all I felt was the usual numbness. Part of me wished it would spread to my mind: the one place where I could still feel something. But what would be left of my humanity without that? The pain I experienced each time I saw Ella's sorrow was what drove me forward, determined to break through to her.

It was then I noticed a black Audi driving past. It slowed as it reached my house, but the car's tinted windows stopped me from getting a good view inside. A few minutes later it was back, coming from the other direction this time, and it pulled up on the opposite side of the road. I was curious now, so I got up to cross the street, hoping to get a closer look and to find out who was in there. Just then another car, a navy Ford Fiesta I didn't recognize, pulled up at speed and swerved on to my drive.

'Bloody hell,' I shouted, diving to one side and narrowly avoiding the car's path. I didn't know what would happen if a moving vehicle hit me; it wasn't something I particularly wanted to find out. I picked myself up to see the Audi disappearing into the distance and a young, slightly taller version of my mother stepping out of the driver's side of the Fiesta. 'Lauren,' I said. 'I might have known.'

My sister had always been a crazy driver. You'd have thought she might have toned it down a bit after her younger brother's death in a road accident, but that would have been far too sensible. Fifteen years of living in the Netherlands also meant she was out of practice at driving on the left-hand side, so goodness knows how many near misses there had been on the way from the airport.

Lauren's husband Xander, a six-foot-six-inch Dutch giant with floppy brown hair in a centre parting, prised himself out of the front passenger seat and strode over to ring the bell of the front door.

'I don't think anyone's home,' he announced eventually.

Lauren, who had the boot open and was rooting through her case for something, swore loudly. 'I don't believe this. Mum said they'd be here; otherwise we could have gone straight to their place. Hang on, I'll give her a call.'

'Hello, sis,' I said loudly into her ear as she dug her mobile out of a coat pocket. 'Long time no see. Can you hear me? I'm still here, you know. I'm a spirit these days.'

She held the phone up to her ear. 'Mum? Hi, it's Lauren
... No, we're at Will's house already ... Yeah, it was fine,
thanks ... No, we decided to hire a car instead ... Oh,
okay. Good. See you soon.'

'Where are they?' Xander asked.

'Supermarket. They'll be back in ten minutes.'

It felt strange to see Lauren. I knew she was coming,
as I'd heard Mum and Dad talking to her on the phone,
but I hadn't seen her for months. She was immaculately
turned out, as usual, effortlessly stylish in a tunic top and
tailored trousers, her chestnut hair in a sleek bob. She
looked much younger than her thirty-eight years, her elfin
features still fresh and largely untroubled by wrinkles.
She'd never had any difficulty passing herself off as my
younger sister, even though she was the eldest, especially
once my premature grey hair set in.

There were only two years between us and, although
we had the usual sibling rows while growing up, we'd
always got on pretty well. She'd looked out for me at
school and had been happy to dish out advice on girl-
friends or to help with homework. In our early teens we
started socializing a bit together, enjoying the same bands
and clubs, and even dating some of each other's friends.
But then came an awful period when things changed for
a while. We eventually got past all that nastiness, but not
long afterwards she met her future husband and he
whisked her away to live with him in a small Dutch village
near the town of Gouda. She'd been there ever since.

Even that had been okay to start with. She made two or
three visits home a year and I went out there a few times

33

to stay with her. But then she and Xander set up a small business together, designing and marketing bespoke wedding stationery, which took over their lives. Lauren's visits home became few and far between. She and Xander seemed to prefer to spend what little free time they had on jetting to tropical islands, rather than visiting the UK. And after one terrible trip to see them, when I spent half of my stay alone while they worked, I made the decision not to return.

Once Ella was born I had hoped that Lauren would make more of an effort. When my wife died and I was struggling to manage as a single dad, I thought my big sister would be there for me. However, nothing changed. It was hard to forgive her for that.

The irony was that Lauren and Xander had been brilliant with Ella on the few occasions they had seen her. They'd never had children, nor shown any inclination to do so, and Xander was an only child, so there were no other nieces or nephews on the scene. They'd always lavished Ella with affection before disappearing back to their work-fuelled lives with barely a backward glance.

I was still glad to see them now, though. Lauren had done far worse things in the past than being too busy for me, so I knew from experience that I could never stop loving her. She'd always be my big sister. And even though it was Xander who had taken her abroad, he was a good bloke.

When she first saw them after school, Ella got upset, bursting into tears and running to her room. It was too much for her, that was all, but it made Lauren cry too.

Mum put an arm around her as Dad went upstairs to check on Ella. 'It doesn't mean anything, Lauren. Don't take it personally. That little girl's been through so much over the past few days, it's to be expected. Her emotions are all over the place. She's grieving like the rest of us.'

'Sorry,' Lauren said, dabbing her eyes with a tissue. 'I know that. I don't know why I let it upset me. I'm all over the place – you ask Xander. I've been biting his head off or crying on his shoulder ever since I heard. I can't believe Will's gone. I never even got to say goodbye. I've been a crap sister, especially the last few years, and I wish I could say sorry. I wish I could tell him how much I love him.'

'You just did,' I whispered.

I left Mum comforting Lauren and followed Dad upstairs, where I found him kneeling in front of Ella's princess castle, the door of which was zipped tightly shut. There was a sobbing sound coming from within the tent.

'Are you all right, love?' Dad puffed, out of breath. 'What's wrong? You can tell Grandad.'

He didn't get a reply to start with but continued to coax her into talking.

'I feel sad,' Ella replied eventually in a tear-filled voice. 'Seeing Auntie Lauren reminded me of Daddy. I miss him a lot.'

Dad ran a hand through his neatly cropped hair, which had held on to its dark brown colour far longer than mine, meaning we were now about the same shade of grey. 'Oh, Ella. Of course you do. I miss him too.'

'Nana said I'll only get to see him again when I go to Heaven, so how come he's in my dreams sometimes?'

My ears pricked up. Did this mean I was somehow getting through to her?

Dad shifted awkwardly into a sitting position, wincing as he straightened his knees. 'Um, Nana's right what she told you. Dreams are complicated. They seem real when you're in them, but they're not. They're created by your mind. It's your memories of your dad that you're seeing. That doesn't mean you can't enjoy them, but you need to remember that it's not really him.'

I sighed, wishing he hadn't told her that, even though it was something I would have said once.

Ella unzipped the tent door and looked out with red eyes. 'Do you think Daddy might come back to visit me before I go to Heaven? I don't think I can wait that long.'

'I wish I could tell you that he would. I really do, but that's not how it works. It's like Nana told you. You're not alone, though. You mustn't forget that. We're here for you whenever you need us.' Dad spread his arms wide. 'Come here, princess. There's a big hug waiting for you.'

After a while he persuaded Ella to go back downstairs with him. I stayed behind, a cocktail of emotions swirling around my head. I was annoyed at what Dad had told her. But what else could he have said? And what should I make of the fact Ella remembered seeing me in her dreams? Was that really something to take strength from, or was it just like Dad had told her? The unanswered questions were stacking up. I was tempted to call for Lizzie again but didn't allow myself. There was no point. It would only be like last time. Instead, I calmed myself down and returned to my role as a silent observer.

CHAPTER 5

THIRTEEN DAYS DEAD

When the day I'd been dreading finally arrived, I wanted to get it over and done with as soon as possible. My funeral had been delayed by the need for a post-mortem, which had found the cause of my death to be severe head and chest injuries. However, the arrangements were quickly finalized once the coroner released my body.

That morning I found myself wandering aimlessly around the house as everyone got ready to say their goodbyes to me.

'There's no need to cry,' I said to Mum as she shed a silent tear while applying her make-up. 'I've not gone anywhere. I'm still right here. It's just that none of you can see me.'

I wandered down to the kitchen. Sam was lying in his bed. He looked at me when I entered, yawned and then averted his gaze. 'Hello?' I said. 'You can't even be bothered to bark at me any more? Brilliant. The only one who can see me has lost interest.'

I heard someone on the stairs behind me and turned to see Ella descending in a knee-length black dress. Mum had bought it for her a couple of days ago, as all the other clothes in her wardrobe were in bright, girly colours. It hadn't been easy to find, but Mum's determination – a welcome distraction from her grief – had eventually paid off. Ella looked really pretty, her curls tamed in a tight plait. But her skin looked too pale next to the dark material of the dress and there was a terrible sadness in her eyes. She sat on the bottom step and stared blankly at the front door.

'My precious girl,' I said, kneeling before her. 'I wish you didn't have to go through this.' I placed my right hand above hers, just far enough away to avoid being repelled, and told her how much I loved her. 'You won't know it, darling, but I'll be right by your side all day. We'll get through this together.'

I thought back to all the mornings I'd seen Ella sit on this step before school. I remembered the fruity shampoo smell of her hair as I'd lean over to help her put her shoes on, planting a kiss on her forehead. The two of us had always had such a close bond; I missed that more than anything.

The bell rang as two black silhouettes, one much taller than the other, appeared on the other side of the door's frosted glass panel. Ella let in Lauren and Xander, who were staying at Mum and Dad's place while they remained here with Ella.

'Hello, gorgeous,' Lauren said to her, picking her up and giving her a big hug. 'You look lovely – especially your hair. Did Nana do that for you?'

Ella nodded shyly.

'Well, it looks fantastic. Your daddy would have loved it. And the dress too. It's very beautiful, isn't it, Xander?'

'Yes, definitely. You look great, Ella. We'd call you a "*mooi meisje*" in Dutch.'

'Thank you,' Ella said, perking up. 'Do you speak Dutch all the time in Holland?'

'Of course. Lauren and I tend to speak English when we're alone, though. We always have, because she didn't speak any Dutch when we met.'

'Do you speak Dutch now, Auntie Lauren?'

'*Een beetje.*'

'Eh? Is that Dutch? What does it mean?'

'It means "a little bit".'

'She's being modest,' Xander said. 'She speaks it very well. Maybe we can teach you a few words.'

Ella smiled.

Dad appeared on the landing. After years of having to dress up for work, he rarely wore anything other than jeans since retiring, although today called for his black suit. It was a snug fit; the jacket wasn't getting buttoned up any time soon. 'Everything okay at the house?' he asked his daughter and son-in-law, coughing his way downstairs.

'Fine,' Lauren replied, reaching inside her handbag. 'Here. I've got those cufflinks you wanted.'

'Thanks. I'll grab them in a minute. I'm just popping outside for a smoke.'

'Sounds like you could do without it,' Lauren said, her words falling on deaf ears.

Once Mum appeared, looking anxious in a smart jacket and skirt, the conversation turned to practicalities regarding the day's arrangements. I followed Ella to the lounge and watched her pick up a school reading book about the Loch Ness Monster.

'I went to Loch Ness once with your mummy,' I said. 'You were just a twinkle in my eye then.' I'd got into the habit of chatting to Ella as if she could hear me. Although she clearly couldn't, I found it comforting.

I felt badly underdressed. Everyone was in black – suits and smart frocks – apart from me, still stuck in my frayed jeans and T-shirt. They ought to have been filthy and stinking of sweat after all this time, but they didn't look any different from when I'd first found myself on the pavement watching the paramedics try to revive the old me. I couldn't say what they smelled like, due to my whole sensory deprivation thing, but my guess was that spirits and their clothes didn't smell of anything.

I walked over to the long mirror on the wall near the front door. I could remember hanging it there last year. Ella had wanted to help me and had plonked herself on the laminate floor by my toolbox, passing me each drill bit, screw or wall plug as I needed it. That was the best and the worst thing about being in this house. There were memories everywhere; sometimes they made me smile, but mostly they made me long to have my old life back.

I liked being able to see my reflection, even though no one else could. I'd tried several times with Ella, despite the failed attempt with my parents, but it hadn't worked. All the same, I found it a good way to assert my existence when being invisible got on top of me.

I looked exactly as I must have looked just before the accident. My thick hair was windswept, which I wasn't able to change, and my nose and cheeks were slightly reddened by the sun that had beamed down on me on that fateful day. I permanently had a day's stubble, which I was actually quite pleased about, as I'd always thought that suited me. Not that there was any point in vanity now. I suppose I was lucky not to be walking around battered and bloody, like my body was when I saw it in front of me. Still not a great look for a funeral, though, particularly when I was to be the guest of honour.

Lizzie's face appeared behind me in the mirror, giving me one hell of a fright.

'Sorry,' she said. 'Didn't mean to scare you.'

'What are you doing here?'

'I thought you might like me to accompany you to the funeral.'

'What about some answers to my questions? I need to know how to get through to my daughter.'

'You've not made any progress with that?'

'What do you care? You don't even want me to be here any more.'

'It's not a matter of what I want or don't want; it never has been. My views don't come into it. I'm just doing my job. In this case, that means attending your funeral. It's not usually a good time to be on your own.'

'So you've been to a few funerals before?'

'Of course.'

'How many?'

'I couldn't give you an exact number.'

'A ballpark figure, then. Dozens? Hundreds? Thousands?'

41

'A few hundred, I suppose. Don't look so shocked. This is what I do.'

'You must have been at it a while. How come you look so young?'

'I was only twenty-seven when I died. My appearance is the same now as it was then. That was back in nineteen ninety.'

'Wow. So you're older than I thought. And you were human once?'

'Yes. Does that surprise you?'

'Um, no. I guess not. I just … there's so much to take in. Have you been doing this ever since you died?'

'More or less. It wasn't long after I passed over that I chose to train as a guide.'

'What happened? If it's as incredible as you say on the other side, why would you want to leave? Did you get bored or something?'

'It is incredible. And, no, I didn't get bored. I had a calling. I wanted to help people like you.'

'I thought most people moved on straight away. You made out that I was unusual in wanting to stay here.'

'Most spirits do cross over quickly, although you also get a few who hang around for a while. Staying until the funeral isn't uncommon. I suppose it's a type of closure. It happens in maybe a quarter of cases. But normally that only takes a few days. Yours took longer because of the accident.'

'Hold on. Wait a minute. I see what's going on now. You're not here to hold my hand; you're hoping I'll want to come with you afterwards. Well, sorry, I'm not interested. I'd rather you left.'

'You want me to go?'

'That's right.'

'Are you sure?'

'One hundred per cent.'

'Would you like me to smarten you up first? Jeans and a T-shirt isn't exactly typical funeral attire.'

'What does it matter? No one can see me. I don't need your help.'

'Very well, but if you change your mind, give me a shout. I know this is a difficult day for you.'

'Please go,' I said, turning away from her.

'Okay. One last thing. I was going to wait until afterwards, but now will have to do. The deadline for your grace period has been set at two months from today, which is actually very generous. Remember, if you don't cross over by then, you'll never be able to, so please give it some careful thought. I'm on your side, William, whatever you might think. I hope it goes smoothly today.'

With that, she was gone. Seconds later, everyone was putting their coats on and heading out of the door. I'd assumed that they'd be going in two cars, hopefully leaving room for me to slip in somewhere. Then I saw them all piling into Dad's silver BMW and I realized that I had a problem. With him and Xander in the front and Ella on her booster seat in the back, next to Mum and Lauren, there was nowhere for me to squeeze in. The doors slammed shut.

'Hang on a minute,' I said, trying desperately to bang my hand down on the car roof, but feeling and hearing nothing. 'What about me? It's my funeral. You can't leave me here.'

CHAPTER 6

'Shit!' I shouted at the top of my lungs. 'Bollocks! What the hell do I do now?'

The funeral was being held in the village where I'd grown up – and my parents still lived – about twelve miles further out from the city. They'd decided against holding it here, on the grounds that I had no ties with any local churches. Like many of my generation, I'd drifted away from organized religion after leaving home. And yet the core belief that had been ingrained in my younger self had never entirely left me, so a church send-off felt right. The village church I'd attended as a boy, and where Mum and Dad remained regulars, was the obvious choice.

The big problem now was how to get there. There was no way I'd make it on time by foot. I feared for a moment that I'd have to eat humble pie with Lizzie and ask for her help. Then I heard the answer to my problem trundle past on the main road a couple of streets away; I raced to the bus stop.

The service I needed ran every ten minutes and would drop me just a short walk away from the church. I missed the first one to pass, as I was alone in the shelter and the driver didn't stop. Luckily, the next bus pulled up to let a passenger off. I jumped on just as the door jerked shut, and found myself a seat near the back of the empty top deck.

As the bus wound its way out of the suburbs and into the countryside, the landscape opened up into an autumnal spread of glorious reds, yellows and golden browns. My mind started to drift. How will it feel to attend my own funeral? I wondered. What if hardly anyone turns up? All of a sudden I felt incredibly nervous.

I moved downstairs once the bus entered my parents' village. Someone rang the bell for the stop prior to mine, so I got off with them in case the driver skipped the next one. I jogged to the church in five minutes and was relieved to see the front door open and people still making their way inside.

The scene that awaited me when I entered the church came as a shock. It was jam-packed with more family, friends and colleagues than I'd ever dreamed would come. There were faces from throughout my whole life: primary and secondary school, university, the various stages of my journalistic career, and everything else along the way. It jolted my mind back for an instant to my wife Alice's funeral. There had also been a huge attendance that day, although I'd hardly acknowledged anyone. I'd been a mess, thanks to the combination of my grief and the terrible guilt I felt for what I'd done to her. Everything had been a blur.

45

Back in the moment, standing at the rear of this church, panic got its claws into me. This is wrong, I thought. I shouldn't be here. My plan had been to find Ella, who was no doubt somewhere near the front with Mum and Dad, and to stay with her throughout the service. But it was all too much. Before I knew what I was doing, I found myself outside once more, watching the last few stragglers make their way into the church, the door shutting behind them.

What am I doing? I thought. I've just travelled all the way over here by bus so that I can hang around in the churchyard and miss the service. But it was too late now. Unless someone opened the door, I couldn't go back inside even if I wanted to.

I took a seat on a green bench that overlooked the sprawling graveyard. I could hear the muffled sound of voices singing 'All Things Bright and Beautiful' behind me as I stared into the distance.

'Are you on the lookout for other spirits?' a croaky voice said, startling me.

I looked to my right and a friendly face I'd not seen since childhood was beaming at me. 'I was wondering where you were, William. Mind if I join you?'

'Huh?' I was utterly confused.

'Sorry. Didn't mean to frighten you,' he chuckled. 'You look like you've seen a ghost.'

'Arthur,' I replied.

'Ah, you remember me.'

'Of course. But … what's going on? How are you here? You died when I was a boy.'

'All in good time, lad. Let's focus on you for now. It's your funeral.'

Arthur had been caretaker at the village primary school, which was a hundred yards down the road from the church. When I was a pupil, I'd thought of him with his white hair and wrinkles as being pretty ancient. Now, still as I remembered him but viewed from an adult's perspective, he looked to be in his early sixties.

I'd always been fond of Arthur. All the kids had. He was a lovely chap – almost like an adopted grandad to us all. He took care of much more than the school premises, fixing cuts and grazes with his tin pot of plasters and magic tube of antiseptic cream, and mending broken smiles with his endless supply of jokes and tall tales. Officially we were supposed to call him Mr Brown, but he'd laugh at us if we said that, refusing to answer to anything other than Arthur. We'd all been so shocked and upset when he'd died halfway through my final year.

I looked at him, sitting next to me in the maroon cardigan I remembered and the thick brown glasses with a plaster around the bridge, and I couldn't help but smile. 'It's good to see you, Arthur.'

'You too, lad. Sorry about … you know, the whole dying thing. It takes a bit of getting used to, doesn't it?'

'Yeah, you could say that. But I don't understand how you can be here. Lizzie, my guide, says you can only stay for a certain amount of time before you have to move on. Otherwise you—'

'Like I said, William, let's not get into that right now. You're the one with a funeral going on in there. Which brings me to a rather important question: what are you doing out here?'

'I don't know. I guess I panicked. I walked inside and ... seeing all those people there because of me, it was too much.'

'You should be proud. I've seen a lot of funerals at this church over the years – I was churchwarden at one time – and I can tell you that not everyone gets such a big turnout. You must have done something right over the years.'

I shrugged. 'Did you go to yours?'

'Yes. It was overwhelming. I do see where you're coming from. I understand that you left a young daughter.'

'That's right. Ella. She's six.'

'How's she coping?'

'It's hard to say. She's very up and down. One minute she's behaving like nothing has happened; the next, she gets upset or goes very quiet. She's finding her own way to grieve, I expect. I just wish I could let her know that I'm still here. I don't suppose you could help with that, could you? Lizzie's no use at all.'

Arthur paused before answering: 'I may be able to give you some advice later, but first let's focus on what's happening now. Are you sure you wouldn't rather be in the church with Ella than out here with me?'

'Um, yeah. I should be, but the door's shut. I can't get in.'

'Don't worry about that.' Arthur squeezed my hand and I was back inside, sitting on a pew next to Ella. Astonished, I looked around and spotted Arthur standing at the back, near the door, a gentle smile on his face.

48

'Hello, darling,' I whispered to my daughter. She was staring stoically at the front of the church, where my sister was climbing the steps of the pulpit, a crumpled piece of paper in one hand.

'I wanted to say a few words about my little brother,' she said, her voice faltering. 'I loved him very much. I hope he knew that. I still can't take in the idea that he's gone. It seems so cruel. So unfair.' She took a deep breath. 'Will was the best brother anyone could ever ask for. He was a wonderful son to our parents and an incredible father to his beautiful daughter. He did such an amazing job of bringing Ella up as a single father, even while he was consumed by grief over the loss of his beloved wife, Alice. He gave up a high-flying job in London to focus on raising Ella and he never looked back. He loved every second he spent with her. She was his life; she brought him so much joy. It's that little girl who needs us all right now. As Will's family and friends, we owe it to him – each and every one of us – to give her as much of our love and care as we can.'

All eyes were on Ella, who was staring at the ground, ashen-faced. One of her hands was tightly wrapped around Mum's left thumb; the other was clenched into a tiny white fist. Listening to the eulogy made me feel uncomfortable. I desperately wanted to leave, but seeing my little girl struggling to cope, I knew that wasn't possible. 'Come on, Ella,' I whispered into her ear. 'You're doing great.'

I looked over at Arthur but couldn't catch his eye, as he was staring intently at the pulpit from which my sister was still speaking.

'As awful as it is that my brother is dead, I think it's important that we all take a moment today to reflect on the happy memories we have of him. That's what he'd want us to remember; not the terrible way that he was taken from us. We need to celebrate his life as well as mourn his death. I'd like to share one of my own memories with you and then we'll have a minute's silence for you each to think back to some of your own.'

Lauren cleared her throat and took another deep breath before continuing. 'A lot of my favourite memories of Will are from our childhood. When I was considering which one to mention here, there were so many it was hard to choose. But one story kept coming to mind. My first thought was that it was too silly to repeat at a funeral, but – well – I decided Will would have liked it. It always made him giggle.

'We were away on holiday with Mum and Dad one summer. I think I was twelve, which would have made Will ten. We were staying in a caravan in France and we'd both just been to the campsite shop to spend our pocket money. I'd bought some French magazine I'd never be able to read and he'd got some sweets. Back at the caravan, where Mum and Dad had unwisely left us alone for half an hour, I was trying to persuade him to give me a couple of his orange Tic Tacs. He said I could have one if I closed my eyes and opened my mouth. Foolishly I did, upon which he promptly stuck one up each of my nostrils.'

She smiled as there was a rumble of laughter from the pews. 'Charming, I know. That was the kind of prank my mischievous brother used to love playing on me. I, of course, went mad, panicking when I couldn't dislodge the sweets and threatening all sorts in retaliation. The two of us spent ages extracting them from my nose with a hand mirror and pair of tweezers. You'd be surprised what a good fit those Tic Tacs were. One was particularly wedged in, but eventually we got it out. I agreed not to tell Mum and Dad; the cost of my silence was the rest of his sweets and a quarter of his holiday pocket money. For years afterwards, if Will and I ever fell out about something, he'd always buy me a pack of orange Tic Tacs to make things up between us. It never failed to work.'

She reached inside a pocket and pulled out a pack of the tiny sweets, shaking it into the microphone. 'Now it's my turn. Will, I'm sorry. Sorry I've not been around much for the last few years. Sorry I've not been a better sister. I love you so much, now and forever.'

'I love you too, sis,' I said in a shaky voice.

Lauren wiped away a tear. 'Now let's have that minute's silence for you all to dwell on your own fond memories of Will.'

My sister remained in the pulpit while the sixty seconds ticked away and everyone sat still in quiet reflection. Then she said a simple 'thank you' before returning to sit next to Xander as the vicar took back the reins. For the rest of the service I kept my attention focused on Ella, whispering regular words of encouragement into her ear, hoping they might subconsciously help her get through the day.

Afterwards, it was on to the crematorium, a ten-minute drive away, although Arthur whisked us both there in an instant.

51

'That's some trick,' I said as we appeared on the front lawn. 'I could have done with that earlier when I missed my lift and had to get the bus. How does it work?'

He chuckled. 'That would be telling. It does come in handy, though. How are you holding up?'

'I'm okay. I felt awkward in the church, like I was eavesdropping, but I was glad to be there for Ella, even though she didn't know it.'

'Good. One final hurdle.' He nodded towards the chimney. I'd chosen to be cremated, like Alice had been, as it had felt like a better option than leaving my corpse to rot underground. Now I wasn't so sure. As I imagined my body – the last physical link to my old life – ablaze in a furnace, I felt distressed. It was tough to accept that I'd never need it again.

'It's just skin and bone,' Arthur said, as if he could read my mind. 'An empty shell. There's no part of you in there any more.'

'I know. It feels weird, that's all.'

'I didn't say it would be easy. Just to warn you, the crematorium service is often the hardest bit for your loved ones. It's when people usually say their goodbyes.'

I decided to change the subject while we waited for everyone to arrive. 'Earlier, when we met outside the church, you asked if I was looking for other spirits.'

'That's right.'

'Well, I wasn't. Not until you said it. But it's got me thinking. There weren't any apart from us. Not that I could see. How come? Isn't a graveyard the sort of place you would expect spirits to hang out?'

'Hmm, maybe in films. In reality, it's the last place most spirits want to be after their funeral. Who needs a constant reminder of their death?'

'Why were you there, then?'

Arthur smiled. 'I like to keep an eye on the place; the school too. I was responsible for them both when I was alive. I suppose I've never let go.'

'How did you know it was my funeral today?'

'A little bird told me.'

'Who?'

'Someone who cares about you and was concerned you might not cope alone.'

'Lizzie? Did she ask you to come?'

'You shouldn't be so hard on her. She only wants to help.'

'To help me move on. I've told her I want to stay here, but she's not interested. She won't answer any of my questions.'

'No? I'm sure she's doing all she can.'

Before I had a chance to reply, the hearse containing my coffin pulled into the car park followed by Dad's BMW. Arthur grabbed my hand and I found myself on the front pew of the crematorium chapel, staring straight at the curtain through which my coffin would soon make its final journey.

CHAPTER 7

I don't want to talk much about what happened in the crematorium, other than to say it was horrible. Arthur had been right to warn me about how my family might react. I'd not realized how much everyone had been bottling up their feelings so far – particularly Mum and Dad – until they came flooding out in a torrent of tears at the end of the short service in the chapel. As hard as it was to witness, I was at least prepared for it with Ella, Mum and Lauren. I wasn't expecting to see Dad cry. That sight caught me completely unawares. He'd never been a man to show much emotion and was usually the family's pillar of strength. So watching him lose control like that – so vulnerable, so human – was horrendous.

I don't know whether my body was burned straight afterwards or not. Previously, I'd worried that I might somehow feel the flames eating away at my flesh, but such fears paled into insignificance once I witnessed my family's suffering. Whenever the cremation did happen, I wasn't aware of it. I felt no physical sensation at all.

Arthur found me as the others were getting ready to head back to my parents' house for the wake. I was still sitting on the front pew, shell-shocked. 'The worst is over now, lad,' he said gently. 'How are you feeling?'

'Dreadful. Totally drained. That was far worse than I expected. Seeing them all like that, I can't help blaming myself for what happened. I keep thinking that if I'd not taken my bike that day, or if I'd left a couple of minutes earlier, or if I'd worn a cycle helmet—'

'Stop. Don't do that to yourself. It wasn't your fault. Sometimes terrible things happen. You can't beat yourself up about it. That won't change anything and it won't help anyone. Come on, let's get out of here. I'll take you to the wake.'

He made to grab my hand, but I stopped him. 'Wait. Is there any chance we could go somewhere else first? Somewhere peaceful where I can get my head together.'

'Of course,' he said. I blinked and we were back on the bench overlooking the churchyard where he'd found me earlier. 'How's this?'

'Perfect. Thank you.'

'No problem. Listen, I have to go now. I've got some business I need to attend to. Can you manage to make your own way to your parents' house?'

'Oh, um … yes, it's only a two-minute walk. But I was hoping to talk with you some more. I've got a million questions.'

'Another day. Give me a shout. And well done, lad. I mean that.'

'Thanks. How do I—'

Before I could finish, Arthur had gone.

'Great,' I said. 'Another one with the sudden exits.'

I stayed on the bench, enjoying the silence, for some time. My mind drifted back to Alice's funeral again. I wondered if she had been around like this – watching me grieve and beg forgiveness for how I'd betrayed her – or whether she'd moved on straight away. I still missed her terribly. I remembered the raw pain I'd felt at the time; the hopelessness and sense of injustice. Was that how my family were feeling now?

My pain over losing Alice had never gone away. I'd gradually learned to cope with it and the initial angry intensity had faded, but going through that wasn't something I'd wish on my worst enemy. It was caring for Ella that had kept me together. At the time, having to cope with that on top of everything else had seemed impossibly unfair. But that routine – that purpose – was what stopped me falling into a bottomless pit of hopelessness and self-pity. I realized that a part of my wife was able to live on through Ella. Her appearance and many little things she did reminded me of Alice: from the way her nose crinkled up when she laughed to the stubborn streak I could already see forming in her personality. She was an intelligent little girl too. I could picture her following in her mother's footsteps as a dentist. That or some other equally prestigious career.

I was surprised – and touched – to see Alice's parents in the congregation at my funeral. Margaret and Ron lived in Spain these days, so I hadn't expected them to make the trip. Mind you, they'd always been good about keeping in touch with their granddaughter. They made an effort to see her at least twice a year and gave generous gifts on her birthday and at Christmas. She would never be as close to them as she was to my parents, but at least they were still in her life.

The sound of a car starting up jerked my mind back to the present. I'd assumed everyone from the funeral had gone by now and I'd not seen anyone visiting any of the graves, so I wondered who it might be. I stood up and walked to where the car park was visible. A black Audi with tinted windows was turning round. It looked like the same car I'd seen lingering outside my house the other day, which bothered me. Instinctively, I ran towards it.

Hey,' I shouted. 'Who are you? What do you want?'

But the car pulled away before I could reach it. I continued my pursuit as it stopped to turn on to the main road, but again it drove off before I caught up. I watched it disappear into the distance. 'Damn,' I said. 'Who the hell is that?'

I headed to my parents' place: the roomy four-bedroom detached house that I'd grown up in. It was located on a quiet, leafy street full of similar homes, all built in the early 1970s. There were lots of cars parked outside and I could see the silhouettes of countless visitors sipping drinks in the front room. The front door was shut, but at the back I found the patio doors open and Dad lighting a large cigar with his friend Larry, who lived two doors along.

'The church service was lovely,' Larry was saying. 'A fitting send-off. Everyone said so. How did it go at the crematorium?'

'Oh, you know,' Dad replied, exhaling a thick cloud of smoke. 'As well as could be expected.' He'd regained his composure but had a vacant, exhausted look about him. 'Thanks for your help with the catering, Larry. Ann and I appreciate it.'

'You're welcome. Sylvia did most of the work, anyway. You'll let us know if there's anything else we can do, won't you?'

'Yes. Thanks. You're good friends.'

'Are you staying here tonight with Ella?'

'That's the plan. We'll be moving her here full time in the next few days. We were concerned about uprooting her so soon, but we've had several chats with her and she seems okay about it. She's stayed here plenty of times before and I think it helps knowing that her dad grew up here.'

'Poor thing. First her mother and now her father. No child should have to go through that.'

'I know. I'm amazed she's coping as well as she is. God knows what's going on inside that little head of hers.'

Larry nodded, slowly puffing on his cigar. 'It only seems five minutes ago that Will was that age, asking for his ball from our garden. He was such a polite lad. Always had plenty to chat about. Ella's the same, isn't she? Sylvia and I were only saying the other day how well she talks. She's a real credit to her father.'

'She is that.'

'Any news about what's going to happen to the, um, driver?'

'She's been charged with causing death by dangerous driving. That's good, as we had feared she might only face death by careless driving, which is less serious. But there's still a long road ahead. She'll only plead guilty to the lesser offence, so there will have to be a full trial. It could be a year before it gets to the crown court.'

'A year? That's ridiculous.'

'It may be less, but I'm not holding my breath.'

'Will she go to prison?'

'If she's found guilty. The top penalty's fourteen years, although I doubt she'd get anything like that. It would be four years at the most, I reckon.'

I generally tried not to think about the crash and the woman who'd caused it, because it made my blood boil yet achieved nothing. Where was she today when my body was burning? I wondered. But I didn't let the thought process go any further. Instead I moved inside, away from the conversation, and forced myself to refocus.

The dining room and lounge were bustling with people, which I found uncomfortable, especially since I was the topic on most of their lips. I darted into each room, carefully wending my way between bodies to avoid getting repelled, but Ella was nowhere to be seen. I could hear Mum's voice coming from the kitchen, so I made that my next port of call. She was in there pouring drinks with Alice's mother, Margaret, and Larry's wife, Sylvia.

'Why don't you go and mingle, Ann?' Sylvia said. 'I can take care of this.'

'Don't be silly,' Mum replied. 'You've already done more than enough. This is my house. I'm not going to sit around and watch other people do all the work at my son's wake. It wouldn't be right.'

'I'll stay and help Sylvia,' Margaret said. 'She's right. You shouldn't feel like you have to do everything. I know how awful you must be feeling right now. I remember what I was like after Alice—'

'I said I'm fine,' Mum snapped, promptly bursting into tears.

As the other two rallied round to comfort her, I left to continue my hunt for Ella. It was too distressing to see Mum like that – and it wasn't like I could do anything to help her. I narrowly avoided bumping into Xander in the hall. He'd just returned from walking the dog and was busy hanging up his coat and changing his shoes. Sam started barking at me. He strained at his lead, nearly toppling my brother-in-law in the process. Xander, who managed to hold on to him with one finger, said something aggressive-sounding in Dutch, which I assumed was a request for him to shut up.

'Hello, boy,' I said to Sam, glad of the attention. 'So you're interested in me again, are you? How did you get here? I thought you were still at my place. Did Xander go and pick you up?'

He continued barking.

'Hmm. Unfortunately, I've no idea what that means, Sam. It's ironic, considering you're the only one who has any idea that I'm here.'

He barked again.

'Where's Ella, boy? I can't find her?'

Sam switched to growling.

'Charming. I'll check upstairs, shall I?'

Before reaching the landing I heard the sound of my daughter's pain through the closed door of her new bedroom. Of course I'd heard her cry countless times before – from urgent tears after falling and grazing her knees to crocodile tears over not getting her own way. But this was different. It was a terrible low-pitched wail of despair. Such a bleak, battered sound had no business coming from the throat of a child.

My parental instinct kicked in. I needed to take her in my arms and comfort her; to soothe her pain. Yet already, as I raced to her door, I knew that wasn't possible. If I could just get close to her, I thought, to stand by her side and whisper some comforting words. But no. A newly varnished door stood in my way, firmly shut and – despite being flimsy enough for me to have punched a hole in as a teenager – as secure as a bank vault from me now.

I lay down and stretched out on the light green carpet of the landing, putting one ear to the small gap at the base of the door. I could hear that gut-wrenching sound more clearly now, but also, thankfully, the quiet voice of my sister. At least that meant Ella wasn't alone.

'That's right. Let it all out,' I heard Lauren say. 'You've been such a brave girl, but sometimes you need to have a good cry. That's how you deal with your emotions.'

The crying continued for some time, but it gradually began to fade as Lauren's calm words soothed her niece. Eventually it was little more than a sob. I heard someone climbing the stairs and quickly rolled away from the door when I saw Xander approach.

'Lauren?' he called. 'Are you in there?'

'I'm with Ella,' she replied through the door. 'Give us a second.'

Xander waited silently in front of the bedroom door, oblivious to my presence as I got up from the floor and stood next to him. 'All right, big guy?' I said. 'Ella's not doing so well. Lauren's been comforting her.'

Lauren opened the door and beckoned her husband inside. She whispered something to him in Dutch as I slipped past. Ella was lying on the bed, staring at the ceiling through puffy red eyes. I knelt down next to her.

'My gorgeous girl. You poor thing. Today must have been hell for you. I'm sorry I couldn't get here sooner. I wanted to, but I was stuck on the landing. Are you feeling a bit better?'

No sooner had I said that than a strange thing happened. Ella jerked her head in my direction and stared straight at the spot where I was kneeling, her eyes screwed up quizzically. She slowly sat up in bed, keeping her gaze directed at me.

'Ella?' I said. 'Can you see me? Can you hear me? Don't be scared. It's Daddy.'

'What's the matter, Ella?' Lauren said after looking away from Xander and noticing her trance-like pose. She called her name again, more firmly, and Ella blinked twice before giving her head a little shake and turning towards her auntie.

'What?'

'I asked you what was wrong, because you were staring at the wall. What were you looking at?'

'I don't know. I'm not sure. I thought I—'

'Is everything all right?' Dad said, bursting through the door. 'We were wondering where you'd got to.'

'We're fine, Dad,' Lauren replied. 'Ella and I were just having a time-out. We'll be down soon.'

'Good. I thought I'd best check up on you, that's all. Are you okay, Xander?'

'Yes, Tom. You?'

'Fine. Thanks for picking up Sam, by the way. I appreciate it.'

'Ella?' I said. 'You could sense me before, couldn't you? Can you hear me now? Look this way again if you can.'

But she didn't. She gave no sign that she could sense me at all. The moment was gone; the spell broken.

'Come on!' I shouted. 'This isn't fair. Why can't any of you see that I'm right here?' I ran from person to person, screaming in each of their faces, waving my hands wildly in front of their eyes. 'Why can't you see me? The bloody dog can do it, for God's sake. Why can't you?'

Finally I knelt down again by Ella's bed, holding my hands up in supplication. 'Please, darling. Please give me something more. I know you could sense me just now. I'm so lonely here without you, Ella. I'm begging you.'

But it was futile. As far as my family was concerned, I was gone. I no longer existed.

I suppose I ought to have taken strength from the fact that Ella had sensed me again. It was, after all, my first sign of a breakthrough since the time she'd answered me in her sleep. For some reason, though, it had the opposite effect. I felt dejected, like there was no point in going on. The whole being dead thing seemed far more real – and final – now the funeral was over. The only definite in my future was Lizzie's deadline.

CHAPTER 8

THIRTY-NINE DAYS LEFT

I sank into depression and the days slipped by. Lauren and Xander returned to the Netherlands and Ella moved in with Mum and Dad. I went too and kept trying to get through to her, but my heart wasn't in it. I made no progress and, although I thought about seeking Arthur's advice, I couldn't motivate myself to find him. I felt paralysed. Then one rainy morning, when Mum and Dad had taken Ella to school and I was alone in my childhood home, something snapped. It dawned on me that more than three weeks had passed since my funeral. There were just five and a half weeks left now until my deadline. Then I would have to decide whether to stay or go forever.

Despite what I'd told Lizzie, I knew deep down that there was a serious choice to make. It was hard to admit, as I was desperate to stay here with Ella, but I knew I had to at least consider the idea of moving on if things didn't change. The problem was that I had no idea who or what I might find on the other side. Nor did I know the full implications of staying here for all eternity as a spirit. A paranoid part of me wondered whether I could take Lizzie's word as gospel truth. What if she wasn't who she said she was? That might explain her unhelpfulness. Then I recalled Arthur saying she'd asked him to attend my funeral. Perhaps I couldn't trust him either.

Stop being ridiculous, I thought, reminding myself of Arthur's support. He was the closest thing I had to a friend in this in-between world I occupied. I needed to contact him and, with the clock ticking, now was as good a time as any. So as soon as Mum and Dad returned home and I was able to slip out, I walked to the church. I found Arthur under the lych gate, sheltering from the rain.

'Hello, lad. How are you doing? I expected to hear from you sooner.'

'Hello, Arthur. I let things get on top of me for a bit, but I'm here now. I've got a lot of questions. Any chance we could have a chat?'

'Of course. Let's get somewhere a bit drier.'

He held out his hand and, as soon as I took it, we appeared together on a pew inside the empty church.

'Hold on,' I said. 'Why did you want to get out of the rain? Why were you hiding from it under the lych gate?'

'It's coming down quite hard, in case you hadn't noticed.'

'I had, but only because I can see it. I can't feel it at all. I can't feel anything. Can you?'

'That's an interesting question,' Arthur replied. 'The answer is complicated.'

'I'm in no rush.'

'No. I don't suppose you are. I assume you have other things to ask too.'

'I do.'

'Okay. How about I start by summing up all the important stuff? You listen and then, afterwards, you can fire away with any questions you've still got. What do you say?'

'That sounds good.'

'Excellent. I'm not sure how much you've already been told, but I'm guessing not a lot, so I'll start with the basics. When we die, our souls are released from our bodies. It's the same for all humans. What differs is where they go to next, which depends on what each person got up to during their life. Some are invited upstairs and some go downstairs.'

'Heaven and Hell?'

'Essentially, although those are just names. I prefer not to use them any more. The reality of what happens after we die isn't as simple as folk like to think.'

'How do you mean?'

'Well, look at you and me – detached spirits in the land of the living. Where do we fit into Christian doctrine?' Arthur ran one hand through his white hair. 'It's only the really bad apples who go downstairs. The rest get another chance, although I'm not the one to tell you about what happens up there. I'm as clueless as you on that score.'

'How—'

'Bear with me, lad. Listen now; ask questions later. The big difference is that the bad apples don't get any say. Their souls are marched away – and that's it. The option to stay here is strictly an upstairs thing. You've earned the right to retain your free will. Hence you get to choose whether you want to move on or not. Most do, of course. Otherwise, there would be spirits walking around all over the place. How long do you have left to decide?'

'Until December the twelfth.'

'That's generous. The situation with your daughter has obviously been taken into account. Anyway, I'm sure it's already been made clear to you that, should you choose to stay after that point, there's no second chance. You'll be stuck here for good.'

'Like you?'

'Yes, like me.'

'Why—'

'Later. Let me finish. You asked if I could feel anything. Well, yes, some things. Not like I could when I was alive, but to a degree. How to describe it? I suppose it's a bit like touching something when you're wearing rubber gloves.'

He paused for a second before adding: 'For you it's like walking around in a bubble. Physically you can't feel anything, yes?'

I nodded. 'Apart from when I interact with you. Or Lizzie, my guide. That's because you're dead too, right?'

'Exactly. The rest of it – that's because you're a visitor. You're here on a kind of guest pass, which only affords certain privileges. You get more freedom if you choose to stay for good.'

'So you can touch? You can open doors and move things around? You can interact with people?'

'Hold your horses. I didn't say that. I said I could feel some things, such as the rain. It's more of a reminder, an echo, than a proper sensation. I don't actually get wet or cold or anything like that, although I do find the rain a bit unpleasant. It sort of … itches. But I'm still a spirit with no physical presence. I can't occupy the same space as a living person any more than you can. Don't kid yourself. It's not like everything goes back to normal if you decide to stay. You're still dead; all you get is a taste of what you used to have.'

'But what about that transporting thing that you do?'

Arthur laughed. 'Impressive, isn't it? That's one perk you do get as a permanent spirit – and it does help with staying out of folk's way – but that's pretty much it.'

'What about communicating with people? You know how desperate I am to contact Ella.'

'That's a bit of a grey area. Officially, none of us are supposed to be able to communicate with the living, regardless of the permanency or otherwise of our status. However, that's not to say it can't happen. A lot depends on the living person involved: whether they're tuned into that kind of thing or not and how strong a bond there is between them and the deceased.'

I recounted the two occasions on which Ella had appeared to sense me. 'Does that mean there's a chance of something more?'

'Maybe. It's definitely something to work with. The fact that she's so young is likely to help. Children tend to be far more receptive than adults. Their minds aren't cluttered with the kind of junk that blinkers most folk.'

'So what next?'

'If you're a hundred per cent sure that you want to contact Ella; that it's the right thing to do—'

I held up one hand to stop him. 'Hang on a second. What does that mean? Why wouldn't it be? She's my only daughter. I disappeared without saying goodbye. First her mother and then me. She thinks I broke my promise never to leave her.'

'Yes, I know that. But don't forget that she's just said goodbye to you. If this works – and there's no guarantee it will – hearing from you now, from beyond the grave, will at the very least be confusing for her. You've had time to get used to what you are; she hasn't. How often have you told her there are no such things as ghosts?'

He paused for a moment, his eyes widening as they stared deep inside me. 'See what I mean? You'll be messing with the normal grieving process and putting her through a whole new rollercoaster of emotions. I'm not saying it's wrong. I'm simply warning you that if you go ahead with this, you need to do so with your eyes open. Be sure it's the best thing for Ella.'

At that moment I heard a rattling from the back of the church, which startled me. 'Looks like we've got company,' Arthur said. 'It's probably the vicar. We don't need him distracting us. Here, take my hand.'

I did as he asked and found myself inside a large wooden shed-like building. I looked around and saw a pile of cricket stumps and balls, a stack of hurdles, a rusty netball post and other sports equipment. There were no windows, but the gloomy day outside peeked in through two water-streaked skylights. Rain was beating down on the roof.

'Grab a seat,' Arthur said, gesturing to a pile of mildew-flecked cricket pads as he plonked himself down on a ragged deckchair.

'Where are we?'

'Don't you recognize it?'

Puzzled, I looked around again and the penny dropped. 'Of course. The cricket pavilion.'

That had been the somewhat misleading title attributed to the storage shed on the sports field at my old primary school. 'Do they still call it that?'

Arthur smiled. 'They do, although it's lucky to still be standing, if you ask me. The new caretaker doesn't creosote it anywhere near often enough. It smells so damp these days.'

'You can smell?'

'Yes. Sorry, I didn't mention that, did I? That comes back too if you stay. Again, it's not the same as it was, but it's better than nothing. It's a bit like having a heavy cold the whole time.'

'And taste? Do you get that back?'

Arthur laughed. 'I wish. No, that's gone for good, along with eating or drinking anything. The smell is the closest I get to food these days. Sometimes it kills me, getting a whiff of hot buttered toast or freshly brewed coffee. Bacon's the worst, mind. I still get cravings after all these years. I used to love my food. Not that it did me any good. It was clogging up my arteries that caused the heart attack that killed me. That and the fags, although I don't miss them at all – horrible things.'

'Do you think you still get to eat and drink on the other side?' I asked. 'You know, if you pass over.'

'I've often wondered that myself,' Arthur replied. 'I like to think you do; that you can eat whatever you like, whenever

71

you like, as often as you like, with no negative consequences.'
He licked his lips. 'Now that would be bliss.'

'So why did you stay?'

He fell silent for a moment before replying: 'I had my
reasons. But don't you think for a second that I chose not
to go because of what it's like over there. By all accounts
it's the most perfect place imaginable. I stayed here because
I had to. It's not something I'd recommend.'

'It's not all that bad, is it? You seem to be doing okay.'

He snorted. 'Do you really want to pass the rest of
your days watching the world go by around you? Haven't
you felt the loneliness yet?'

He stared at me, awaiting an answer. 'Yes, I do feel it
sometimes,' I replied eventually.

'It only gets worse,' he said. 'That horrible feeling of
being invisible gradually eats away at you. It's like
you've lost your identity, your purpose, your self-worth.
Many spirits over the years have let it get on top of
them and lost their minds. Those are the ones that give
us lot a bad name, carrying out the hauntings and so
on. Maybe I'll end up that way one day. I've come close
before now.'

'But don't you keep each other company? Don't you
have any spirit friends?'

Arthur shook his head sadly. 'Nice idea, lad, but it
doesn't work like that. Those of us that choose to stay
all have our reasons for doing so. You could probably
call them our obsessions. We each have our little corners
of the world and we rarely stray from them. Being a spirit
here is a solitary life.'

'So what are you saying, Arthur? Is your advice to abandon my six-year-old daughter and take the elevator upstairs without looking back? That's what you'd do, is it? This is bullshit. I thought you were here to help.'

'Calm down, lad. I wouldn't feel qualified to offer such advice. I'm simply laying out all the cards in front of you. I didn't mean—'

Arthur stopped mid-sentence. His eyebrows crinkled into a look of concern and his pupils flicked from side to side as he appeared to listen for something.

'What's the matt—' I started to ask before he held one finger up to his mouth.

'Got to go,' he whispered, looking backwards and then vanishing.

I rushed to my feet. 'Arthur? Arthur? What the hell?'

A dark shadow fell across the skylights.

CHAPTER 9

I didn't utter another word. I was too afraid. Someone or something was out there and Arthur's disappearance didn't bode well. As the shadow remained across the skylights, I could hear the muffled sound of movement on the other side of the pavilion's timber walls. I cowered into a corner, terrified without knowing why. Leave me alone, I thought. But it didn't. The presence moved slowly along the perimeter of the building, rustling here and scratching there, until it eventually stopped by the entrance, darkening the gaps around the doorframe.

I closed my eyes, gritted my teeth and held my head in my hands, half trying to hide and half bracing myself for whatever might happen next. When I opened my eyes again, I saw the door handle turning. Please, no, I thought. Why did you abandon me, Arthur? You knew what was coming and you left me.

The locked door shook in its frame for a few terrifying seconds and then the handle rose again. The shadow sank to the bottom half of the door and there was an irregular sniffing sound that seemed to go on forever. I heard more movement as whatever it was circled the pavilion once more, tapping the wall here and there as it went. And then there was silence. The shadow lifted from across the skylights and I was alone again.

'Bloody hell,' I said, standing up. I felt utterly exhausted. 'What the hell was that? What just happened?'

I expected Arthur to return, but after a few minutes there was still no sign of him. 'Hello, Arthur, can you hear me?' I called. 'It's safe to come back. You do realize that I can't get out of here by myself, don't you?'

But he didn't return.

A bell rang outside and, a few minutes later, I could hear the sound of children playing. I walked over to the door and peered through a crack. I could just about make out the schoolyard and a blur of different coloured coats running to and fro. It made me think of Ella. Was it also break time at her school? Would she be playing with her friends or standing alone? The former, I hoped, but her teacher had told Mum and Dad that she'd become introverted since my death. They had discussed moving her here now that she was living at their house, but they'd decided not to, fearing she might struggle to make new friends in her current state of mind.

What are the chances of anyone coming in here today? I wondered, staring at the locked door. Not likely at this time of year, as most of the equipment I could see lying around was for summer sports.

I called Arthur again, but there was still no response, which left me with only one option. I looked up through the skylights. 'Lizzie? Are you around? I'm in a fix. I need your help.'

'You called,' a voice said from behind me.

I turned to face my guide. 'Hi, Lizzie. Thanks for coming. I was afraid you might not bother after last time.'

'That's water under the bridge,' she said with a dismissive wave of her hand. 'What can I do for you?'

'Um, well, I need some help getting out of here.'

She scanned the pavilion. 'I see. How did you get yourself trapped in this strange little hut?'

'Long story. Arthur brought me here and then got called away.'

'Arthur?'

'Yes. Arthur Brown. You know, from my funeral.'

She gave me a blank look. 'You've lost me. Anyhow, let's get you home.'

She tapped my shoulder and we both appeared on my parents' empty driveway. 'How's that?'

'Perfect. Thanks a million.'

'Would you like me to let you inside the house too? It looks like no one's home.'

'That would be wonderf—'

Another tap on my shoulder and we were inside, sitting together on the sofa.

'How's living here working out, William?'

'Fine. My place is empty and will be up for sale soon. I go where Ella goes.'

'Are you keeping an eye on the clock?'

'What do you mean?'

'The deadline – for your grace period.'

'I've got thirty-nine days left, I believe.'

She raised an eyebrow. 'Good. I see you are keeping track. Any thoughts or questions?'

'What's the point? You never give me a straight answer.'

'That's not true. I tell you what I can. And I did just drop everything to rescue you.'

'Sorry, I didn't mean to snap. It was a bit hairy back there before you arrived, that's all.'

'Because you couldn't get out?'

I contemplated telling her about the strange presence that had scared me so much, but I decided against it, especially as she was denying any knowledge of Arthur. I felt like I ought to discuss it with him first. He might have left me there, but he had been a big help beforehand. I still hoped to get more information from him about communicating with Ella. I also had a feeling there was something not quite right about what had happened. Had Arthur got himself into some kind of trouble? If so, I didn't want to make it worse for him by telling the wrong person. So I kept quiet. 'Yes. That's right.'

'Okay,' she said slowly, her eyes scrutinizing mine. 'That was all?'

'Uh-huh. I've never been good in enclosed spaces.'

'I see. And do you feel any closer to moving on yet – now the funeral is out of the way? You don't have to wait until the deadline. I can come for you any time you like. To be honest, I was hoping that might be what you wanted now.'

'I've told you: I want to stay with my daughter. How can you not understand that? You've never been a parent, have you?'

Lizzie shook her head.

'I didn't think so. How old did you say you were when you died?'

'I was twenty-seven.'

'Right. And wasn't there anyone you didn't want to leave behind: a husband or a boyfriend perhaps?'

'No one serious. I was never very lucky in love.'

'What about your mum and dad; a brother or sister maybe?'

'Sure. I left my parents and a younger brother. Friends too. But it never occurred to me to stay.'

'Your situation was very different to mine,' I said. 'Maybe that's part of the problem here.'

'You need to focus on what's important, William. I died a long time ago and I've been a guide for many years since then. I've been in this situation a lot of times before with all sorts of different people. I understand how difficult it can be to part with loved ones. I feel your pain, whether you believe that or not. But I also know what's best for you and for Ella – and this isn't it.'

'We'll have to agree to disagree about that,' I told her.

Three days later I went looking for Arthur. I was surprised he hadn't contacted me after abandoning me like he had. So when I found him leaning casually against the church entrance, as if he didn't have a care in the world, I saw red.

'There you are,' I snapped. 'Remember me? The guy you left stranded. The guy you threw to the wolves.'

He turned, startled. 'W-w-william,' he stuttered. 'I meant to come and see you.'

'Really? So why didn't you? For all you knew, I could have still been stuck in the cricket pavilion.'

'No, that's not true. I came back to get you, but you'd already gone.'

'Why the hell did you leave me there in the first place? And what on earth was that thing you were running away from? It scared me out of my wits.'

Arthur's eyes widened. 'There was something there?'

'Oh, don't give me that. You knew it was coming. That's why you left.'

'Did you see it?'

I shook my head. 'It circled around outside for a while. It even sniffed at the door, but then it left, like it couldn't find whatever, or whoever, it was looking for. It was terrifying. What was it? You must know.'

Arthur was bent forward, his head cradled in his right hand. After a short silence, he looked up at me. 'Some kind of enforcer, I suppose. It wouldn't have harmed you, though. That's why I left you. It was only after me. I wasn't supposed to be talking to you. I shouldn't be now either.'

'What? Why not?'

'Permanent spirits are forbidden from communicating with temporary spirits.'

'I don't understand.'

He shrugged. 'I don't make the rules. I just break them. Well, not usually, but when Lizzie asked for my help, I said I'd do what I could. Especially since you and I already knew each other.'

'When I mentioned you to Lizzie, she claimed not to know you.'

'She has to say that, lad, to protect herself. It's best you don't discuss me with her. Don't you worry, though, she knows me well enough. If it wasn't for her covering my tracks, I'd have been caught by now.'

'Is that what nearly happened at the pavilion?'

Arthur nodded.

'And what would your punishment be?'

'Nothing good.'

'But what's so awful about the two of us talking?'

'They want you to pass over. That's what your guide is there for: to lead you across to the other side. They don't want you getting mixed messages. They don't want me trying to convince you to stay.'

'Or helping me to get through to my daughter.'

'Exactly.'

'So why did Lizzie involve you? Doesn't she want me to pass over?'

'Oh, she wants that more than anything. She just realizes you need to find your own way there.'

'Does that mean you'll help me make contact with Ella? The last thing I want is to get you into trouble, but I need to know. I need to try.'

Arthur closed his eyes for a moment before replying. 'Okay. I think we'll be all right for a little while. Are you sure this is what you want?'

'I'm sure.'

'Then you'd better have a seat.'

As I watched Mum read Ella a bedtime story that evening, I felt excited and scared. Arthur's words of advice were running through my head. I was desperate to try them out. But what if they didn't work? What then?

'Right. That's it for tonight,' Mum said, putting down *Kitty Power*, a novel about three superhero kittens.

Ella had loved cats for as long as I could remember. She was always finding one to stroke and she'd amassed quite a collection of feline-themed books and toys. Although she'd begged me countless times to let her have a cat of her own, I'd always said no, not wanting the hassle. I'd have probably given in eventually; it saddened me to think that I'd never get the chance now.

'Can I not have just one more chapter? Pleeease, Nana.'

'No, darling. You said that after the last one. It's time to sleep.'

'Oh, go on. Grandad always lets me.'

'That's because he's a soft touch and you've got him wrapped around your little finger. No, Ella. I mean it. Time for bed now. You've got school tomorrow.'

'Can I go to the toilet first?'

'Do you really need to?'

Ella nodded.

'Go on then. But be quick.'

'Will you come with me, Nana?'

I stood quietly by the window, peering outside through a crack in the curtains, as they disappeared to the bathroom together. It wasn't long until they returned. Mum gave her a kiss and disappeared downstairs to fetch Dad.

'Goodnight, princess,' he said after hefting his bulky frame up the stairs.

'Yuk!' Ella said as he leaned over to give her a kiss. 'You stink.'

'Charming,' he replied. 'Sorry. I've just been outside for a smoke.'

'You shouldn't do that, Grandad. Mrs Afzal says smoking is really bad for you and only stupid people do it.'

Dad chuckled. 'She's right, love. I'm a silly old man who should know better. It's hard to stop, though, once you've started. Make sure you never start.'

'I won't. It's disgusting.'

'Good girl.'

An anxious look appeared on Ella's face. 'What was that?'

Dad looked confused. 'What was what?'

'That noise. Like a knocking sound. There it is again.'

'Oh,' he replied, wrapping a large arm around his grand-daughter. 'That's just the central heating, love. The pipes can be noisy as they get hot and cold. They always have. I hardly notice it any more. It's nothing to worry about, honestly.'

'It's not bats?'

'Bats? Of course not. Why would you think that?'

'It was in a programme I saw on telly. This girl found them in her loft.'

He raised one eyebrow. 'I see. Well, you shouldn't be watching programmes like that. Anyhow, listen, I was in the loft the other day. There's plenty of old junk up there, but nothing else. Definitely no bats.'

'Promise?'

'Cross my heart.'

'Thanks, Grandad.'

'No problem. Okay now?'

Ella nodded and he tucked her in before heading for the door. 'Sleep tight.'

'Don't forget the bugs, Grandad.'

'Of course. Sorry. Don't let the bedbugs bite.'

'I won't. Grandad?'

'Yes.'

'You won't turn the landing light off, will you?'

'No, love. Of course not. Sweet dreams.'

I'd decided to leave it for a couple of hours, to ensure she was in a deep enough sleep, but the waiting was hell. To kill time, I hung around in the lounge with my parents, who were sitting together on the couch watching TV.

At one point I saw Mum try to snuggle into Dad, only for him to push her gently away. 'Sorry, love. Do you mind not doing that? I'm feeling a bit stiff today.'

'Why's that?' she asked.

'I don't know. Probably moving Ella's stuff the other day.' Dad erupted into a smoker's coughing fit.

'Are you all right, Tom?' Mum asked as Dad continued to hack up his lungs. 'Maybe it's time you knocked the smoking on the head. There are all sorts of new ways of giving up, you know. They said on the radio—'

'No, thanks,' Dad spluttered. He took a large swig from a glass of whisky – one of his expensive single malts, no doubt – before adding: 'I've got a heavy cold, that's all. I'm as fit as a fiddle.'

Eventually, after barely taking my eyes off the silver carriage clock on the mantelpiece, I decided enough time had passed. It wasn't quite as long as I'd planned, but I couldn't wait any more. I climbed the stairs back to Ella's bedroom. Then I strode to the foot of her bed.

CHAPTER 10

THIRTY-SIX DAYS LEFT

'Ella?' I whispered.

No response, but that was hardly a surprise. She wouldn't have been able to hear me even if she was still awake. I desperately hoped that might change tonight. But Arthur had warned me it might take some time. 'It's a gradual process,' he'd said. 'Think of it like tuning a radio into a station with a weak signal. You need a steady hand and plenty of patience.'

He had made much of the radio analogy, claiming it was all about focusing Ella's brainwaves on the right frequency to see and hear me. 'You're still here, lad. You know that and I know that. Even your parents' dog knows that. The problem is that you're on a slightly different plane of exist-ence, which is beyond most human folk's perception. The spirit level, I call it. People sometimes get a glimpse of it, usually at moments of heightened emotion or when they're not fully conscious. That's probably what happened with Ella, which is a good start. Now you've got to get her locked on.'

'So what do I do?' I asked.

'The best starting point I know of is sleep. That's when the mind is most receptive.'

'You're saying I should talk to her when she's asleep? I've done that plenty already, but there's been no progress since that one time she said goodnight.'

'Oh, I'm talking about much more than speaking to her. You need to get yourself into one of her dreams.'

Arthur's words still fresh in my mind, I peered over the bed to see whether Ella was asleep. She seemed to be. She hadn't moved for a while and her breathing was deep and steady. She was curled up on her side, face to the wall. Kitten, her favourite soft toy, was squeezed under her left arm. I crept up to the side of the bed and leaned over to get a closer look at her face. Her eyes were shut and the tip of her thumb was resting on the bottom lip of her open mouth. She looked so peaceful that I hesitated for a moment, wondering whether I ought to leave it until later.

No, just do it, I told myself. Don't screw up your big chance of a breakthrough.

'Please let this work,' I whispered.

Carefully following Arthur's instructions, I knelt at the side of the bed and placed the open palm of one of my hands on top of the other. I held them just above Ella's head, closed my eyes and focused on my daughter. As Arthur had told me to, I tried to blank my mind of everything else. I pictured Ella standing there in front of me, eyes twinkling and that gappy smile she'd developed after losing her first few milk teeth. I imagined myself ruffling her beautiful blond curls before lifting her into a hug. I thought back to some of the best times we'd spent together, just the two of us: her wide-eyed face watching elephants at the zoo; waving goodbye on her first day at school; playing computer games together. But nothing happened.

My arms were aching, so I lowered them and opened my eyes. 'Come on,' I whispered. 'This has to work. Don't give up so easily.'

I was startled by a noise from behind me, which turned out to be Mum peeping around the open door, checking Ella was asleep. 'Sweet dreams, darling,' she said with a wistful smile before heading back downstairs.

I raised my arms and started the process again. Ella, Ella, Ella, I thought. Nothing else. Blank out everything else. It had the opposite effect at first, bringing other thoughts to the fore. They teased and tested me as they jostled for centre stage. Occasionally one would succeed for a moment, grabbing prominence and flooding my mind with distracting images. But as I kept calm and continued to focus on Ella, she grew and grew in my mind until there was no room for anything else.

I moved beyond images and memories to emotions. I focused on the sheer strength of my love for Ella: an iron bond that surpassed anything else I'd ever felt. I promised never to leave you and I haven't, I thought. If only you knew I was here by your side, watching over you. If only …

The world appeared to fold in on itself, swallowing me whole. My stomach lurched. I was falling. I was upside down. I opened my eyes but everything was black. I panicked. Had something gone wrong?

'No!' I screamed. 'Help me. Someone please help me. This isn't supposed to be happening.'

I kept falling.

Down.

Down.

Down.

I could feel again. Things were brushing up against me as I tumbled. Plummeted.

Lower.

Lower.

Lower.

They made my skin crawl. Slimy. Wriggling. Alive? What was happening to me? Where was I going?

The darkness around me seemed to flex, to warp, to contract, to suck me in deeper and then to spit me back out. My stomach lurched again as I flew sideways, a cold wind rushing past my skin. I was terrified. I squeezed my eyes tightly shut and prayed for it to end.

It did.

I opened my eyes. It was still dark, but not like before. I was lying on a hard surface. There was a glimmer of light in the distance. As I pulled myself to my feet, the first thing I noticed was the cool, rough feel of the floor under my hands. It was some kind of stone. I could feel it, like when I was alive. I took a breath and grinned at the incredible sensation of cold air rushing into my lungs. There was a damp, fishy smell that shocked me at first with its intensity. I ran my hands along the rocky walls on either side of me and on the low ceiling above. Where was I? It felt like some kind of narrow cave, which my eyes confirmed as they adjusted to the dark and black became grey. Was that the sea I could hear in the distance? I headed towards the sound. Slowly the darkness lifted and stale air was replaced by a warm breeze. But it was a longer walk than I'd anticipated. More of a tunnel than a cave, the walls of my unfamiliar surroundings twisted and turned as the ceiling rose and fell. I had to lower myself to a crouch and wade through some shallow pools of tepid water before finally reaching the opening. Then I walked out on to a vast sandy beach. It was daytime and, although still in the shadow of a towering cliff, I could feel the intense heat of the sun pounding down like midsummer. Cornwall, I thought. This is like one of the beaches Ella and I visited in May when we stayed in Bude with Mum and Dad. The weather was just like this then – a mini heatwave – the beach awash with picnicking families and stripy wind-breaks, damp dogs and surfer dudes. Now, in stark contrast, the expanse of sand was deserted.

I stepped forward into the sun, noticing for the first time that I was in different clothes: a pair of light chinos and a short-sleeved checked shirt. I kicked off my trainers and socks, eager to feel the warm sand between my toes, and strode to the choppy sea. The waves looked perfect for body boarding, I thought, until I rolled up my trouser legs and let the outgoing tide spill over my bare feet. I gasped at the chill. It focused my mind, which I realized had been seduced by this beautiful scene when I ought to have been questioning it. What is this place? What's going on? I puzzled, scouring the scene with my eyes. Am I really inside Ella's dream?

And then I saw it. Way in the distance along the sand: a pink blur. A feeling in my gut sent me running towards it.

I was still a few hundred yards away when I recognized what I was heading for and it made me run even faster. It was Ella's princess castle: the play tent she'd brought to her new bedroom at Mum and Dad's and in which she'd spent so much time since my death.

'Ella?' I screamed at the top of my lungs. 'Are you there?'

Time slowed as I approached the tent and saw the door being unzipped from the inside by a little hand. Then my daughter's head popped out and she beamed at me. 'Daddy!' she yelled, racing out on to the sand in her favourite red and white polka dot swimsuit.

She jumped into my arms and I pulled her into a huge hug. Our warm tears flowed together as I held her soft cheek against my own and took a deep breath of sea air, savouring the moment for as long as I could. Then, eventually, I placed her down on the sand and knelt in front of her so we were face to face.

'Hello, my darling,' I said, ruffling her curls before pulling her into another embrace. With one finger I wiped away the tears from under her swollen eyes and looked into them, their pale green beauty shining through the redness and reminding me of her mother.

'I knew you'd come,' she said.

'Oh, Ella. I've missed you so much. You don't know what it's been like, watching you every day without you being able to see me.'

She screwed her face up, puzzled. 'What do you mean?'

'Sorry. I need to explain, don't I? Give me a moment to get my head around all of this, darling, and then I will. I promise. It's just so good to see you. And this place. It's … wow. I can't believe I'm really here with you. It's so vivid. Amazing.'

Thank you, Arthur, I thought. Thank you from the bottom of my heart.

'Just don't get too comfortable,' I remembered him warning me. 'Breaking through to Ella's subconscious is only the first stage. That doesn't guarantee anything once she wakes up again.'

Ella was staring at me, a quizzical look still etched on her face.

'What's wrong, darling?' I asked.

'Nothing. It's just—' She looked down at her feet. 'Um, I don't know. You're … different.'

'Different to what?'

'When we meeted here before.'

'In your dreams, you mean?'

'Yes.'

I took a deep breath, still relishing the feeling of fresh air in my lungs. 'There's a reason for that, my love …'

After I'd done my best to explain the situation to her, Ella fell silent. She stared out over the incoming waves. 'But Grandad said dreams aren't true. He told me it's not really you here.'

'Usually it's not,' I replied. 'But – well – this time it is. It's hard to understand, I know, but you said yourself that I seem different this time.'

She gave a tiny nod of her head. 'Does it still hurt?'

'Sorry?'

'You know. From the accident.'

'Oh, Ella. I'm fine. I'm not in any pain now.'

'Is that why there's no blood or anything?'

I shrugged. 'I guess so.'

'That's good,' she said, smiling. She hesitated before adding: 'Did it hurt when it happened?'

'Only for a moment. And then it was all over. Listen, Ella. I'm so sorry that I let you down. I know I promised never to leave you. And the thing is—'

'It's okay, Daddy. I know it wasn't your fault. Nana said it was a terrible accident.'

'I've missed you so much, my beautiful girl.'

Ella's eyes welled up. 'I love you, Daddy.'

I hugged her again. It felt wonderful.

'Daddy?' she said. 'Will you come and see me every night in my dreams?'

'I'm hoping to do better than that, darling. The thing is, er, I never really went away.'

I'd not explained that part of the story to her yet and she looked at me incredulously. 'That's not true, Daddy. Don't tell lies. You died.'

'I know. You're right, of course, darling. I did die. But I'm not lying. I've been following you around the whole time since it happened. I was there with you on the day of the accident: when you were waiting in school with Mrs Afzal. I was sitting next to you at the funeral. I was at your bedside tonight when Nana read you some of that book I bought you, *Kitty Power*. I didn't leave you. I couldn't. The problem is that no one can see me.'

'Like a ghost?'

'Sort of, but not in a scary way. More like a spirit.'

'What's that?'

'Um, well, kind of like a good ghost.'

'But I thought ghosts weren't real.'

'Like I said, I'm not a ghost: I'm a spirit. Do you understand?'

'Not really. But I am glad you're here. Would you like to come to Cat Land? There's this flying cat. She's purple with a huge fluffy tail – and she lets me ride on her back. That's how I get there. I'm sure she'd let you come too.'

'I'd love to do that later with you,' I replied. 'But we need to talk more first. Why don't we have a stroll along the shore? We can chat as we go.'

Ella nodded. She reached up, squeezing her little hand into mine and it felt fantastic. Choked with a rush of emotion, I had to fight to compose myself before continuing.

'If we work as a team,' I said eventually, 'I think we could be together in the real world.'

'Like before you died?'

'Sort of, but different. You won't be able to touch me. Not like here. So we won't be able to hug and things like that, but hopefully you'll be able to see and hear me.'

'Nana and Grandad will be happy. They miss you loads too.'

'They won't be able to see me. It'll just be you, my love. And, well, you won't be able to tell them about it.'

'Why?'

'Because adults aren't as good as children at under-standing new things. They'll think it's just your imagination

– and it might make them worry about you. It'll have to be our secret. Okay?'

Ella nodded. 'Like when the policeman told you off for driving too fast?'

I laughed. 'Yes, I suppose so. Trust you to remember that, cheeky monkey. The thing is, I've been trying to make contact with you for ages and, so far, I've not had much luck. There were two occasions, though, when I thought you sensed me.'

'When?'

'First time you were asleep; you said "night night" after I told you some stories. It gave me hope.'

She shook her head. 'I don't remember.'

'The other time was on the day of my funeral. You were in your bedroom afterwards with Auntie Lauren. I came inside with Xander. I said something and you stared at me, like you were in a trance. It definitely felt like you could sense me. Then you snapped out of it and the moment was gone.'

Ella clasped a hand to her mouth. 'That was you?'

'Yes. What did you see? What do you remember?'

'Um, nothing really. I just felt … weird.'

'How do you mean?'

'Sort of shivery. And there was a strange feeling in my tummy, like the butterflies I get when I'm nervous.'

'Try to remember exactly how you felt.'

'I told you.'

'That's fine, darling. You're doing great. I just want you to recognize the feeling, so next time you'll know it's me. Come on, we can do this. All I want you to do is

93

think of me when that feeling comes back. Imagine me talking to you like I am now. And then focus on something we did together before I died. We need to pick one specific moment, so I can think of it too. Any ideas?'

She screwed up her face in concentration. 'Um, I don't know. What do you think?'

I looked up and down the deserted beach, so reminiscent of our holiday in Bude, and an idea struck me. 'Do you remember when we built the sand cat on the beach in Cornwall?'

Ella smiled. 'Oh yeah. That was brilliant. We called it Mog.'

'Exactly. The pointy ears were the hardest bit. They kept crumbling away until I used stones to hold them in place.'

'I remember.'

'Good girl. That's our moment. When the time comes, think of it as hard as you can. I'll do the same and, if we're lucky, we'll have a breakthrough.'

'Then will I be able to see you again, Daddy?'

'I really hope so. I can't say for sure, as I've never done this before, but a friend of mine told me to try it. He was the one who led me here.'

'Who's your friend, Daddy? Is he dead too?'

'Yes.'

'What about Mummy? Have you seen her? Have you been to Heaven?'

'Easy, tiger,' I said. 'That's a lot of questions.'

A large shadow fell over me, instantly blocking out the sun's warmth. 'What's that?' I said, looking up and half expecting to see the flying cat Ella had mentioned. Instead I saw a large black cloud.

'What's what?' Ella asked.

'That cloud.'

'What do you mean? What cloud?'

Her hand fell away from mine and I started shivering. 'You can't see it?'

'Daddy, what's happening to you? You look like you're fading away.'

Oh, shit, I thought. This must be what Arthur warned me about. I'd meant to give Ella a heads up, so she didn't worry, but it had come sooner than expected.

'You can only be there for a short while,' Arthur had said. 'It'll feel longer than it actually is, as time works differently in dreams. But your daughter's brain will eventually identify you as a foreign object that doesn't belong. It will take measures to rectify the situation. You'll get thrown out.'

The darkness was all around me now. I couldn't see Ella any more; I could just make out the sound of her screaming my name. 'Don't worry,' I shouted, hoping she could still hear me. 'Everything will be okay. This is normal. Remember—'

My body convulsed. I felt that sickening feeling again of everything folding in on itself and swallowing me whole. I shot upwards – a human cannonball fired into the black unknown. Out of the darkness, as I continued to rise, a series of disjointed images and sounds flashed in front of me. First a grainy glimpse of Ella laughing as she played in a park with my parents and their dog. Then she was

95

hysterical as Sam ran out in front of a speeding car. Next Ella was alone in the school playground late at night. Then she was in the empty shell of her old bedroom. It had been stripped of all her things; she was standing there in just her pyjamas, pale and shivering.

'What is this?' I cried as the montage moved on to a stark vision of Ella running out of a dark cave, eyes wide with fear, followed by a colony of bats. The sound of their flapping wings was deafening.

Then nothingness.

I lurched backwards and forwards, left and right.

Up again.

Down again.

My eyes were glued shut when it finally came to an end. I forced them open and found myself face down on Ella's bedroom carpet. I breathed a sigh of relief. It was a fake breath again – a spirit's breath – and I immediately mourned the loss of sensation in my body. But at least I'd made it back in one piece.

I stood up and peered over at Ella's bed. She was still fast asleep, but her eyelids were twitching and her body was jerking about under the quilt.

'Wake up, darling,' I said, leaning towards her, my mouth as close to her ear as I dared. I repeated it several times, but she showed no sign of having heard me. She did, however, start to settle after a few minutes, so I thought it best to back off.

Looking around the bedroom, nothing appeared any different, which felt wrong considering the enormity of what had just happened. How long had I been gone? I wondered. There wasn't a clock in Ella's room, but her watch was on the bedside table. I moved to look at it and a wave of dizziness crashed over me. I tried to steady myself but was so tired all of a sudden that I collapsed on to the carpet and sank into a deep, dreamless sleep. It grabbed hold of me and refused to let go. By the time I finally escaped its clutches, bright light was streaming in through the open curtains of Ella's bedroom window. Her bed was empty and already made up. The house was silent.

CHAPTER 11

THIRTY-THREE DAYS LEFT

'So what now?'

'How long is it since you entered Ella's dream?'

'By tonight it will be seventy-two hours.'

'And nothing's changed?'

'Not that I can see. She still looks straight through me.'

'Not even a glimmer of … something? You know, some kind of recognition, like you had before?'

'No. Zilch.'

Arthur scratched his head. 'But you say the process of entering her dream went well?'

'Yes. Amazing. We were together and it was like being alive again. I could breathe. I could feel. I could hold her in my arms. I could smell her hair.'

'Ah, yes. Dreams can have that effect.'

'The thing is,' I said. 'It's made me want this even more than before. I had it in my grasp and, like an idiot, I let it slip away. Now I'm tearing my hair out. If only I'd not passed out like I did. I should have been there when she woke up.'

'Don't beat yourself up, William. It's only normal what happened. What you did – where you went – would be exhausting for even the most experienced spirit. It couldn't be helped.'

'When I was with Ella, I told her pretty much everything we discussed. But she's not showing any sign of remembering it. Was it all for nothing?'

'I doubt that. I suspect it's there in her mind somewhere. What we need to do is find a way to help her tap into it.'

'We? You mean me?'

'Look, I'm doing my best to help you here, lad.'

'Sorry, Arthur. I don't mean to take it out on you. I know you're sticking your neck out to help me. Is everything all right on that front? That, um, thing from the pavilion: it's not caught up with you or anything? You're not putting yourself in danger by talking to me now, are you?'

'Don't fret about me, lad. I'm being extra careful. You shouldn't have experienced what you did. That was my mistake and it won't happen again.'

'But I can't just forget. I—'

'It's not something you need to worry about. Seriously, you've enough on your plate. I'm sorry you had to go through that, but you weren't the target and you were never at risk. It's my problem – and it's under control. Concentrate on Ella. What's the next step?'

'Fine. Do you think I should try again? Should I go into another dream?'

'No. I don't think that would be wise. Not yet.'

Arthur and I were sitting on a pair of old deckchairs on a flat section of roof out of sight at the back of my old primary school. I'd found him watching the current caretaker polish the hall floor, taking great pleasure in criticizing his 'shoddy' work. When I'd asked for somewhere quiet to chat, he'd whizzed us up to this old haunt of his. It was a dry day, but all the people I'd passed in the street had been wrapped up to fend off the cold. It made my jeans and T-shirt combo look especially out of place. Just as well I couldn't feel anything.

'Why not?' I asked as a cluster of fallen leaves waltzed around the playground, the wind tricking their orange and brown curls into a false promise of new life. 'What have I got to lose? The clock's ticking. I need a breakthrough and I need it soon.'

Arthur, his hands bunched up in the pockets of his cardigan, gave me a pinched smile. 'I understand. As I explained before, though, you need to leave enough time so that her brain doesn't spot you straight away. Go in too soon and you'll have an even longer wait before the coast is clear again.'

'So how long would you recommend?'

'I'd give it at least a week.'

'From today?'

'No, from when you last went in. That was Sunday night, right? Today's Wednesday, so only a few days to go.'

'I'm not sure I can wait that long, Arthur. Is there nothing else I can do?'

'Not really, other than staying close to Ella and hoping that she remembers something. Memory's unpredictable.

It can be triggered by the slightest thing. Keep your fingers crossed that Lady Luck's on your side.'

Waiting was hard. Really hard. But I forced myself to do it. In the meantime, I stuck by Ella's side like a second shadow, hoping and praying that something might click. The only time I kept my distance was when she was at school. I went with her, but during lessons I stayed outside the classroom, knowing that she wouldn't like me watching her at work. I'd return to her side at break times when she was still, unfortunately, in the habit of wandering around the yard alone rather than playing with her classmates. Her friend Jada, a timid but nice girl who used to come over for tea at our house, would often try to coax her into joining a game. But Ella invariably declined.

I overheard some girls from the year above laughing at her and branding her a 'weirdo' on a couple of occasions, which made my blood boil. I hoped she hadn't heard, although I knew in my heart that she must have. Then on Friday lunchtime the ringleader – a plump girl called Kaylee with blotchy skin, short ginger hair and thick glasses – stuck out her leg as Ella walked past, tripping her over so she grazed both knees. 'Oops!' she said sarcastically. 'You should look where you're going, weirdo.'

'What happened, love?' the kindly dinner lady asked after patching up my daughter and wiping away her tears.

'Tell her, darling,' I said, still raging and wishing I could wring Kaylee's neck. 'Don't let that evil dwarf get away with it.'

But Ella shrugged her shoulders and muttered that she'd tripped.

'Are you sure that's what happened?' the dinner lady asked. 'You mustn't be afraid to tell the truth.'

'It was an accident,' Ella whispered, eyes on the ground.

'Ella!' I shouted, louder than intended. 'Why are you protecting her?'

She looked in my direction for an instant, a puzzled look on her face, but then looked away again.

'Ella?' I said. 'You heard me, didn't you?'

I repeated the question several times, but once again it was useless. The moment, fleeting as always, had passed.

By Saturday I was itching to go back into Ella's dreamland. I couldn't focus my mind on anything else. I was desperate to talk to her again – to iron out whatever had gone wrong the first time – but I still had another day to wait.

It was just after 11 a.m. Mum had gone to the hairdresser, leaving Dad and Ella at home. It was wet and windy outside and the two of them were playing Connect Four in the lounge. I was staring out of the front window at the waterlogged garden when a dark blur on the road beyond caught my attention. I looked up and could see a black car with dark windows crawling past. It stopped a little further on from my parents' house, but the exhaust pipe kept smoking. It looked to be the same Audi that I'd seen at the church on the day of my funeral.

'You again. Who are you?' I tried to read the number plate, having berated myself for not noting it previously, but it was obscured by a bush in next door's front garden.

All I could make out was the initial D3. I wanted to run outside to get a close look at the car and, if possible, a glimpse inside. But I had no chance of getting past the front door without someone to open it for me, so I decided to run upstairs instead, hoping to get a better view from one of the front bedrooms.

I was halfway up the stairs when I heard a crash and the sound of Ella screaming. I froze. My mind was racing, desperately trying to calculate what might have happened. I felt like some unseen force was sucking me to the spot; holding me there as clocks stopped and the world ground to a halt around me. Then I heard Ella again. 'Grandad!' she shouted, her voice brimming with terror. 'Grandad, what's wrong?'

I pulled myself together and rushed to the lounge.

Ella was standing over Dad, who was slumped across the floor. The coffee table was on its side next to him with pieces from the Connect Four game scattered all over the carpet.

'Oh my God,' I said.

My first thought was that Dad was unconscious. But when I reached his side I heard him groaning and could see that he was struggling to get back up. He slurred what sounded like Ella's name followed by: 'Hewpmeup.'

She stared at him, horrified. 'Grandad. What's wrong? You're scaring me. I can't understand you. Why are you speaking like that? What's wrong? I don't know what to do.'

'Hewpmeup. Pliz,' he slurred again. 'Filldizzy.'

'He wants you to help him up, Ella,' I said, desperate to assist her, although she still couldn't hear me. 'Don't

103

panic. Keep a calm head. You're going to need to call for help.'

Meanwhile, Dad had managed to pull himself on to the couch. He was sitting there, blinking, a confused look on his face. His hands were palms down either side of him on the seat, as if to steady himself.

'Grandad?' Ella said. 'Are you okay?'

He frowned. 'What?'

'Are you all right, Grandad?'

He stared at her in silence for a moment, blinking a few more times, before replying: 'Water.'

Ella raced to the kitchen. 'Back in a second.'

Dad lifted one hand to wipe away some drool from the side of his mouth and took several deep breaths. I knelt down to get a proper look at him. He still seemed unsteady and confused, but there was clarity in his eyes.

Ella returned with the water and held it up to his mouth for him to sip. I remembered her doing the same for me when I had the flu once and she enthusiastically volunteered to be my nurse. 'Here you go, Grandad.'

'Thanks, love,' he replied, only a hint of a slur left in his voice.

'Are you feeling better?'

'Yes. I'll be fine.'

My daughter's little face visibly relaxed. 'That's good.'

An hour later, when Mum returned from the hairdresser, Dad seemed normal. An hour after that he was out in the garden puffing on a cigarette. He'd explained away the episode to Ella as a bout of dizziness brought on by lack of sleep. 'I need an early night tonight,' he'd told her. 'That's all. It's nothing to be concerned about. You won't mention it to Nana, will you? There's no need to worry her.'

'Don't be so stupid,' I shouted at Dad. 'You shouldn't be asking a little girl to keep secrets for you like that. You need to get yourself checked out at the hospital. You can't sweep this under the carpet.'

I feared he had suffered a mini-stroke. I was no doctor, but I'd written a health feature about this during the summer news lull and the symptoms rang alarm bells. It was also known as a TIA, I recalled, although what that stood for escaped me. What I did remember writing was that although a TIA generally resulted in only short-term symptoms, it often preceded a full stroke. And Dad was a prime candidate for a stroke, what with all the smoking and drinking, lack of exercise and being so overweight.

I had to do something.

As Ella got ready for bed that evening, I prepared myself for another journey into the world of her dreams. I'd been weighing up my options all day and it seemed to be the only way forward. By Arthur's reckoning it was still too soon, but if I was right about what had happened to Dad earlier, that was a risk I had to take. For such an intelligent man, I couldn't believe how stupid he was being, burying his head in the sand like this. I wasn't about to stand idly by and watch another member of my family die before his time.

After the bath, stories and goodnight kisses were all out of the way, I stood silently by the side of Ella's bed, waiting for her to drop off. She was restless, tossing and

105

turning, unable to find the right position from which to fall asleep. Then she sat up in bed, eyes wide open, and started sobbing.

'Oh, Ella,' I whispered into her ear, silently cursing my father again for the stress he was putting her through. 'Don't cry. Please don't cry. I'm here, right next to you. Why can't you see me? Why can't you remember?'

Tears streamed down her cheeks as she let out all her pain, her fears and her frustration in a cascade of sorrow. I hoped that Mum or Dad might hear and come to comfort her, but the TV was playing loudly below and it must have drowned out the sound.

'God?' Ella whispered eventually after the flow of tears had eased. 'Are you there? I spoke to you before. You didn't answer, but ... I know you're busy.' She paused before adding: 'The thing is, I really need your help now. Something happened to Grandad today and I'm so scared. He made me promise not to tell Nana, but I'm worried if I don't, he might die – like my daddy did. Then it will be my fault.'

She started to cry again.

'No,' I said. 'No, no, no. You mustn't think like that. Not even for a second. Whatever happens to him, it's not your fault.'

I was so frustrated, I felt like I was about to explode. 'For fuck's sake!' I shouted, shaking my hands up in the air. 'What the hell am I supposed to do? Why can't she see me? This is so bloody frustrating.'

I turned and saw Ella staring at me, her eyes wide like two CDs. 'What is that? Is someone there?'

'Ella?' I said slowly, wishing I'd not used such bad language in my outburst. 'It's Daddy. Can you hear me?'

She continued to stare.

'I'll take that as a no. But you can sense something, right? Do you feel shivery, like last time? Butterflies in your tummy? Focus on it. Try to remember what it means. You can do it, Ella. I know you can.'

'God? Is that you?'

'No, darling. It's Daddy. Focus. Think hard what this means.'

Ella kept staring. I didn't once see her blink. Slowly, I started to move towards her; she sat back slightly as I did, a wary expression forming on her face. 'Who's there?' she asked, a sense of urgency in her voice now. 'Don't come any closer. You're scaring me.'

I stopped.

'It's all right,' I said gently. 'Stay calm. I won't move any further. But keep looking at me. What can you see? What can you feel?'

Remaining still and silent for a moment, I watched Ella. Her fast, shallow breathing was the only sound in the room. She frowned. I could tell from the darting movement of her eyes that she was busy thinking; remembering, I hoped. 'That's it, darling. Dig deep.'

I didn't dare to move any closer for fear of alarming her and breaking her concentration. Instead, I tried to focus my thoughts. I imagined beaming them over to her: hundreds of happy memories of the two of us together. And then I concentrated on that single memory – the one we'd chosen – of us building a sand cat. Praying Ella was doing the same, I pictured us on the beach in Cornwall, trying to recall every little detail of the scene, from the reflection of the sea in her pale green eyes to the candyfloss clouds in the blue sky above. I thought of nothing else. I lived in that moment.

And then she said it. Five simple words that brought me hurtling back into the present and changed everything.

'Is that really you, Daddy?'

CHAPTER 12

THIRTY DAYS LEFT

'You can see me?'

She nodded.

I moved towards her but stopped when I saw her flinch. 'There's nothing to be afraid of, Ella.'

'Are you … a ghost?'

'I'm a spirit, like I told you in your dream. You remember that, right? We had a long talk on the beach. You asked if I still felt any pain from the accident; I told you I didn't. You wanted me to come to Cat Land with you, but I never got the chance. I explained how I was still here. That I never left you.'

Ella stared at me, mouth agape but offering no reply.

'We chose a happy memory to think about,' I said, 'as a way to help you recognize me. It was building—'

'The sand cat,' she replied. 'When we were on holiday in Cornwall.'

Her eyes lit up – like a huge weight had been lifted – and suddenly my daughter was grinning at me.

'You remember?'

'Yes. I think I forgot. I don't know why, but I remember everything now.'

'Oh, Ella. That's incredible. It's me. It really is. I promise.'

'I know,' she said.

Instinctively, I got up and raced over to the bed to give her a big hug. But when I tried to touch her, I was hurled back into the bedroom wall.

'Daddy? Are you all right?' Ella yelped, racing to my side. 'What happened?'

'It's okay,' I replied, holding my palms out in front of me to stop her coming too close. 'I'm fine. We can't touch, that's all. I was so excited that I forgot.'

'Why not?' she asked, her little mouth turning down at the corners.

I shrugged, slowly rising back to my feet. 'That's just how it works. I've no idea why. How did it feel when it happened?'

She scrunched up her nose. 'Um, sort of tingly. Only a tiny bit, though. Are you hurt?'

'No. Not at all. I'm totally numb. It's like I'm surrounded by a bubble that stops me from feeling anything. How do I look?'

'Like I remember before, um, you know.'

'Before I died. You needn't be afraid to say it. It's a fact. So you can't see a bubble or anything?'

Ella giggled. 'No, Daddy. You do look a bit see-through, though.'

'Really?'

'Yeah. And aren't you cold in a T-shirt?'

'Like I said, darling, I can't feel anything. I've been stuck in this outfit since I died.'

I smiled at my daughter. I couldn't stop smiling. I was so happy. Finally I could communicate with her again. I could be a father again. It felt amazing.

'How did it happen when you first saw me?' I asked Ella after we'd been chatting for a while.

'Well I was really sad and scared about Grandad. Then, er, it was weird. I got this funny feeling like something was there but I didn't know what.'

'And after that I suddenly appeared?'

'Kind of, but I could only see you a bit at first. You got clearer and clearer.'

'Wow. I can't believe we've finally done it after all this time.'

Ella stifled a yawn.

'You're tired,' I said. 'I'd better not keep you talking much longer.'

'I'm not that tired.'

'Don't give me that. You look shattered.'

'Are you sure I'll still be able to see you in the morning?'

'As sure as I can be. It's not like I've done this before. I think you will, though. You're tuned into me now.'

'But no one else can see you?'

'That's right. You mustn't tell anyone about me and you should only talk to me when no one else is around.'

Despite further protests that she wasn't tired, Ella was asleep in no time. I stayed by her side and it felt fantastic when I saw her peek sleepily at me a couple of times as she was dropping off.

111

We had spoken a little about her dilemma regarding Dad, but I'd not wanted to busy her mind before sleep. I told her not to worry and promised we'd deal with it first thing tomorrow.

'Morning, sleepyhead.'

Ella grinned, still able to see me, thank goodness. 'Hi, Daddy. What time is it?'

'Oh, I'm only joking. It's not late. Almost seven thirty.'

'When did you wake up?'

'About an hour ago.'

'Why didn't you wake me?'

'You need your sleep, darling. It's especially important at your age. Did you have nice dreams?'

'Oh, I don't remember, actually.' She rubbed her eyes. 'I'm so glad you're still here, Daddy.'

I smiled. 'Me too.'

'Is Grandad already awake?'

'Yes, he and Nana are both up and about. After breakfast I'll help you talk to Nana about what happened. Is that okay?'

'Yes.'

'Good. We'll do it when she's brushing your teeth. And don't forget that you mustn't talk to me in front of anyone else. You'll need to pretend I'm not here.'

A nervous look flashed across Ella's face. 'I'll do my best.'

'I know you will, darling. That's all I ever ask of you. Don't worry. It'll be fine.'

'Morning, love.' Mum bustled into the room. 'I thought I could hear you. Were you calling me?'

'Um, yes … I was,' Ella replied, looking at me out of the corner of her eye. 'Is it time to get up yet?'

'It is. I thought it might be nice if we all went to church this morning.'

'Okay, Nana.'

'Good girl. I'll see you downstairs in a few minutes.'

My parents had taken Ella to the Sunday service a couple of times now. Apart from wanting to share their belief with her, I think they were hoping she'd meet some children her age. It would be nice for her to have some playmates nearby; it would also make it easier for her to settle in at the local school if and when they decided to move her.

'Why did we never go to church, Daddy?' she asked me when Mum was out of hearing range.

I smiled at how good it felt to be able to answer my daughter's questions again. 'We did go occasionally. At Christmas and so on.'

'But not like Nana and Grandad do. They go a lot.'

'I know. I used to go with them when I was little. I just grew out of it, I suppose. I found it hard after your mum died.'

'What do you mean?'

I heard the sound of footsteps. 'Later,' I whispered as Dad walked into the room.

'Good morning, princess,' he said. 'Good sleep?'

'Yes, thanks. What about you, Grandad? Are you feeling better today?'

He gave her a grin and a wink. 'Never more so. Come on. It's time for breakfast.'

I didn't buy it. He looked tired and his skin had a grey

tinge to it. The sooner we get him to a hospital, the better, I thought.

'Is he really all right?' Ella whispered as she put on her pink fluffy dressing gown, ready to follow him downstairs.

'I'm not a doctor, but I think he ought to see one to get himself checked out. Nana will know what to do once we tell her.'

'We?'

'Well, you. But I'll be right there next to you, helping you with what to say.'

'That's good.'

Just then I heard Mum cry out: 'Tom? Oh God. What's wrong?'

Ella and I looked at each other, panic-stricken, before rushing down the stairs and into the kitchen to see what had happened. I knew what we'd find before we got there.

Dad was slumped on a chair at the kitchen table, his back to the door, and Mum was leaning over him anxiously. Sam was sitting to attention in his bed, head tipped to one side and big brown eyes glued on my parents. He only looked away for a second when Ella and I walked into the room before snapping his attention back to the matter at hand.

'What's wrong, Nana?' Ella asked.

'Quick. Grab me the phone,' Mum snapped. 'We need an ambulance.'

As Ella ran into the lounge, I circled the table to get a proper view of Dad. He looked awful. His face was covered in sweat and twisted out of shape, his right eye and the same side of his mouth drooping heavily. He was trying to speak, but all that came out was an unintelligible slur. When he attempted to stand, his right leg gave way underneath him and he fell back into the seat.

'Just stay where you are, love. Don't fight it,' Mum told him as Ella returned with the cordless handset. 'We'll get help.'

She grabbed the phone, uttering a quick 'good girl' to Ella while dialling 999.

I could see tears welling up in Ella's eyes. 'You mustn't worry, darling,' I whispered into her ear, doing my best to sound convincing. 'Everything's going to be okay. And don't you go blaming yourself. This is not your fault.'

'But I—'

'Shh! You can't talk to me now. Not in front of other people, remember.'

She looked down at the ground in silence, fighting back the tears, as Mum told the emergency call operator where to send the ambulance.

'It's all right, Ella,' I said. 'No one noticed this time, but you must remember to be careful.'

She gave me a slight nod. 'That's my girl,' I said. 'Now you stay strong. Nana's going to need you by her side.'

As soon as I'd said it, I felt bad. It was a lot to expect of a six-year-old, especially one who'd already been through so much. 'And don't forget that I'm here at *your* side,' I added. 'I'm not going anywhere.'

The ambulance arrived in minutes and Dad was rushed to hospital. The rest of us followed in the car, which I managed to squeeze into with a little help from Ella.

It wasn't until Ella was in bed that evening that she and I got to have a proper talk. As I'd feared, Dad had suffered a full-blown stroke. We'd left him at the hospital after spending most of the day there. He was in a bad way, but at least he was now under proper medical supervision.

The stroke, which had been confirmed by a brain scan, had affected much of Dad's right side as well as his speech. He'd been admitted to the stroke unit and put on special clot-busting drugs, which they were hopeful would help, but it was too early yet to know how well he'd recover.

'You did everything right,' a doctor had told Mum. 'Time's crucial after a stroke and you got him here to us straight away, giving him the best possible chance you could.'

His words may have provided some comfort to Mum, but they made me feel worse, knowing that the alarm could have been raised a day earlier.

'You did really well today, Ella,' I said. 'You've been a brave girl.'

'That's what Nana said,' she replied, 'but when I told her what happened yesterday, she was disappointed. I could tell. I could have stopped it, couldn't I?'

'You mustn't think like that. Of course Nana's not disappointed with you. Grandad had no business asking you to keep quiet and it was me that told you not to say anything until the morning. You're not to blame at all.'

'I wish you could give me a hug, Daddy, like you used to.'

'Oh, darling,' I said, longing to be able to comfort her. Then I had an idea. 'Sit up a minute … that's right. Now move your bum forward a little more and keep really still.'

I sat behind her on the bed and gently moved my arms into position around her. We weren't quite touching; I was

116

careful to leave just enough space so as not to be repelled. 'There you go,' I whispered into her ear. 'How's that?'

'Nice,' she replied in a small voice. 'I love you, Daddy.'

'Me too, beautiful. More than anything.'

We stayed silent for a few moments, taking solace in each other's company. Then Ella started with the questions I'd been expecting.

'Daddy, is Grandad going to die?'

'No, darling. I don't think so. Not for a good while yet, anyway. We all die one day, but hopefully that won't be for a long time in Grandad's case.'

'So he'll get better?'

'It's hard to know with a stroke, but the doctors were really pleased with how quickly we got him to hospital.'

'Why did his face go all funny?'

'That's one of the things that can happen with a stroke,' I replied. 'Some parts of Grandad's body aren't working properly at the moment.'

'It looked like he was sad on one side, didn't it?'

'Yes, I suppose it did.'

'But he will be able to talk properly again, won't he?'

'Let's hope so. Like I said, it's too early yet to know how well he'll recover.'

'Um … what is a stroke, Daddy? I thought that's what you do to dogs and cats.'

'It's the same word,' I said, 'but it has a totally different meaning. What happened to Grandad isn't in any way related to stroking an animal. A stroke in this case means that the blood supply to Grandad's brain got cut off, causing some damage.'

'To his brain?'

'Exactly.'

'That's bad. We learned at school that your brain is the most important organism in your whole body. It controls everything else.'

'Very good. I'm impressed,' I said, not having the heart to correct her wrong choice of word. 'That's why he's having problems talking and moving parts of his body. It's because his brain's not working properly.'

'Will they have to put plaster on his head, like Jada had on her arm when that was broken?'

I stifled a laugh. 'No, it doesn't work like that with your brain. Because it's so important, it's much more complicated to fix than an arm or a leg. It's like a really powerful computer.'

'I know. That's what Mrs Afzal said.' She paused. 'But I still don't see why they call it a stroke.'

'They just do, Ella. Don't ask me why. How are things at school, by the way?'

'Good.'

'What about with Kaylee?' I asked, seizing the opportunity to bring up the bullying I'd witnessed in the playground.

Ella blushed and looked away from me. She didn't reply.

'I was there when she tripped you up at school the other day,' I explained. 'You ought to have told the dinner lady what happened. She shouldn't have got away with it. Has she done anything since then?'

Ella shook her head. 'I'm keeping away from her. She's mean. I don't know why she doesn't like me.'

'She jealous, darling. That's all.'

Ella looked at me like I was crazy. 'What do you mean?'

'Look at you and look at her. You're beautiful. She's a little—'

I stopped myself short of calling her any of the derogatory names I had in my head, realizing that wouldn't be a responsible thing for a father to say to his six-year-old. Instead, I explained as best as I could how children could be cruel to others to make up for their own inadequacies.

'She's a bully,' I added. 'And the only way to beat a bully is to stand up to them. You mustn't be afraid of her. You're twice her size and probably twice as strong. If she tries anything again, don't stand for it. If she pushes you, push her back harder. Do that and she won't try it again. Trust me.'

'How do you know?' she asked. 'What if all her friends are there?'

'That doesn't matter. If you stand up for yourself, they'll leave you alone too.'

I knew I probably ought to be advising her to speak to a teacher instead, but experience told me that this technique would be far more effective in the long run.

'I was bullied for a while when I was at primary school,' I said. 'This stupid little kid called Ricky Adams kept calling me "Stick Insect".'

Ella giggled.

'It might sound amusing now, but it wasn't back then. I was the tallest and skinniest in the class and it really used to bother me. Ricky called me that name at every opportunity, using it as a way to make fun of me. He used to trip me up, just like Kaylee did to you. Then he and his mates would laugh at me and he'd shout something like: "Stick Insect fell over himself." It made me miserable. But one day he pushed me too far. I'd got this new lunchbox. It was an *A-Team* one, which was this TV show everyone thought was very cool at the time. I was really proud of it. Anyway, Ricky snatched it off me and he and his friends started throwing it around. I went crazy. I stormed up to him, shouting what an idiot he was, and then I shoved him to the floor. He was loads smaller than me, you see, so it wasn't hard and he immediately started crying. Everyone saw him for what he was after that and I never had any more problems.'

I kept the pep talk going for a bit longer, hoping it was sinking in. Then Ella started yawning, so I told her it was time to go to sleep. I climbed carefully out of the bed and let her lie back down.

'That's it. You get nice and cosy,' I said. 'It's been a long day and you've got school tomorrow.'

'Nana said I might not be going. She said we'd see how Grandad was doing.'

'All the same, you need your sleep. You're a growing girl.'

'Can I have a story?'

'No, darling. Nana read you one earlier and it's too late now.'

'Okay. You're sure she's not cross with me?'

'Totally. Now goodnight. Sleep tight. Don't let the bedbugs bite.'

'I won't.'

I headed to the door. 'Where are you going?' Ella asked. 'Aren't you staying in here with me?'

'I'm going to check on Nana. Don't worry, I'll be back later.'

The truth was that Mum had been disappointed when Ella had told her about Dad's mini-stroke. She'd not said anything, but a look had flashed across her face. I'd noticed it just like Ella had. It wasn't fair, but Mum wasn't herself right now. She was in shock. Here was a woman who'd just lost her son and been thrust back into raising a young child at the age of sixty. Now this body blow. I desperately wished there was something I could do to help.

I found her lying on the couch, staring blank-faced at some period drama on the box.

'How are you holding up, Mum?' I said, kneeling in front of her. The answer was obvious. For a start, I don't think I'd ever seen her sprawled across the couch like that before. When I was a teenager, she was forever telling me not to do it. 'Sit up, for goodness' sake,' she'd say. 'You look so slovenly. If you want to lie down, you should go up to bed.'

She looked exhausted. Beaten.

So I stayed with her, speaking words of encouragement that I hoped might penetrate her subconscious. When the programme ended and the credits started to roll, Mum heaved herself up and trudged through to the kitchen, so I followed. She put the kettle on and let Sam, who'd been eyeing me suspiciously, out into the garden. 'You still don't trust me, do you?' I shouted after the dog, who replied with a loud bark.

'Be quiet, Sam,' Mum snapped. 'You'll disturb the neighbours.'

While Sam was outside getting his last exercise before bed, Mum sat down at the kitchen table. She stared at a plastic bag she'd brought back from the hospital containing Dad's personal items. She looked so alone; I wished she knew I was there with her.

After the kettle had boiled and she'd made herself a cup of tea, she let Sam back inside and sat down again at the table. She pulled the bag over to her and peered inside before pulling out Dad's mobile. It was one of the latest touchscreen smartphones, which he'd taken great pleasure in treating himself to and spent weeks, and many phone calls to me, trying to understand. Mum then pulled out another phone that I didn't recognize: a small black clamshell. She held it up and stared at it. After a while she let out a long sigh. Very carefully – as if the phone might explode in her hands – she flipped it open.

'Oh, Tom,' she said softly. 'What have you been up to?'

CHAPTER 13

TWENTY-NINE DAYS LEFT

I watched over Mum's shoulder as she opened up the text messages Dad had received on his secret second phone. I saw line after line of damning evidence.

> *Thanks for amazing night xxx*
> *How's my big hunk?*
> *Can u slip out later for quickie?*
> *Told her yet Tom?*

There were loads of them, dating back almost a year. I couldn't believe my eyes. I'd never have thought that of my father in a million years. He and Mum were a constant. They had the strongest marriage of anyone I knew. At least I thought they did.

The latest message – sent, as they all were, from a mobile number saved simply as 'X' – was from 10 p.m. last night. *Pls can we meet again?* it read. *Miss u sooo much!*

Mum, whose face had turned ice white but remained bare of emotion, flicked around the phone looking for Dad's replies. The Sent folder had been emptied, although she eventually found two unsent messages in Drafts. The first read: *Okay. Miss you too. Will try to arrange.* The second stated: *Can't do this any more. Please. It's over.*

Mum stared at this last message for some time before snapping the phone shut and putting it back in the bag on the table. She stood up, poured the cold remains of her tea down the plughole, turned off the lights and trudged upstairs.

'Mum?' I said, following her into the bathroom. 'Are you all right? You're not going to do anything stupid, are you?'

She ignored me, as oblivious as ever to my presence. But I carried on. I didn't know what else to do. 'Don't panic, Mum. There might be some innocent explanation,' I said. How stupid that sounded.

I watched Mum brush her teeth and remove her make-up. It was mechanical the way she did it, like she was on autopilot. Her face gave nothing away; her eyes were a void. I walked to the landing. What now? I wondered. There's no way I can say anything about this to Ella, but if I don't, how can I help Mum to deal with it?

I paced around the house for most of the night. I couldn't comprehend Dad's betrayal. I'd never expected that of him. Although the affair had clearly been going on for a while, I hadn't had a clue. Was it his first or had there been many over the years? He'd certainly spent his share of late nights at the office when he was still working.

124

And he'd never been afraid of going to the pub by himself of an evening.

My mind jumped back to a scene from my own past. Kissing someone I shouldn't have. The thought was intrusive and unwelcome – a time I wished I could forget – so I pushed it away before it had a chance to play out.

At least it explained why I wasn't angry at Dad, although I felt I should be. How could I judge him in light of my own behaviour? No, what I felt was more surprise and disappointment. But most of all I was sorry for Mum. She didn't deserve this. Especially not now. I worried how she'd cope and how it would affect things: not just between her and Dad, but also for Ella.

Then there was the identity of X. Who the hell was she? I couldn't picture Dad with his old secretary – a prim spinster who'd probably never turned a head in her life – and none of the neighbours seemed likely. So who?

'What's up, Daddy?' Ella asked me the next morning.

'What do you mean?'

'You look grumpy and I heard you talking to yourself before.'

'When?'

'Some time during the night. I woke up and noticed that you weren't here. Then I heard you on the landing.'

'Really? What was I saying?'

'I couldn't tell. I was too sleepy.'

'Sorry. I guess I got into the habit of thinking out loud. I didn't mean to disturb you.'

'That's okay. Did something happen to Grandad after I went to bed?'

'No, darling.'

'Good,' she sighed, running her fingers through the matted fuzz of her slept-on curls. 'So why are you grumpy?'

'I couldn't sleep and now I'm tired. That's all.'

Ella twisted her legs round to the side of the bed before standing up with a stretch and a yawn. 'What time is it?'

'Just after seven.'

'Is Nana awake yet?'

'Yes, she is,' Mum said, bustling into the room. 'Who are you talking to?'

Ella went bright red. 'Oh, um … Kitten. Sorry. I pretend she's real sometimes.'

Mum smiled. 'That's all right, love. I used to do the same with my dolls when I was your age. Are you ready for breakfast? You've got school this morning.'

'Am I still going? I thought you were going to see how Grandad's doing first.'

'He'll be fine,' Mum replied a little too quickly. 'They'd have called me if not. I can go to the hospital after I've dropped you off. School's important.'

Later, in the car on the way there, I whispered: 'Ella. Don't look over at me or Nana will see. Blink once for yes and twice for no. Will you manage on your own at school today if I go with Nana? I'd like to see how Grandad's doing.'

Ella blinked once.

'Good girl. I'll come and pick you up with Nana at home time.'

I'd expected Mum to drive straight to the hospital from Ella's school, so it threw me when, instead, she pulled her red Corsa up on to the drive of my old house.

'What are we doing here?' I asked, staring at the big For Sale sign in the front garden, then making a quick, carefully timed exit from the car, so as not to collide with Mum or to get shut inside. It was the first time I'd been here since they'd put it on the market. I'd tried not to think about it, but now it was unavoidable. A wave of sadness passed over me as I followed Mum through the front door.

Robot-like, her face still refusing to reveal any emotion, Mum made her way all over the house. She walked into each room and had a nosy around like a potential buyer. She tidied as she went: moving stray books on to shelves, smoothing the quilt on my bed, shutting the toilet lid and dusting the odd surface.

Much of my furniture was still there. I recalled a conversation Dad had had with an estate agent, who'd said it would be more likely to sell if it looked lived-in.

'Buyers are always suspicious of empty properties,' the man had explained. 'They think there must be something wrong.'

So apart from Ella's room, which was bare, everything else looked more or less the same as I'd left it.

As I followed Mum into the lounge, her inspection complete, I looked fondly at my old desk in the back corner. I pictured myself sitting there, as I had on countless occasions, hammering an article into my laptop to meet the latest deadline. Then Mum slumped on to the couch and started bawling her eyes out.

'You poor thing,' I said. 'That's right – let it all out. Bottling it up never helps.'

'Why?' she asked eventually. 'Why me? What did I ever do to deserve all of this?'

She walked over to my desk and picked up a framed photo of me and Ella. 'I miss you so much, Will,' she said, reviving the flow of tears down her flushed, mascara-stained cheeks.

'Me too, Mum,' I whispered as a rush of emotion caught me unawares. 'I miss our chats. I miss being able to come to you for advice. And right now I really miss your smile.'

Ever since I was a little boy, Mum had been the one I went to first when things went wrong. Dad was a firm advocate of keeping a stiff upper lip, while she liked to talk things through and deal with emotions head on. After Alice died, she'd taught me the A to Z of raising a little girl, as well as persuading me to have grief counselling, which had proved a godsend. One of the most powerful tools in Mum's armoury had always been her positivity, rooted in a firm belief that everything would turn out all right in the end. That had taken a battering of late and its absence was the most heart-wrenching thing of all. Mum just wasn't Mum in her current state.

Taking a seat on the desk chair, she ran her hands over what used to be my work space and closed her eyes. 'I wish you were still here, my love. It's not right for a parent to outlive their child. If I could take your place, I'd do it in a flash. It wasn't your time. You should still be here with Ella. I'm doing my best with her, but it's her father she needs.'

She let out a long sigh. 'There's me feeling sorry for myself when that poor little girl's lost everything: orphaned at six years old.'

'Don't be so hard on yourself, Mum,' I said.

'The thing is, Will, I'm in a fix. I learned something about your father last night and I don't know what to do about it – especially after the stroke. I know your sister will be here soon, but I wish I could talk to you. We grew so close over the last few years; we were on the same wavelength.'

She snapped open her eyes. 'Listen to me, for goodness' sake. I sound like a crazy woman, talking to you like you're still around; talking to myself. What am I doing here, anyway, when I should be at the hospital?'

She jumped to her feet and disappeared into the bathroom, re-emerging a few minutes later looking much fresher, although still a little puffy-eyed.

'It's not as crazy as you might think to talk to your dead son,' I told her as she locked the front door. 'You're doing really well, Mum. I'm proud of you.'

Looking over at the For Sale sign, my mind drifted back to when I'd first looked around the house. Ella was still a baby at the time and had spent most of the visit asleep on my shoulder, only to fill her nappy as I was about to leave. The vendor, who had a baby herself, was kind enough to let me use her changing mat and even to give me a nappy. I already liked the house, a typical 1930s suburban semi, which had been gutted a couple of years earlier and fitted with all the mod cons. But it was when Ella gave me a huge grin as I changed her that I made up my mind to buy the place.

The car door slammed shut interrupting my memories. 'Oh, you've got to be joking. Not again,' I said as Mum started up the engine and I watched the Corsa disappear down the road. I couldn't believe how stupid I'd been to get caught out like that.

A neighbour I vaguely knew walked past the drive with his chocolate Labrador. 'Morning,' I said automatically, but only the dog acknowledged me, barking a couple of times in my direction and pulling on her lead.

'Come on, girl,' the man said, tugging his pet away as he looked straight through me. 'There's nothing there.'

'Yes there is, actually,' I said, eliciting another bark. 'I'm here. You just can't see me. Anyhow, you have a good life. Our days of exchanging small talk are over.'

Wondering what to do next, I toyed with making my own way to the hospital, until it dawned on me that I had no clue how to get there. And it wasn't like I could ask anyone or go on the internet to find out. Returning to Ella's school seemed a better idea, but then I remembered how they shut all the gates after first bell. The only way in now would be through the front entrance, which operated on a buzzer system. I could wait around for another visitor, but that might take forever. Then there were all the internal doors I'd have to negotiate once inside. Maybe not, I thought. Besides, it could get complicated now that Ella could see me.

All I could think of was to take the bus back to Mum and Dad's. But rather than heading straight to the bus stop, I decided to take a detour. I walked back to the place where my life as I knew it had been ripped to shreds. I recalled the awful screeching sound that had been my death knell. I winced at the memory of the agonizing pain as I blacked out. And I wondered whether traces of my blood still remained on the road where my broken body had lain.

But when I got there, there was no sign that anything significant had happened, apart from a withered bunch of flowers attached to a lamppost. Not even one of those police witness appeal signs. My death had made no permanent impression on this busy road. The vehicles flowed by in either direction as they always had.

Then one car caught my eye: a silver 4x4 similar to the black one that had smashed into me. Ended me.

The fury was instant and all-consuming. 'Bitch!' I screamed. 'You killed me!'

I stormed out into the traffic and stood on the centre line, blaring out every obscenity I could think of, my arms outstretched like a mad scarecrow. Then, before I knew what I was doing, I ran head on into the first available vehicle. The white transit van, which had three workmen in the front and a copy of the *Daily Star* wedged between the windscreen and dashboard, drove on like nothing had happened. I was smashed effortlessly out of the way, like a sponge ball that had bounced into the van's path. There was no pain, but I felt a darkness envelop my mind.

When my brain – or whatever it was at the helm these days – rebooted, I was sprawled on the pavement like an idiot. The anger had passed and I hadn't got the foggiest why I'd just done what I had. At least it had clarified what would happen if I was hit by a moving vehicle. I knew from experience that travelling inside one was no problem. Apparently getting in its path was a whole different matter. Doing so appeared to have the same repellent effect as when I tried to share space with a living person, albeit with a bit more oomph. It was as if motion brought the vehicle to life, transforming a safe stationary object into something to avoid. Nice of Lizzie and Arthur to warn me.

Sheepishly, I picked myself up and walked towards the bus stop. It's good to be invisible sometimes, I thought.

CHAPTER 14

TWENTY-EIGHT DAYS LEFT

'Arthur, where are you hiding?'

I'd tried all the usual places – first at the church and now the school – but I couldn't find him. Where was he?

'Come on, Arthur,' I shouted up from the school field to the flat roof where we'd last spoken. I could see that he wasn't there, but I was out of ideas and starting to worry about what might have happened to him. 'I've got good news about Ella.'

I went to try the church again, which I was surprised to find had got busy in the short time I'd been away. The car park was nearly full and dozens of people were streaming through the lych gate up to the main entrance. Their dark attire and sombre expressions left little doubt that they were there to attend a funeral.

Ah, I thought. That must be why I've not been able to find Arthur. But when I slipped inside, I couldn't see him anywhere. The congregation, although substantial, was smaller than at my own send-off; I cringed at my pride about this fact. Popping outside again, I circled the building, but there was still no sign of him. 'Where are you, Arthur?' I shouted. 'I've looked everywhere.'

As I plodded back towards the entrance, still calling out to Arthur, I spotted two men chatting. They were the only ones left outside. One of the pair – a portly, elderly chap in a three-piece charcoal suit – scowled in my direction before whispering something to his companion. The younger man – tall and slim, dressed in a black trench coat with matching trilby – looked over at me and nodded. Then they marched inside the church, shutting the door behind them.

'Hey,' I called after them. 'Who are you? You can see me, can't you? What's going on? Where's Art—'

My mouth kept moving, but there was no longer any sound emerging. Baffled, I tried again and again to make a sound – screaming at what should have been the top of my lungs – but nothing came out. It was like I'd been muted.

Oh my God, I thought. This is a disaster. What if I can't ever speak again? How will I communicate with Ella? I felt a rising sense of panic but forced myself to suppress it. I walked to the bench where Arthur and I had spoken and sat down. I needed to think, so I could work out what was happening to me.

It had to be something to do with those two men. Somehow they could see me and, from the scowl, it wasn't hard to deduce that they were unhappy about my presence. Shit, I thought. If they can see me, they can probably hear me too. I'd never have shouted like that at a funeral if I'd known anyone was listening. So who or what were those men? And what had they done to my voice?

134

Waiting for the funeral to end and for them to come back outside appeared to be all I could do. So I listened to the muffled sound of the service going on behind me. It brought back memories of my own ceremony: Ella's little hand wrapped around Mum's thumb; Lauren in the pulpit, wiping away a tear. I wondered whose funeral this was. Then it clicked.

The elderly guy walked alongside his pallbearers as they carried his coffin towards its final resting place. At one point he looked nervously back at his companion, who gave him an encouraging smile. The younger man then peeled away from the procession to approach me.

'Can I trust you to behave?' he said in a quiet baritone.

I nodded and he took a seat next to me on the bench, removing his hat to reveal a head of white-blond hair, slicked back to one side. His hand touched mine for an instant and my voice was back.

'Thanks,' I whispered.

'I hope you understand why it was necessary.'

I stared at his sea-grey eyes, which beamed back at me with an unnerving intensity. 'I do. Sorry about that. I didn't realize. Please could you pass on my apologies?'

'I will.'

After it was over and all the mourners had walked back down to their cars, the two men remained at the graveside. I was close enough to see what they were doing but not to hear what they said. As I watched, the one I'd spoken to, whose trilby was back in place, said something to the other; he nodded before looking over at me and raising his right hand to his temple in an informal salute. I understood his meaning and waved back to say thank

135

you. I felt as though I should leave after that, not wishing to further intrude, so I stood up and started walking round to the front of the church.

Before turning the corner, I couldn't resist snatching another glance. The pair of them had their backs to me, but I could see that they were standing next to each other, perfectly still, faces up to the sky. The next minute, the guy in the trilby reached over and put his arm around the other man's shoulders. No sooner had he done this than a faint glow surrounded them. I rubbed my eyes to check they weren't deceiving me, but the glow got brighter and brighter by the second. Soon the two men were enveloped in a fierce, pulsating white light. I was mesmerized. Shielding my eyes with my hands, I fought to keep them locked on the spectacle – determined to see what would happen next. But it was too intense. I looked away for an instant and it was over. The light was gone – and the two figures had vanished with it.

Dazed, I watched a glowing after-image dance through the air in front of me, gradually fading away. I willed it to stay. It was so pure, like nothing I'd ever seen before. Just looking into it had affected me profoundly. It was as if my soul had been caressed; my doubts and fears cleansed. I turned towards the church and saw a reflection of my face – eyes wide and mouth stretched into a grin – in a stained-glass window. Was that what I think it was? I wondered. Did I just witness someone passing over to the other side?

'What happened today, Daddy?' Ella asked me later. Mum was cooking tea in the kitchen and we were in the lounge watching cartoons on TV.

'What do you mean?'

'Well, you didn't come with Nana to pick me up from school. And, er, now you seem a bit ... weird.'

'Oh?' I said, playing ignorant, although I knew I'd been walking around with my head in the clouds since the incident in the churchyard.

'Is it about Grandad? Nana said he was walking in the water or something.'

I smiled to myself. 'Treading water.'

'Yes. What is that?'

'Treading water is literally swimming in one spot. You move your arms and legs in such a way that you don't go anywhere. You stay afloat in one place.'

'Oh yeah. I've seen children doing that at swimming. It looks tricky.' Ella frowned. 'But what's that got to do with Grandad? Is there a pool at the hospital?'

'No, darling. It's just an expression. It means Grandad's stayed the same: he's not any better, but he's not any worse either.'

'Is that good or bad?'

'Well, it can take a while to recover from a stroke. It's definitely good that he's not had another one.'

I should have chosen my words more carefully; Ella's eyes stretched wide with panic. 'Another stroke? Would he die then?'

'He hasn't had another one, darling. I'm sure he'll be fine now that he's in the hospital getting the right treatment.'

'I hope so. I miss him.'

'I'm sure Nana will take you to visit him soon,' I said, my attention drawn to the TV as the volume rose for the adverts.

'Look, Daddy,' Ella said, pointing at a make-up kit in the shape of a cat's head, which was being fawned over on screen by a group of excited girls. 'Jada's got one of those. She says it's amazing.'

'Wow. That looks good,' I said, knowing exactly what the next question would be.

'Do you think I could get one, Daddy?'

'You never know. Maybe Father Christmas will get you one, if you're good.'

'But Christmas is ages away,' she moaned.

'It'll be here before you know it,' I replied, smiling to hide the sadness I felt as it struck me that I'd play no part in Santa's gifts this year.

Ella jumped back to her original question. 'So what did happen to you today, Daddy? Why weren't you there after school?'

I couldn't bring myself to tell her about the white light. I suppose I didn't like the implications of how it had made me feel. 'There's not much to it,' I said. 'Nana got into the car before I had the chance to slip in and I got left behind.'

'At the hospital?'

'No. I never made it that far. She stopped off at our house on the way to check everything was okay. That's when it happened.'

Ella's mouth drooped at the edges. 'Have they sold it?'

'Not yet, love.'

'I don't like the idea of someone else living there.'

'I know. Me neither, but that's how it has to be. This is your home now. You do like it here, don't you?'

138

'I do, but I still miss our house.'

'At least all of your things are here,' I added. 'Hey, guess how I got back?'

'How?'

'On the bus.'

She giggled. 'Really? How come?'

'Well, it would have taken me forever if I'd tried to walk. So I waited for one to stop, slipped on – no charge since the driver couldn't see me – and grabbed an empty seat on the top deck.'

Ella had always loved travelling by bus; especially if it was a double-decker and she could sit upstairs. 'You're lucky,' she said. 'I wish I could have come. I've not been on a bus for ages.'

'You'll have to ask Nana to take you on one sometime,' I replied, wishing I could do it myself.

Stop being so negative, I thought. It wasn't long ago that you couldn't even communicate with her. Now here you are, chatting away, and you're still feeling sorry for yourself. It was a struggle, though. Seeing that incredible light earlier – that glimpse of something amazing – had altered my perception. It had flicked on a switch in my mind that I couldn't turn back off. I wasn't sure I even wanted to.

'What's it like, Daddy, walking around and doing things when no one can see you?'

'You can see me.'

'I know, but no one else can. Isn't that weird?'

'A bit. Especially at first. I suppose I've got used to it now.'

'Aren't there any others like you?'

139

'Spirits? Of course. I've met a couple. They look like normal people to me, so I may have seen others and not known what they were.'

Ella threw me a puzzled look. 'Don't they look see-through, like you do?'

'No. But I don't see myself like that either.'

'Strange.' She paused before adding: 'Will I see them too?'

I shrugged my shoulders. 'I'm honestly not sure, love.' Up to now, it wasn't something I'd even considered.

CHAPTER 15

TWENTY-SEVEN DAYS LEFT

Mum was sitting at the kitchen table. Sam started a low-pitched growl as I walked into the room. 'You silly dog,' she said. 'Why are you growling?'

'Easy there, Sammy, old chum,' I added. 'I thought we'd got past all that.'

He eyeballed me and growled some more.

'Enough, Sam,' Mum snapped. 'Put a sock in it, for goodness' sake.'

It was then I noticed what she was doing. She had the mysterious black clamshell phone open in front of her. X's number was displayed on the screen and Mum's finger was hanging over the green call key. The pained look on her face – the result of Dad's betrayal – stirred demons within me; roused memories of my own guilt.

Then the phone rang and the pair of us nearly jumped through the ceiling in shock.

It wasn't the clamshell, though; it was the landline. Mum had brought the cordless handset through from the lounge.

'Hello?' she said, answering it after taking a moment to compose herself. 'Oh, hi, Lauren. How are you? Have you landed already?'

Ella appeared at the kitchen door as Mum hung up. 'Was that the hospital? Is Grandad okay?'

'It was Auntie Lauren, darling. She's at the airport and about to get a taxi, so she'll be here soon.'

'How many minutes?'

'Ooh, about forty-five, I'd say.'

'Goody. Is she going to have tea with us?'

'It'll be a bit late by then. I've got fish fingers and chips in the oven for you. They'll be ready in a few minutes.'

'Yummy,' she replied, grinning in my direction for a second before correcting herself and turning away.

Mum gestured for Ella to sit on her knee. She pulled her up and kissed her forehead. 'Listen, you mustn't worry about Grandad. Leave that to the adults.'

'I don't want him to die. That's all.'

'I know, Ella, but worrying about it won't make a jot of difference. He is very poorly, but hopefully he's through the worst.'

'Have you got a new phone?' Ella asked as the mobile on the table caught her eye.

Mum reached over, snapped it shut and stashed it in her trouser pocket. 'No, no. It's just an old one I was using for something.'

'I'll have it if you don't want it any more. There's a boy in my class who's got his own mobile.'

Mum looked horrified. 'A mobile phone? At six years old? Goodness me. Whatever next.'

'Don't be ridiculous, Ella,' I said, drawing a scowl. 'You're far too young to have a mobile and you shouldn't be asking for one.'

Ella was finishing a bowl of chocolate ice cream when the front doorbell sounded. Lauren bustled in with two large suitcases and a tired, anxious look on her face.

'Auntie Lauren,' Ella said, sprinting over to her and squeezing her tightly around the waist.

'My favourite niece,' Lauren replied, picking her up and showering her with kisses.

'I'm really glad you're back,' Ella said. 'I missed you loads.'

'Me too, sweetheart.'

'Where's Uncle Xander?'

'He's still in Holland. One of us had to stay behind to run the business.'

'Grandad's really poorly. He's in hospital. He can't talk properly. He got stroked.'

Lauren put her down, ruffling her hair. 'I know. That's why I'm here. As well as to see you, of course.'

You wait, sis, I thought. Dad's stroke's only half the story.

I wondered how long it would take Mum to tell Lauren about the secret mobile and Dad's mystery lover. I suspected she might wait a bit. Over the years she and Dad had often tried to shelter the two of us from bad news. When I was in my early twenties, for instance, Mum had gone through a cancer scare, although it wasn't until well after she'd been given the all-clear that she told Lauren and me. At the time I couldn't understand why

143

she'd not said anything earlier. But having my own child had opened my eyes.

As it turned out, Mum told Lauren everything later that night. She obviously needed someone to confide in. An hour or so after Ella had gone to bed, they were chatting over a glass of wine in the lounge under my watchful eye. Lauren asked Mum how she was coping; she burst into a flood of tears and the whole story came gushing out.

Lauren was as surprised as I was to learn that Dad had been cheating. 'Are you absolutely sure?' she asked Mum. 'Is there no other explanation? What if it's not his phone? Perhaps he found it somewhere or was looking after it for someone.'

Mum, her face still bright red and glistening from all the crying, slowly shook her head. 'She refers to him as Tom in some of the texts.'

'That's not conclusive proof,' Lauren said half-heartedly, clutching at straws. 'It's a common name.'

Then Mum explained how she'd also noted some of the dates Dad and his mistress had arranged to meet and cross-referenced them with the calendar. 'Several corresponded with supposed arrangements of his,' she sighed. 'Things he did alone, like having lunch with an old colleague or watching a cricket match.'

Lauren's face hardened. 'Oh.'

More tears flowed as Mum continued: 'It's the idea that he lied to me so much that hurts the most. I didn't think he was capable of that. I thought I knew him better than anyone else and there he was living a sordid secret life behind my back.'

'You poor thing, Mum. I can't believe he'd do this to you; to all of us. It's … disgusting.'

'I didn't know how to face him today. I delayed going to the hospital for as long as I could. Then when I got there, I stayed in the car for ages before building up the courage to go inside.'

'And what did you say when you saw him?'

'Nothing. He was asleep. I only stayed for a short while and left before he woke up. It's so hard. I don't know what to do. I want to shout and scream at him; to force him to explain himself. But how can I when he's in such a state?'

'How bad is he?'

'Like I said on the phone, it was a major stroke. It's affected most of his right side and his speech. God knows how long he'll need caring for. He may never fully recover. I know that he needs me, but I'm completely lost, Lauren. I'm still mourning my son and doing my best to raise my granddaughter. How can I handle this too? It's like God's punishing me. I keep thinking that somehow I must have brought this all on myself.'

Lauren scowled. 'Don't be ridiculous, Mum. None of this is your fault.'

'Maybe I'm a bad wife; a bad mother.'

'No. You're a wonderful wife and the best mum ever. There's only one person at fault here and that's Dad. If anyone's got what they deserve, it's him.'

I couldn't believe what I'd just heard.

'Don't say that, Lauren,' Mum replied. 'Whatever he's done, he doesn't deserve this.'

'Well, I'm not having anything to do with him,' Lauren added, steely-eyed. 'I'll stay here to help you and Ella, but I'm not going to visit him. How could I, knowing what I do now? I'll never forgive him.'

Mum stayed quiet. Like me, she probably thought Lauren needed time to calm down.

'Who is she, anyway?' my sister asked. 'Who is this tart he's having his dirty affair with?'

Mum explained that she didn't know and hadn't yet got up the courage to ring the number.

'Why not? Where's the phone? Give it to me. I'll give that family wrecker a piece of my mind.'

Mum hesitated but eventually removed the phone from her pocket and handed it to Lauren. 'What are you going to say?'

'I don't know. I'll see what comes out when she answers.'

She stood up and flipped open the black clamshell. After taking a second to locate X's number, she selected it. With no pause for thought, she jammed her thumb into the green dial button and held the phone up to her ear.

The whole room was silent and then Lauren erupted: 'This is the daughter of Tom Curtis. I know you've been having an affair with my dad and I think you're the scum of the earth. I'm calling to tell you that it's over. For good. If you ever try to contact him again, I will hunt you down and make your life even more miserable than you've made ours. Don't test me or, mark my words, you'll be sorry. Leave. Him. Alone.'

146

Lauren swung her hand away from her ear, slammed the mobile shut and tossed it on to the couch next to Mum. 'Voicemail. Still don't know who she is, but hopefully she'll get the message and leave well alone now.'

Mum gaped back at her, aghast. 'Lauren, what did you just do? I can't believe what you said.'

'It needed saying.'

'But—'

'But nothing. I sorted it. That's all. We can still find out who she is, if you like. We can call again.'

'You were so ... aggressive,' Mum said. 'So threatening.'

'Well, it's nothing she doesn't deserve. Don't you feel angry? You should do.'

Mum put her head in her hands. 'I'm not sure how I feel, Lauren. These last few weeks have been hell. Most of the time I feel numb. Every so often I get a flood of emotion and then I pack it away again. I have to, for Ella's sake.'

I shared Mum's surprise at the way Lauren had dealt with X. I hadn't seen her get that angry for ages. Not since the wild period of her late teens and early twenties when, after years of being a model student, she went off the rails good and proper. I'd heard her rant and rave plenty back then. Usually at my parents; sometimes at me. She went off to uni to study modern languages but dropped out at the end of the first year after spending most of the time off her head on drugs and sleeping her way around the campus.

She moved back home for a hellish few months of rows, which didn't exactly help me focus on my A levels.

Then she fell in with a rough crowd. She moved in with one of them, a nasty piece of work called Ed, who introduced her to heroin. A nightmare catalogue of incidents followed, leading up to her stealing our late grandmother's engagement ring from Mum's jewellery box and selling it to fund her habit. That proved the final straw for my parents. I'd gone off to uni myself by then, determined to make the most of it and not to follow the same path my sister had. But I'd never forget the phone call I got from Dad, warning me not to let her in if she visited.

'We've had to cut her off,' he told me, his voice brimming with pain. 'She's out of control. We've told her she's not welcome at the house any more. I've warned her not to contact us again unless she says goodbye to that bloody boyfriend and goes into rehab.'

My eighteen-year-old self was glad. Having had Lauren dominate family discussions and spark fight after fight for more than a year, I'd grown to resent her. She'd shattered the closeness we'd once had as siblings and I welcomed the hard line my parents were taking with her.

Now, as a parent myself, I wondered how Mum and Dad had had the strength of character to act like they did. It was the right thing to do; I'd never doubted that. But would I have been able to do the same with Ella in that situation? It must have been horrendous for them.

Luckily, Lauren never did come to visit me at uni. None of us heard from her or saw her again for nearly eighteen months. Mum and Dad put on a brave face, but I could see that it was killing them. We didn't have a clue where she was, although we later found out that she'd spent

148

most of that time up in Scotland. She and Ed had moved into a squat in his home city of Glasgow. Then one day, after Ed moved on from verbal abuse to physical abuse, she finally saw sense. She sought refuge in a women's centre where a kind member of staff took her under her wing. She guided Lauren into rehab and, after that, back into the arms of her family, her health thankfully still intact.

There were a few hiccups along the way, but Lauren was determined to succeed, so she did. It took a long time before any of us trusted her again, but that too came eventually. Then she met Xander – a well-educated, eloquent Dutchman – while InterRailing around Europe. He was the antithesis of Ed; Mum and Dad were over the moon, even when she decided to move to the Netherlands to be with him. I liked him too, although I would have preferred it if he'd come to live here instead. I'd just got used to having my sister back, only for her to go away again.

I remembered wondering whether I ought to have chosen Lauren and Xander to be Ella's guardians at the time when I wrote my will. They were much younger than Mum and Dad and likely to be around longer, but I'd been put off by the fact they lived abroad and didn't see Ella that often. She didn't know them nearly as well as her grandparents.

'You're not really going to refuse to see your father, are you?' Mum asked. 'He needs his family right now – all of us. As hard as it might be, we can't desert him. None of us can. If you find it hard, imagine how tough it is for me. Families stick together at times of crisis, no matter what. And if anyone should be able to forgive him, you should. He forgave you enough. We all did.'

Lauren looked sheepishly across the room, tears in her eyes. 'That was a low blow.'

'It needed saying.'

'Why are you, of all people, defending him?'

'Someone has to – and he is still my husband. You'll feel different when you've seen what a state he's in.'

'Look, maybe I was a bit harsh, but this has come as such a shock. I feel like Dad's totally let me down.'

'I understand that, believe me, but he's been a very good father to you over the years. You can't just write him off.'

Lauren paced up and down the room a few times before sitting next to Mum on the couch and giving her a hug. 'Sorry. I'm not helping, am I?'

Mum shook her head.

'What do you want me to do? How can I help?'

'Ditch the anger for a start. I don't need conflict. It's been really hard doing everything alone. Now you're here, what I need most is your support.'

'Fine. You've got it. But how are you going to play things with Dad? He won't always be asleep. Sooner or later you'll have to talk to him. Are you going to tell him what you know?'

Mum sat back with a sigh. 'I honestly have no idea. It's like there are two voices in my head. One tells me that I've got to do it: that the last thing we need is more lies. But the other says I should wait until he's better. Otherwise I might harm his recovery. Even if I do tell

150

him, it's not like he'll be able to respond properly in his current state. I'll have to sleep on it, I suppose; see how I feel in the morning.'

I stayed with them as they chatted some more and watched a little mindless TV. They were talking about going up to bed when we were all startled by a blood-curdling scream from upstairs.

'Daddy!' Ella's voice cried in terror. 'Get off my daddy!'

I tried to race upstairs but ran straight into the path of Mum and Lauren – also on their feet – who unknowingly repelled me. I found myself slammed into the nearest wall with even greater force than usual. It must have been because we were all moving so quickly. It left me stunned – but still conscious at least, unlike the earlier incident with the transit van. By the time I'd got back up and brushed myself off, I was a couple of minutes behind the other two.

Upstairs I found Mum sitting on the edge of the bed, leaning over Ella and stroking her hair, while Lauren knelt at her niece's side, whispering soothing words into her ear. Ella was still whimpering. Her tired eyes gave a flicker of recognition when I entered, but she heeded the finger I held in front of my mouth and looked away.

'There, there, little one,' Lauren said. 'Are you feeling a bit calmer now?'

Ella nodded against her pillow and slipped her thumb into her mouth.

'It was just a bad dream,' Mum said. 'It's only normal. It's your mind's way of dealing with things. You know none of it was real, don't you?'

151

Ella nodded again. 'Yes, I know,' she said, slipping her thumb out of her mouth so Mum and Lauren could understand her. 'I think I'm ready to go back to sleep again.'

Lauren planted a kiss on her cheek. 'Would you like one of us to stay with you until you drop off?'

'No. I'm okay.'

I took care to stand well aside as they left the room and then padded over to the bedside. 'Hi, Ella.'

'Why are you whispering, Daddy? No one can hear you apart from me.'

'I know. I just wanted to make sure that you kept it down too. They might still be listening.'

'I will.'

'You had a nightmare?'

'Yes. About you.'

'What happened?'

'You were outside Nana and Grandad's church.'

'Where my funeral was held?'

'Yes. Someone was trying to take you away from me.'

'Who?'

'I don't know. I couldn't see. They were in a black car. They pulled you inside and drove away. I thought it was real.'

A sliver of fear sliced through me.

'Well, don't worry,' I said. 'It wasn't real. I'm here and no one's taking me anywhere. It was just a bad dream. Are you feeling better?'

'I think so,' she said, stifling a yawn. 'Will you stay with me?'

'Of course. I'm tired anyway. I'm sure a good sleep will do us both the world of good.'

Ella pulled the quilt around her, tucking herself into a cosy foetal position from which she could gaze at me as she dropped off.

I smiled. 'Goodnight, my love. Sleep tight. Don't let the bedbugs bite.'

'I won't.'

CHAPTER 16

TWENTY-SIX DAYS LEFT

Arthur was on my mind the next morning. It was very odd that I'd not been able to find him. Where could he have been? As far as I knew, he spent almost all of his time at the church and the school. Unless he didn't want to be found. Perhaps it wasn't safe for him to meet me at the moment or – perish the thought – that thing from the cricket pavilion had caught up with him. I prayed that wasn't the case. Despite Arthur's reassurances, the memory of being trapped alone there, so close to that terrifying presence, still spooked me.

I wanted to look for Arthur again today, but I was torn, as I knew I ought to check up on Dad at the hospital. In the end, it was Dad who won. He was family and, what's more, Ella had specifically asked me to visit him while she was at school.

'I don't trust Nana to tell me the truth,' she said precociously. 'She thinks I can't handle it, but I can. Really. You'll tell me, won't you?'

154

'Yes,' I replied.

'Promise?'

'I promise.'

'Will Auntie Lauren be going to the hospital too?'

'I'm not sure.'

At that moment Lauren walked into Ella's room, brushing her teeth. 'What was that, Ella? Did you want me?'

Ella went bright red. 'I, um, was just telling Kitten that you'd come to stay,' she said, snatching her favourite cuddly toy from the bed and waving it in the air.

'Hello, Kitten,' Lauren replied through a mouthful of toothpaste. 'Is that all right with you?'

Ella held Kitten's mouth to her ear. 'Yes. She says she likes you.'

'Purrfect,' Lauren said with a grin.

An hour later, after dropping Ella off at school, Mum drove into the hospital car park. Lauren was in the front passenger seat and I was in the back. Mum found a space and turned off the engine. 'So. Here we are.'

Lauren nodded. The pair of them looked terrified.

'Come on,' I said, as if they could hear me. 'You can do this. You have to.'

I followed them as they headed up to the stroke unit, staying close to avoid getting left behind at any of the doors we passed through along the way. I'd never much liked hospitals. I particularly hated that stink of disinfectant covering up all kinds of nastiness, so for once I was glad not to be able to smell anything.

We were greeted by a friendly but no-nonsense ward sister with short hair and a stocky frame. 'Hello. It's

Mrs Curtis, isn't it? Tom's wife.'

'That's right,' Mum replied. 'And this is our daughter Lauren.'

She gave Lauren a curt nod of recognition before turning her attention back to Mum. 'The physio is with him at the moment. We need to leave them to it. Maybe we could use the opportunity to have a quick chat about how he's doing.'

'Oh, um, yes. Of course,' Mum replied, throwing an anxious glance in Lauren's direction.

'Very good. If you'd like to come through to my office.'

She led the way down the corridor to a box room; I just managed to squeeze inside behind the others.

'Is there a problem?' Mum blurted out as soon as the sister shut the door.

'No, no,' she replied, sitting down on the opposite side of her chock-a-block desk. 'Sorry, I didn't mean to alarm you. This is something we always try to do in these circumstances. Recovering from a stroke can be a long process. We find it really helps for patients' families to be as informed as possible right from the start.'

'I see,' Mum replied, shuffling in her seat.

'That sounds like a good idea,' Lauren said, nodding at the sister, encouraging her to continue.

She launched into a detailed explanation of the type of stroke Dad had suffered, from cause and effect to treatment and recovery. She handed them a selection of leaflets to look through before asking if they had any questions.

'Where does my dad fit into things?' Lauren asked. 'Is he one of the people likely to make a full recovery or not? How long do you expect he'll need to be in here?'

The sister peered back at her apologetically. 'I wish I could give you proper answers to those questions, but I'm afraid I can't. Not at this early stage. It always takes some time before we can estimate the length of a patient's recovery.'

'How is he at the moment?' Mum asked.

'Well, I'm glad to say there has been an improvement, as he now has some movement in his right leg.'

Mum's eyes lit up. 'Really? So he's getting better?'

'It's a good sign, but these are early days,' the sister replied. 'The upper right side of his body is still in paralysis. The important thing is that he's in the right place to have the best possible chance of recovery. He's surrounded by specialists, who'll make sure he receives the most suitable medication and therapy to move forward.'

'What about his speech? I couldn't understand him when it happened. Has that improved at all?'

'He's still struggling with it, I'm afraid. The good news is that the doctors say it's a speech disorder rather than a language one.'

'Sorry, what does that mean?' Lauren asked. 'Why is that good news?'

'It means he has difficulty speaking because the relevant muscles aren't working properly, rather than because his language processing has been impaired by the stroke. Consequently, he should still be able to understand you and to communicate in other ways.'

'I see,' Lauren replied. 'And will these muscles start working again?'

157

'Your father will be seeing a speech therapist later today or tomorrow and they should be able to help him.'

'So he could be here for a while? Weeks or even months?'

'That's possible, yes. There are instances where people make miracle recoveries, but it's rare. Getting over a stroke usually takes a lot of time and hard work.'

Later, as I paced up and down the corridor while Mum and Lauren sat waiting for the physio to leave, they had a whispered discussion about Dad's dirty little secret.

'We can't say anything to him now,' Mum said. 'Not while he can't respond properly. It could harm his recovery. We're going to have to pretend we don't know.'

'Are you sure? Can you live with that, Mum? Can you come here every day, knowing what you do, and treat him like he's done nothing wrong?'

Mum let out a long sigh and ran her fingers through her hair. 'I'll have to.'

Lauren sighed too. 'Then I'll support you. If you can do it, so can I. But there will come a day when we have to tell him what we know.'

A few minutes later the sister returned to say that the physiotherapist had left. She led us through to see Dad. He was sitting up in bed, hair ruffled. His face, still drooping on one side, was red and sweaty, and he appeared out of breath. It was horrible to see him like that. I knew my father as a big strong man: someone unstoppable, almost bulletproof. It felt so wrong to see him weak and helpless in a hospital ward. It wasn't as bad as seeing him in the throes of the stroke, but it was close. He'd been robbed of his essence – the imposing presence he was known for – and although I told myself he'd recover, at that moment it was hard to imagine.

'How are you doing?' the sister asked him, darting over to mop his brow with a cloth she seemed to pull out of thin air. 'Did you find the physio strenuous?'

He nodded.

'That's normal. It means it will have done you some good. Anyhow, as you can see, you've got visitors.'

He nodded again and a lopsided grin appeared on his drawn face.

'I'll leave you to it,' she said.

Mum and Lauren shuffled to opposite sides of the bed. They each greeted Dad with a peck on the forehead before pulling over a chair. I could tell they were struggling to suppress what they knew. Lauren, seeing him in this state for the first time, could barely conceal her shock.

I stood at the end of the bed as Mum took his left hand in hers and gave it a squeeze. I was surprised at the tenderness of the gesture. She must really love him, I thought. I wonder if Dad has a clue how lucky he is that she's here?

'How are you, Tom?'

He smiled that newly crooked smile of his again: a look infused more with sadness and pain than happiness. Then he pulled his hand free from Mum's and tilted it from left to right in a so-so gesture.

'I came yesterday, but you were asleep the whole time. I didn't like to wake you. Did they tell you?'

He nodded.

'The sister said you're able to move your leg again.'

Dad nodded and raised it a couple of centimetres off the bed.

'That's great,' Mum said. 'What about your arm? Still nothing?'

He shook his head.

'It's a good thing you're left-handed. Imagine what it would be like if you weren't. Can you talk, Tom?'

He shook his head.

'Not at all?'

He shrugged his left shoulder.

'What happens if you try?' Lauren asked.

He turned to look at her before opening his mouth and then moving it in an awkward, twisted manner. A strained, gurgling noise came out and he started drooling. Lauren's hand flew to her mouth in shock. That was the only time he attempted to speak while we were there and my sister barely said another word either. The rest of the conversation came from Mum. After wiping away the drool, she rattled on about Ella and day-to-day things in between asking questions about Dad's condition and treatment, which he did his best to answer using gestures.

Afterwards, Mum and Lauren walked in silence through the sterile, shiny-floored corridors back to the car park. It was Lauren who eventually said something, but not until we were sitting in the car. 'You were amazing back there, Mum. I'm sorry I was so useless. It just ...'

Lauren started to cry and, as Mum leaned over to comfort her, I saw that she too had tears in her eyes.

'It threw me when I heard Dad try to speak,' Lauren managed eventually. 'And then I couldn't stop thinking about his affair. I don't know how you stayed so strong.'

Mum took a deep breath and slowly exhaled. 'It wasn't easy, but it would have been harder without you there. I tried to blank what I knew out of my mind and pretend it hadn't happened. It feels strange to say it, but I still love him. I hate seeing him like that. How do you feel now?'

'I'm glad I came and I feel awful about saying he deserved this. It was right what you said to me last night. I needed it.' She paused before adding: 'I'm still angry at him, though.'

'Me too,' Mum whispered. 'But now's not the time.'

Mum reached over, took both of Lauren's hands in her own and looked her in the eye. 'Don't worry, I've not forgotten about it. I've no intention of being one of those push-over wives who turns a blind eye to this kind of indiscretion. As soon as your father's up to it, I'll tell him exactly what I know. Then we'll see what he's got to say for himself. But not yet. Now is about a family pulling together in a time of crisis. Okay?'

'Okay.'

'We're a team, right? We need to hold things together and ensure Ella has a happy place to return to every night. Agreed?'

'Yes.'

'Good. Let's go home.'

I couldn't believe Mum's strength. Where had that come from? Only yesterday she'd seemed so broken. Lauren's arrival had made a huge difference. Not as I'd thought it would, though. I'd expected my sister to come in and take over, looking after Mum and advising her on the best way forward. Instead, it was like her presence had reminded Mum of her role as matriarch. Maybe she just needed to know that she wasn't alone; that she had someone else on her side to fill the void left by me and Dad. Either way, one thing was for certain: Mum was standing tall and very much in charge.

To while away the time as she drove us back, I'd been playing a game Ella and I used to enjoy together on long journeys. It involved looking at the number plates of passing or parked cars and using their last three letters to form a silly phrase. For instance, MBS might be 'monkey brain soup' or 'my breath smells'; CLB might be 'cats love bogeys' or 'cabbage leaf breakfast'. As we pulled into Mum and Dad's street, I was looking for one final registration to use when I spotted that bloody black Audi again. It was parked on the opposite side of the street, a few doors down from the house, but it was definitely the same one I'd seen before.

This time I was determined to find out more.

As soon as Mum pulled the Corsa on to the drive, along-side Dad's BMW, I crouched into the gap between the two front seats, ready to make a fast exit. Lauren was the first to undo her seat belt and open the door. As she stepped out of the car, I slipped into the space she'd vacated on the seat and, with practised precision, rolled out behind her.

Right, I thought, time for some answers. I sped off in the direction of the mystery car, expecting it to race away just before I got there, but this time it stayed put. The reason for that was obvious as soon as I pulled up to the side of it and peered in through the windscreen: there was no one inside. There wasn't even anything on display to give me a clue as to the driver's identity.

I walked out into the middle of the street and looked all around, but no one was in sight. At least the car's whole number plate was visible now. The initial D3 I'd noted previously was followed by VLN. It was some kind of personalized registration, with the 3 presumably meant to be read as an E.

'Devln,' I said, trying it out for size. 'Devil in?' It couldn't be, could it?

'Shit,' I said, backing away from the car into the street. My mind was so busy with possibilities that I didn't hear the bicycle coming. The first I knew of it was when it smashed into me at full force, catapulting me into the air, while the cyclist carried on pedalling, none the wiser. Just like with the transit van, I felt nothing but couldn't stop myself from blacking out.

I came round a short while later, face down on a neighbour's front lawn. I was still lying there, getting over the shock of my latest battering, when I noticed a man walking briskly along the pavement towards the Audi. Looking on in silent fascination, I saw the tall, wiry figure pull a key fob out of his trouser pocket and unlock the black car.

So you're the one who's been watching us, I thought.

Who – or what – the hell was he? The figure I could now see swinging open the driver's door certainly looked human, but I wasn't ruling anything out. I didn't recognize him. He looked to be in his early fifties but had the wax-sculpted hairstyle of someone younger, too black to be natural. His navy pinstripe suit and wool overcoat were the clothes of a businessman.

I crawled along the grass to find cover behind a tall conifer. I was taking no chances. What if he wasn't human? That might mean he could see me.

I hunched back into the tree as he looked up and down the street before stepping inside the car. A few seconds later the engine started up. He opened the window and lit a cigarette as the Audi pulled away.

Walking back to the house, I felt bewildered. Seeing the driver hadn't been the revelation I'd expected; I was still in the dark. At least I didn't get stuck outside for ages, as I'd feared, since Lauren took Sam for a walk and I managed to slip in as she left.

Mum was alone in the kitchen making a sandwich and a cup of tea. As the kettle boiled she reached up into a cupboard to get a mug, but it slipped out of her hand, falling on to the worktop and breaking its handle.

'Shit,' she shouted. 'Shit, shit, shit!'

She picked up the damaged mug, hurled it on to the tiled floor and screamed with rage. Then she slid to the ground and burst into tears.

By the time Lauren returned, the smashed mug had been swept up, wrapped in newspaper and stuffed to the bottom of the dustbin. 'Good walk, love?' Mum asked with no sign of her recent anguish.

'Yes, thanks, Mum. Some fresh air was just what the doctor ordered. Sam enjoyed it too.'

'Would you like some lunch now? I've already had a sandwich.'

'No, I'm still not hungry, thanks. I'd love a cuppa, though.'

CHAPTER 17

TWENTY-THREE DAYS LEFT

'Wake up,' Lizzie whispered into my ear. I'd dozed off on the sofa in the lounge after everyone had gone to bed.

'Oh. It's you,' I groaned. 'What time is it?'

'Just gone eleven thirty. I thought you'd still be awake. Most spirits don't sleep a lot.'

'Really? Well, I was only snoozing. I've been busy since we last met. I assume you know what happened to my dad.'

She nodded. 'I'm so sorry. How's everyone coping?'

'As well as can be expected. Mum finding out that he's been having an affair hasn't helped.'

'Oh dear.'

'Yeah ... Is my dad going to be all right? Will he make a full recovery?'

'Sorry, I don't know.'

'Can't you find out?'

She shook her head. 'That's not how it works.'

'Of course. What was I thinking?' I muttered. 'So why are you here, Lizzie, if not to help me?'

166

'Because time's ticking, that's why. Only three weeks and a day now until your deadline.'

'Three weeks and two days, actually. It's still Saturday.'

'Only just. Any closer to a decision?'

I hesitated for a moment, the strong feelings I'd experienced at the churchyard the other day bubbling to the surface again. But I swallowed them back down as I told her: 'I want to stay here with my daughter.'

She leaned forward. 'If you say so. How are things going with Ella?'

'Fine.'

'There's no need to be coy. I know that you managed to get through to her; that she can see you now. That kind of thing doesn't go unnoticed.'

'Oh, right. Um, yeah.'

'So how is it?'

'Great. I couldn't be happier.'

'And how does Ella feel about it?'

'What do you think? She's over the moon. She's got her father back.'

'Right,' Lizzie replied. 'Of course.' She waited a moment, staring at me the whole time, before adding: 'That's not quite true, though, is it? Having you around as a spirit isn't the same as before. You're still dead; you can't do a lot of the things you used to do with her. You can't cook a meal for her, push her on a swing or carry her when she's tired. You can't drive her to a swimming lesson or take her to the doctor when she's ill. You couldn't protect her if, let's say, someone tried to kidnap her.'

I couldn't believe what I was hearing. 'Bloody hell, Lizzie. What a thing to say.' My heart dropped. 'Hold on: why did you say it? Are you trying to warn me about something?'

'No, no. Calm down. That's not it. I was just giving you an example.'

She sighed. 'Listen, I was hoping to avoid this, but I don't think there's any choice.'

'Avoid what?'

'You think it's wonderful that Ella can see you because it's what you wanted. It's your wish come true. That doesn't mean it's the best thing for her. I'm sure she's glad to see you now, but how do you think it's going to affect her in the long run? You've already got her keeping it a secret; lying to her closest living family.'

I could feel the anger rising in my chest. 'What else am I supposed to do? If people see her talking to her dead father, they're going to think she's crazy.'

'Exactly. There are good reasons why people can't usually see the dead.'

'So why did you tell Arth—'

Before I could finish my question, Lizzie grabbed my hand. In the blink of an eye, the world around me changed. I was somewhere else. Everything was different and yet oddly familiar.

'What the hell's going on?'

'You'll see,' Lizzie whispered.

We were sitting on a lipstick-red leather couch. It looked much less comfortable than the navy fabric sofa I'd just slept on, although my lack of sensation meant I could

168

only speculate. Everything in the room looked hard and functional.

'Where are we, Lizzie?' I growled.

She smiled calmly. 'It's less a question of where than when.'

'What's that supposed to mean? Help me out here. I only woke up a few minutes ago. Can't you ever give me a straight answer?'

'The answer's all around you, Will. All you have to do is look.'

'Fine,' I replied like a sulky teenager, jumping to my feet.

I stormed over to the nearest window and peered through a gap in the thick vertical blinds. I gasped. Despite the darkness outside, there was no mistaking the fact I was looking at my parents' front garden.

'What the hell?' I said, turning back to Lizzie and gaping wide-eyed at her.

She frowned.

'Sorry,' I added. 'Bad choice of words. But come on. How ...'

Words failed me as I tried to take everything in. The dimensions of the lounge were the same, but everything else was different. No wonder I'd not recognized it. Gone were my parents' floral wallpaper, carpet, coffee table, curtains, light fittings; you name it. Even the textured ceiling had been replaced with smooth plaster and recessed spotlights. The walls were painted a light grey colour. They were bare but for the floating black hands of a stripped-back analogue clock and a large print of an American painting I'd always liked, *Gas* by Edward Hopper.

169

The floor was covered in some kind of granite-effect material and the furniture – what little there was of it – was angular and simple. The TV had been replaced by a brushed-chrome floor lamp, which stood nearly as tall as me, and the focal point now seemed to be a low glass table in front of the sofa. It was empty apart from an A4-size thin glass sheet lying in one corner. Set into the centre of the table was a silver disc about the size of a CD, which was embossed with a large 'i'.

'What is this thing?' I asked. 'There's no way it's just a table. Come on, Lizzie. You've got to give me some idea what's going on here. I'm totally confused.'

'I already have.'

I thought back to her earlier words: 'It's less a question of where than when.'

The penny finally dropped. 'No way! Are you saying what I think you are?'

Lizzie raised her eyebrows and stared at me.

A few weeks ago I wouldn't have believed it to be possible. But after everything that had happened to me of late, my mind had become a lot more willing to accept extraordinary things. 'So this is—'

I was interrupted by the sound of the door swinging open and my dead wife bursting into the room.

I froze as Alice approached me.

'There you are,' she said, bending down to pick up the A4 glass sheet from the table.

'Sorry?' I replied, flustered. 'What—'

She didn't stop to answer me, turning and darting back out of the room.

'Alice?' I called after her. 'Is that really you?'

I was about to follow her out of the lounge when Lizzie grabbed my hand. 'She wasn't speaking to you. Her words were meant for the object she took. And that's not your wife, William. It's your daughter.'

'What? That's Ella? But she looks just like Alice. How—'

'She's twenty-six years old.'

'We've travelled twenty years into the future?'

'One version of the future.'

'And she can't see me any more?'

'She can't see this version of you. That's against the rules. You're here strictly as a spectator. But she can still see the version of her father from her own time.'

Lizzie nodded towards the door. 'Go and have a look.'

I took one step and then stopped. 'Will he – I mean I, you know, the other one – be able to see me?'

Lizzie shook her head. 'You're safe. Go on.'

I walked into the hall and was guided towards the kitchen by the sound of voices. The other version of me – unaged and still dressed in the same frayed jeans and T-shirt, with rosy cheeks and a day's stubble – was standing by the sink. Opposite him was the older Ella, sitting at a sleek table made of a shiny black material somewhere between plastic and metal. This room was as streamlined and functional as the lounge. The most comfortable-looking thing in there was a furry purple cushion near the back door. A large black cat was fast asleep on it.

'So you're not going to finish in time?' the other me asked Ella.

'No. I don't think I can, Dad,' she replied, running both her hands through her darkened long curls. 'I'm shattered. I've taken too much on.'

I couldn't take my eyes off her. She'd grown so tall and beautiful. It was unsettling how much she looked like her mother: the hair, the pale green eyes, the fair skin and delicate features. Even her voice sounded similar to Alice's, albeit with a slight northern twang.

'You know that I'm here to help,' the other me said. 'Let me know what I can do.'

Ella kept her eyes fixed on the table in front of her. 'I don't need your help, Dad. What I need is for you to give me some space. I know you mean well, but you're always pushing me to take on more work. Now look what's happened.'

'Sorry, I forgot. I don't have your fancy qualifications. I'm just the old newspaper hack; the dinosaur.'

'Dad, I didn't mean it like that. Sometimes I'm best getting on with things myself, that's all. I don't need you constantly on my back.'

'It sounds like you don't need me at all. You should watch what you say. One day you might turn around and find I'm not here any more. Then who will you have? Friends, family? I don't think so. I'm all you've got. And to think of the sacrifice I made to stay here with you.'

'Don't be like that, Dad,' Ella replied as the other me stormed out of the room and disappeared upstairs. I was shocked at what I'd heard. How could I say such things to her? How could I make Ella feel guilty about my choice to stay with her?

172

She picked up the A4 glass sheet from the kitchen table and brought it to life with a quick tap, so it displayed a glowing matrix of colours. After swiping and tapping it some more, she put it back down. To my surprise a crystal-clear hologram of a man's head appeared from the device and started talking. 'Miss Curtis. How can I help you?'

'Hello, Mr Reynolds,' Ella replied with a polite smile. 'Sorry to interrupt your evening, but I don't think I'm going to be able to make the deadline.'

That wasn't the news Mr Reynolds wanted to hear. He launched into a rant that culminated in a pledge never to hire her as a contractor again. Once the call was over, Ella hunched over the table and started to cry.

It was at this point that Lizzie walked into the room. 'Oh dear,' she said to me. 'What's happened?'

'What do you care?'

'That's not very nice, William.'

'Why did you bring me here?' I asked.

'Why do you think?'

'Here we go again. Can't you ever give me a straight answer?'

'You may not believe it, William, but I'm doing my utmost to help you.' She took my arm and led me back to the lounge. 'Do you think this version of Ella is happy with her life? Is what you see here everything you'd wish for her?'

'She seems to be doing okay for herself,' I said.

'On the surface, perhaps, but do you think she's happy?'

'I don't know, Lizzie. I've only seen a glimpse of her life and it's all a bit of a shock, to be honest. Jumping twenty years into the future might be normal for you, but I'm finding it a lot to take in.'

Lizzie held up her palms defensively. 'I get that. I just wanted to give you a chance to see the bigger picture.'

I looked down at the hard, dark floor beneath my feet. 'There did seem to be a bit of friction between the two of them. What happened? How did they – we – get to this point?'

'It's hard to function normally when your dead father is always at your side, watching you.'

'Surely I wasn't there all the time. Why didn't I give her some space?'

Lizzie shrugged.

'Is it true what he – the other me – said about Ella not having any other family and friends?'

'I'm afraid so. Talking to you became so normal for her that she started doing it in public without realizing. People thought she was talking to herself. You can imagine what conclusions they drew. That's why she ended up working from home. It's easier than ever in the twenty thirties. In fact, she barely needs to leave the house at all.'

'Hasn't she got a boyfriend or anything?'

'What do you think?'

'Where are Mum and Dad?'

'Um, a lot can happen in two decades,' Lizzie said. 'I'm afraid your parents have both passed away.'

'Oh, right,' I replied, taken aback. 'What about Lauren and Xander?'

'She speaks to them from time to time – birthdays and so on – but they're not close. Ella never really let them in.'

'I see. And this is my fault? You're saying it's because of me that she's in this situation, right?'

Lizzie reached over and took my hand. 'What you're witnessing here is only one possible path for you and Ella. You control your own future. It doesn't have to turn out this way.'

As she spoke I saw the room around me change, morphing back into the living room I knew of old: the carpet, the navy sofa, the floral wallpaper. 'Wait,' I said. 'Let me check she's all right. I don't want to leave her like that, crying in the kitchen.'

'Shh,' Lizzie whispered in my ear, close enough to pierce my numbness for an instant. It made me shiver. 'Don't worry about her. That's not happened yet. That version of your daughter may never exist.'

'How—'

Lizzie placed a cool palm on my forehead and I collapsed into nothingness.

CHAPTER 18

TWENTY-TWO DAYS LEFT

Ella and I were sitting in her princess castle when a shadow fell across it and I heard the muffled sound of movement on the other side.

'What is that, Daddy?' she asked, terror etched across her face.

I tried to reply, to reassure her, only to find that I was frozen. I couldn't even speak as, to my horror, the presence crept around the tent, rustling here and scratching there, until it eventually stopped by the door. There was an irregular sniffing sound and then the zip started to open.

'I'm scared,' Ella whispered. 'What's happening?'

Despite my own fear, I was desperate to protect my daughter. But it was useless: I was paralysed.

'Daddy!' she cried. 'Wake up!'

My eyes snapped open and I was lying on my parents' couch, Ella standing before me. 'Are you all right? I think you were having a nightmare.'

'Darling,' I replied, stunned for a moment as I shook off the false reality of my dream. 'Thank goodness.'

'Was it a scary one?' Ella asked, making me wish I could pull her into a hug. 'What was it about?'

'Just some nonsense. I'm fine now. What time is it?'

She ran to the silver carriage clock on the mantelpiece and squinted at it. 'Um. The little hand is on six, I think, and the big hand is almost at the top. Is that six o'clock?'

'That sounds right, love. Well done.'

'We've been practising at school. Mrs Afzal said I did a super job.'

I chuckled. 'I'm sure she did. That's early, though. Don't you want to sleep some more?'

'No. I'm wide awake. Can we do something?'

'Are Nana and Auntie Lauren still asleep?'

'Yep. I peeked in on them.'

'Fine. What would you like to do?'

'Can we play Ginger Man?' she asked, jumping up and down on the spot.

She was referring to a video game we used to play together. That wasn't its actual name; she'd called it that when she was younger, because she thought the main character looked like a gingerbread man, and it had stuck.

'I wish we could,' I replied, 'but the console's not set up here. Even if it was, my days of holding a controller are long gone.'

Ella pulled a sad face. 'Not fair.'

'Sorry, darling. I agree, but there's nothing I can do.'

I suggested playing Connect Four instead, as long as she didn't mind making my moves for me.

She agreed, although it was hard not to miss the disappointed look on her face.

We had fun all the same, switching to draughts when we needed a change. Our conversation was comfortably sparse, never straying far from the game at hand. And when thoughts about my trip to the future fluttered into my mind, I told myself that I might have dreamed the whole thing. That was possible, wasn't it?

I looked over at the clock and was surprised to see it was already after 7 a.m. 'I think we'd better call it a day, Ella. The others will be up soon. They might think it a bit odd to see you playing against yourself like this.'

'I'm not playing against myself. I'm playing with you.'

'Of course you are. We both know that, but it's our secret, remember.'

'I remember,' she said, her voice tinged with sadness.

'That was fun, wasn't it?' I said, trying to lift the conversation. 'See. We don't need video games to enjoy ourselves.'

'Daddy,' Ella said. 'Why can't I just tell Nana and Auntie Lauren about you? They'd be so happy if they could see you too.'

'I know, darling, but it's not that easy. Like I told you before, adults aren't as good as children at understanding new things. It was hard enough for me to get through to you; it would be a thousand times harder still to do it with them. If you tell them, they'll think you're imagining it and they'll worry about you.' I hesitated before adding: 'They might even think you're sick and take you to a special doctor.'

'But I thought it was wrong to lie?'

178

'It is, darling, but this is … an exception. You don't necessarily need to lie, anyway. Just don't mention anything in the first place.'

'Okay,' she whispered.

'Good girl,' I replied with feigned assurance as her breathy one-word reply raked at my soul. How can it be right to tell my six-year-old daughter to lie for me? I thought. What kind of a parent am I?

My mind flitted back to the image of a grown-up Ella crying in her futuristic kitchen. Real, imagined, whatever it was, I could picture it as clear as day in my mind's eye. And it haunted me. Even as I justified my actions to myself as necessary and unavoidable, that image said otherwise. It countered my argument with a simple truth: if I wasn't still here, there would be no need for Ella to lie.

Before I had time to rein myself in – to leave my daughter out of this internal conflict – I heard the words falling out of my mouth. 'You do like me being around, don't you, darling? Even though it's not like it was before?'

She looked at me like I was stupid. 'Of course. Why wouldn't I? Having you back is the best thing ever.'

I smiled at her, knowing in that moment more than ever why parents called children their pride and joy. 'I love you so much, Ella. You know that, don't you? You're the best daughter in the world. Probably in the universe, although I can't say for sure as I've never travelled that far.'

Ella giggled as she packed away the board games. 'I love you too, Daddy.'

Mum came down the stairs a few minutes later. 'Good morning, Ella. You're up bright and early. Did you sleep well?'

'Yes, thanks, Nana.' Ella looked straight at me as she picked up a school book and waved it in the air. 'I was doing a bit of reading.'

My heart sank at the deception, no matter how small.

'Good girl,' Mum replied. 'Did you understand all the words?'

Ella nodded. 'I think so.'

'Excellent. Maybe you can read to me later to show me how good you are.'

'Okay, Nana.'

I returned to the church and the school a couple of times over the next few days, but I made no progress in my search for Arthur. There was no sign of him. I was concerned, but other matters also demanded my attention.

There was Dad, for one, still in hospital and showing few signs of improvement beyond the regained use of his leg. There was his mystery woman, who we were no closer to unmasking. Then there was black Audi stalker man, for whom I'd been keeping my eyes peeled without any further sightings. And as if that wasn't enough, playground bully Kaylee had been picking on Ella again.

I'd stayed away from her school recently, figuring she'd integrate better with her classmates if I wasn't around. I hadn't heard any more of Kaylee since our pep talk. Then one evening, out of the blue, she flew into a tantrum about her tea being ready before the end of a TV programme she was watching. She blanked me when I told her to pull herself together. I'd seen her like that before – when she was tired or upset about something – but grandparents usually escaped such behaviour. So the initial reaction from Mum, more used to spoiling Ella than standing her ground with her, was one of shock. I think she was about to back down and let Ella eat in the lounge when Lauren stepped in.

'Come on now, Ella,' she said calmly but firmly, kneeling down so she was eye to eye with her niece. 'Nana's made you a nice tea. The television's going off now and that's that. There's no need for silliness.'

Ella stared at her in silence for a moment, as if weighing up whether or not to do as she said, before walking over to the TV and turning it off.

'Good girl,' Lauren said. 'Come on now. Let's wash your hands and I'll sit down at the table with you.'

Mum looked as impressed as I was. I don't think either of us thought she had it in her.

'Nice one, sis,' I said once Ella was out of earshot. 'You're a natural. Who knew?'

It was also Lauren who got Ella to admit there was something wrong when she put her in the bath that evening. She confessed that Kaylee had been calling her 'Orphan Annie' in the playground for the last few days. That lunchtime she'd had enough and – presumably acting on my advice – she'd pushed Kaylee over. One of the teachers had seen and Ella had got into trouble.

'Was she hurt?' Lauren asked her niece as I peered through the bathroom door, which stood ajar.

181

Ella shook her head. 'She just pretended while the teacher was there.'

'Did you tell the teacher what she'd been calling you?'

'No.'

'And did the teacher punish you?'

'No, but she told me off,' Ella replied, throwing an accusatory glance in my direction. 'And I'm worried she might tell Mr Norris.'

'Who's he?' Lauren asked.

'The head teacher. He sometimes calls naughty children into his office and shouts at them. I don't want him to shout at me.'

'Is that why you got all worked up earlier?'

Ella nodded.

'Well, don't you worry about it any more. I'm coming into school with you tomorrow and I'm going to tell those teachers exactly what's going on. I'm not surprised you pushed over that nasty little girl. It was the least she deserved. I can't believe she'd say such a thing to you after everything you've been through. This Mr Norris ought to be shouting at her.'

Ella protested at first, but Lauren soon persuaded her it was the right course of action.

Standing there on the landing, listening to their conversation, I felt like an outsider. I was proud of my sister for getting to the root of the problem and for the way she intended to defend her niece. But I couldn't help also feeling frustrated that I wasn't able to do those things myself. It reminded me of what Lizzie had said about not being able to protect Ella from being kidnapped.

But had she said that? Or had I actually dreamed that conversation and the subsequent trip to the future? I thought about calling my guide to find out but decided against it. The likelihood was that she wouldn't tell me. Giving straight answers wasn't her speciality. Besides, what did it matter? Whether she'd said it or my subconscious had thought it, the realization was the same: I couldn't be a proper father to Ella like this.

CHAPTER 19

SEVENTEEN DAYS LEFT

By the time Arthur finally showed up again, my deadline was fast approaching. It was too close to ignore. Two weeks and three days were all I had left to decide whether to remain here for eternity as a spirit or to pass over to the other side.

It had seemed such a simple decision at the start. But ... well, it just wasn't straightforward any more. It constantly weighed on my mind. Of course I wanted to stay with my daughter. That had been the driving force behind my post-death existence so far. But now that the reality of my decision was staring me in the face, I could no longer ignore the voice of doubt nagging away in the back of my mind. Would staying here be the right decision? That question seemed to be getting harder to answer by the day.

The idea that my presence might be bad for Ella was the main issue, but it wasn't the only one. As much as I wanted to be completely selfless, it was impossible. I couldn't help imagining what blissful, amazing things might await me if I chose to pass over. Witnessing another spirit's ascension had sparked a fire in me that refused to go out.

I also found myself pondering how lonely my existence here would become once Ella and everyone else I cared about had themselves passed over. It wasn't like I could expect them to stay behind with me, thus forfeiting their own spot in paradise.

I might have been able to ignore these thoughts if I was sure that staying here was best for my daughter. Instead, they grew in strength, voicing their arguments with ever-increasing volume.

Ella's bonding with Lauren further confused matters. Her auntie had gone into school, as promised, regarding Kaylee; the little bully had been duly taken to task by a horrified Mr Norris. Kaylee's parents had been called in and she'd been forced to apologize to Ella for her comments. As a result, Lauren had been elevated to super-hero status in her niece's mind. For the last few days they'd been spending a lot of time together before and after school. I found myself growing jealous and, at one stage, considered saying something about feeling pushed out. But I bit my tongue when I remembered how horrified I'd been to hear my future self playing the guilt card. It's good that they're getting on so well, I told myself. That's probably exactly what Ella needs right now.

Meanwhile, I desperately wanted to talk things through with someone who had an outside perspective. Arthur was my only hope. I'd decided that if I didn't find him now, I'd have to confront Lizzie about what had happened to him.

I headed back to the church, expecting to draw another blank, only to spot him standing in front of the main entrance as soon as the building came into view across a field.

'Arthur!' I shouted.

He turned and, with a smile and a wave, beckoned me over.

My walk turned into a run.

'Hello, William,' he said, leading me over to the usual bench. 'Why the rush?'

'I was keen to catch you, Arthur. I've been looking for you for ages. Where have you been? I was afraid you might be in trouble. I had a dream about that thing from the cricket pavilion. It came after me and Ella.'

Arthur winced. 'That'll never happen for real. Neither of you have anything to fear. Trust me.'

'I know. I do. But since I hadn't seen you for a while, it made me think.'

'Fair enough. I did have to lie low for a bit, but here I am.'

'And everything's okay?'

'Tickety-boo,' he replied with a grin. 'How are things with you, lad? It has been a while. Any luck getting through to your daughter?'

'Yes. It worked. She can see and hear me. I wanted to tell you earlier but—'

'You must be over the moon. How's she taken it? Was she scared to start with?'

'A bit, although it was fine once she remembered meeting me in her dream. Unfortunately, it took my dad getting ill for her to get to that stage.'

I explained to Arthur what had happened.

'Oh dear,' he said. 'Is your father all right?'

'Not really. It was a bad stroke. He's in hospital now.'

'Sorry to hear that, lad. I hope he'll recover.'

'Thanks. Me too. Arthur, why do you think Ella was able to see me when she was – and not before?'

'It's hard to say. There are no textbooks on this kind of thing. She was upset when it happened?'

'Definitely. She was in a right state: terrified her grandad was going to die and that it would be her fault.'

'Poor thing. It was probably her heightened emotions that made the difference.'

'That's what I thought. So how come she didn't see me straight after I died, nor at my funeral? And why hasn't anyone else in my family seen me after all they've been through?'

'You broke through to Ella while she was dreaming. That's when you made the connection. It just needed a kick-start. You've not done that with any of the rest of your family – and, to be honest, the bond you have with them isn't likely to be as strong. Also, as I told you before, children tend to be more receptive than adults. Their minds are open to more possibilities.'

'So it never happens with adults?'

'Oh, I didn't say that. With the right bond and the right person, it can definitely happen.'

Arthur squinted at me, delving into my eyes for answers. 'You look a bit peaky.'

'What do you mean? How do I look anything? My appearance hasn't changed since the day I died.'

187

'Maybe not on the outside, lad, but it's the inside that counts with us spirits. That's where I was looking and you're definitely off your game. It's more than your father, isn't it? Come on, William, what's up? You can talk to me.'

I hesitated for a moment. Then I reminded myself that this was the reason I'd come here. If not him, who was I going to talk to? Ella? Lizzie?

'There is something. It's, um, my deadline.' I took a deep breath and then let the words flow. 'I know I've always been about staying here with Ella, come what may, but … I don't know. It's hard to say it. I've got doubts. They've always been there, but now the deadline's getting so close, they're louder than ever. Sometimes it's like they're screaming in my ear. I do still want to stay with Ella, but the idea of being here forever scares me. I can't help it. I'm afraid of what it might do to me – what I might become – in the long run. And I worry that my presence might actually be bad for Ella.'

'Did that come from Lizzie?'

I nodded.

'Thought so. Did she show you a glimpse of the future?'

That got my attention. 'Yes, although I half convinced myself it was a dream.'

Arthur nodded. 'I thought she might. They often do that with the reluctant souls.'

'The what?'

'Reluctant souls. That's what they class you as upstairs,' he said, staring longingly at the overcast sky. 'I've been there too, don't forget. A guide's main purpose is to help

188

you pass over to the other side. That's what it's all about for them.'

'So what do you think I should do, stay or go?'

'I'm afraid I can't tell you that. You're the only one who can decide. It's tough, I know.'

'You told me that you only stayed here because you had to, Arthur. I remember you said it wasn't something you'd recommend and talked about the loneliness. But I never heard you say that you regretted your choice.'

Arthur stared wistfully into the distance. 'No, you're right. I don't regret what I did. I don't do regrets. There's no point. The important thing once you've made your mind up is to stick with it.'

'But I've not made a decision yet. If you're not going to advise me one way or the other, at least give me the benefit of your experience. Can't you explain why you chose to stay?'

There was a long moment before Arthur answered. I was expecting him to refuse; to be evasive. So I was taken aback when he turned towards me and, with absolute solemnity, said: 'Very well. I'll tell you. Come on, let's take a walk.'

Arthur had the heart attack that killed him one chilly January evening in 1991. He was working late, polishing the wooden floor of the school hall, when it struck. One moment the sixty-two-year-old was clutching his chest and falling to the ground in agony; the next he was standing over his dead body, wondering what on earth was going on.

A lifelong churchgoer with a strong Christian faith, this wasn't exactly what Arthur had expected of the afterlife. He'd always chuckled to himself about people who believed in ghosts. Now what was he supposed to think?

'Is that what I am?' he asked Lizzie after she introduced herself.

'We prefer not to use the G-word. It has too many negative connotations. We're advised to use the term "spirit" instead.'

Arthur wasn't too impressed with his so-called guide to the afterlife. She was so young and nervous, smiling awkwardly every time he asked her a question and churning out stock replies like she'd memorized them from a textbook.

'So if I come with you, you'll take me to Heaven?' Arthur asked.

'Yes, um, that's pretty much it. More or less.'

'Why didn't I go there straight away? Wasn't I deemed worthy?'

'This is how it works for everyone. You have to choose to pass over. It's all about free will.'

'Really? And how do I know you're telling the truth, Lizzie? You could be Satan in disguise, trying to lure me to Hell, for all I know.'

'I can assure you that I am not.'

'Can you prove it?'

'I, um,' she replied, horrified. 'I, um, don't—'

'It's okay, lass,' Arthur said, easing off when he saw she was close to tears. 'If the Devil actually was trying

190

to trick me, I'm sure he'd use a more convincing disguise. You've not been doing this long, have you?'

The next time they met, after Lizzie had given Arthur some time to come to terms with his situation, he had several questions for her.

'How many others have you guided?'

'Um, you're the tenth.'

'I see. That explains a lot. And you were human before?'

She nodded.

'When did you die?'

'Last year.'

'What happened?'

'I'm not sure if I should be—'

'Come on, lass. You want me to trust you. Well, it works both ways.'

'Fine. It was a car accident. I was riding my bike to work and I was hit by a bus.'

'Ouch.'

Lizzie shrugged. 'I don't remember much about it.'

'What did you do?'

'Well, like you, I met my guide and—'

'No, I don't mean that. What was your job? Where were you cycling to?'

'Oh, right. I was a nurse. I was on my way to do a shift at the hospital. I did get there in the end, only it was in the back of an ambulance; I died in the operating theatre.'

'You remember?'

'Only the dying bit. I was unconscious before that. My guide filled in the gaps.'

'You were a nurse?'

'That's right. You're surprised?'

'No. Not at all. It kind of makes sense, actually. I bet that's why you started doing this, isn't it? So you could keep on helping people.'

'Um, I guess so. I just wanted to do something useful. To have a purpose. I was only twenty-seven when it happened. I didn't feel old enough to be dead.'

Arthur winked. 'Not like me, eh?'

'That's not what I meant.'

'So why did they send me a novice? Aren't I worthy of someone more senior?'

'I, er. I'm not sure exactly how it works. I'm sorry if you don't feel I, um. I mean, I can get someone more senior if you like.'

'But that would reflect badly on you, right?'

Her wavy black ponytail bounced on the collar of her mac as she nodded in reply.

'You'll do, then, for now. You've more experience of this than I have; let's try to muddle through together.'

Lizzie managed a smile, but it soon disappeared when Arthur asked his next question. 'What about Peggy?'

He was referring to his wife: the woman he loved with all his heart and who he'd not spent a night apart from in the entire forty years they'd been married. The fact they'd not been blessed with children had hurt when they were younger. Ultimately, though, it had cemented the bond between them; each was unquestionably the most important person in the other's life. Two days earlier she'd been diagnosed with lung cancer after finally heeding his

192

warnings to get her persistent cough and breathlessness checked out by a doctor.

'Don't worry, love,' he'd said, determined to be a rock for her despite the terror and fury he felt inside. 'I'm here for you. We'll get through this together.'

But now he wasn't there for her. He'd abandoned her at the time she needed him most. 'What about my wife?' he asked Lizzie again, desperate for an answer. 'How is she going to manage without me?'

Lizzie knew about Peggy's cancer but hadn't got a clue what to say. Her nose twitched involuntarily. 'I, er, I … I'm not—'

'You're not what? Not sure? Fantastic. Maybe I do need to see one of your superiors after all.' Arthur paused for a moment before adding: 'I've been thinking. You said when we first met that I have to choose to pass over. So that means I can also choose to stay, right?'

And that's how it began.

Despite Lizzie's advice to the contrary, Arthur determined to stay at Peggy's side and to try to make contact with her. It hurt that he was invisible to her, but his pain was nothing compared to what she was going through. At the same time as having to deal with her illness, she was consumed by grief. So much so that she declined the chemotherapy and radiotherapy the doctors offered her. She felt there was no longer anything worth living for now her husband had gone. However, Arthur felt very differently. Knowing what it meant to lose his own life, he desperately wanted her to fight to sustain hers for as long as possible.

193

'You'll never get another chance to live this life again,' he told her over and over, even though he knew she couldn't hear him. 'It's not your time to die yet.'

Although nothing he saw gave him any hope of success, Arthur was determined to get through to his wife. His faith had taken a big knock, but in its place he found blind determination. Lizzie told him it wasn't possible, but he refused to accept it. Day after day he tried everything he could think of to smash down whatever barrier it was that stopped Peggy from sensing him. Such was the fervour of his obsession, which only increased as Peggy's health worsened, that he paid little heed to his guide's warnings about an approaching deadline. Before he knew it, the weeks he had left had turned into just twenty-four hours to make a final decision.

It was soon after Lizzie had reminded him of this fact – even showing him a glimpse of the lonely future he faced if he stayed – that Arthur reached breaking point. He'd persisted day after day, week after week with his attempts to communicate with his wife: talking to her, whispering in her ear, even shouting and screaming at times. He'd followed her everywhere, always at her side, without even the slightest sign of a breakthrough. And all the while she'd been taking less and less care of herself. She'd become weaker and weaker; the cancer had spread.

His mind was reeling that night as he knelt at her bedside and watched her sleep. For the first time, he found himself considering the unthinkable: whether to move on and leave Peggy behind. What's the point in staying? he thought. She hasn't got a clue that I'm here.

194

'Oh, Peggy,' he bawled. 'This is agony. I'm so lost and lonely. Why can't you see that I'm here with you?'

Floods of images of their life together swept in and out of his memory as he remained next to his sleeping wife, paralysed by the weight of his emotions. How could he abandon her at such a time of need? He'd never loved anyone like he loved her and he never would again. Leaning over her inert form, wretched and desperate, he knew he couldn't imagine an existence without her. Then it was like his feelings took on a life of their own. They rose up from deep within his essence, smashing down the barriers that stood in the way, and taking Arthur to a place in Peggy's unconscious mind where they could finally be together again. And when she woke from that beautiful dream, she found her husband waiting for her as he'd said he would be. Everything Arthur had strived for since his death had finally come to fruition and it was without hesitation that he told his guide the next day of his decision to forfeit his place in paradise.

'Are you sure?' Lizzie asked him. 'There's no going back.'

'I'm staying here, where I belong, at my wife's side.'

'What about when her turn comes, Arthur? What then? You won't be able to pass over with her. Or do you want her to miss out on Heaven too?'

'We'll cross that bridge when we come to it. Right now she needs me here. I can help her to keep on living. It's the right thing to do. It's the only thing to do.'

'There's nothing for Peggy to fear in death.'

'That doesn't mean she should suffer alone and die before her time. You only get one life. Mine's gone, but her heart's still beating.'

'Do you realize what you're giving up?'

'I can't miss what I've never known.'

'But is this what she—'

'My mind's made up. There's nothing you can say to change it.'

CHAPTER 20

'And did it work? Did Peggy start getting treatment?'

Arthur looked at me with sad eyes. 'She did, yes. But it was too late. The cancer had too great a hold. Her body was riddled with it.'

'How long did she last?'

I felt awful for not knowing what had happened to his wife. I'd been a child living in the village back then. Before Arthur died I remembered seeing her with him at church, but I'd never really known her like I knew him. I only noticed her because she was with Arthur; alone, I doubt I could have told her apart from all the other white-haired old ladies.

'Almost a year,' he replied. 'She really fought it once she knew I was with her, but it was a battle she could never win.'

'I'm sorry. You deserved more time together.'

'We felt lucky to have that long. It could have only been a few weeks. I've no regrets.'

'Wasn't she in a lot of pain?'

'Only at the very end, when the cancer had spread into her bones and pelvis. She was in a hospice by then and on constant medication to ease her suffering.'

'And what happened when she died?'

'I did what I had to do,' Arthur replied after a long pause.

'What do you mean?'

He closed his eyes and let out a long sigh of anguish. 'Just before she passed away, I told her that she should follow her guide straight away to the other side once they revealed themselves. I told her to trust them implicitly, as they'd take her to Heaven and I'd be waiting there for her. She had nothing else to keep her here, so that's what she did.'

'But ... couldn't she see you once she'd died?'

'I hid from her. There was no other way. If I hadn't, she'd have given up her place on the other side to stay with me. I know she would – and I didn't want that for her. I'd understood by that stage the enormity of what I'd done. I couldn't let her do the same.'

'I don't know what to say.'

'It's okay. I know what you're thinking: it was her choice to make, not mine. Well, I did what I did and that's all there is to it. You asked for my story. Now you have it. I hope it's of some help to you.'

'So you've been alone all those years since she died? Didn't you have any other family?'

Arthur shook his head. 'Peggy and I were both only children. Other than a couple of distant cousins I hardly knew, there was no one.' He gestured back towards the church and over at the primary school. 'I visit lots of places, but here is where I've always felt most at home.'

'What about your old house?'

'That was sold after Peggy died. It didn't feel right to stay once the new owners moved in.'

'You must have been so lonely.'

'Yes,' he replied. 'It eats away at your soul. Staying here definitely isn't the soft option.'

'How do you deal with it?'

He shrugged. 'As best I can.'

I didn't know what to do with myself after I left Arthur. My mind was all over the place and I needed space to think, so I just started walking. I strode into the grounds of the primary school, headed past the main building, then across the playground and on to the field, where the clover-filled grass was still white with frost.

When I reached the end, I squeezed through a gap in the fence that had been there since my school days and continued towards a wide, sloping meadow, eventually joining a dirt path that led down to a small stream. We'd called it a river as children, which made me smile for a moment as I walked alongside the icy water. I stopped when I reached the towering oak tree. Unlike the stream, it seemed as big as ever, the lack of leaves showing off the muscular swell of its ancient branches. There remained a knotted piece of blue rope hanging from one thick branch, allowing kids to swing across the bubbling water. Could it be the same piece of rope I had swung on all those years ago?

There were so many happy childhood memories associated with this place. As I drank in the scene through my two remaining senses, fragments of those golden days fluttered in and out of my thoughts. Perched atop the highest branches, the village a distant carpet miles below, I was Superman, afraid of no one. Later I was 007, licensed to shoot the bully from the class above with my home-made catapult.

Then a more recent memory took hold and pushed the others aside. I was there with Alice, my wife, on a rare visit back up north to visit Mum and Dad. It was a warm summer evening and she'd suggested a walk, just the two of us. I'd never shown her this place before and she loved it.

'Watch this,' I told her as I pulled myself up on to the lowest branch. 'Come on. You too. It's easy.'

She shook her head, beaming a happy grin. 'No, thanks. Don't let me stop you, though, as long as you're sure it's safe.'

'Of course it is,' I said, climbing higher. 'I've been up here a hundred times before.'

'I imagine you're a bit heavier these days.'

'Is that what's stopping you? Look at the size of these branches. They'd hold an elephant. Come on. I dare you to climb up here with me. I'll keep you safe.'

She shook her head again, her long curls flapping from side to side and an even bigger grin on her face. 'No, thanks. Better not.'

'What are you smiling about?' I asked, halfway up now. 'Is it so funny to see your husband climbing a tree?'

'No, not at all.'

'Then get your arse up here.'

'I can't.'

'Why not?'

She paused before replying: 'You have to be careful in my condition.'

'What?' I said, the shock causing me to lose my footing.

'Will! Are you all right?' Alice shouted as my flailing arms managed to grab on to another branch and I pulled myself back to safety.

'I'm fine,' I panted. 'Did you say what I think you just said?'

'I'm not saying another word until you get back down here to safety.'

'Okay, okay. I'm coming.'

I clambered down as quickly as I could, my limbs still quivering from the scare. As soon as I was standing next to her, I asked my question again.

'What do you think I just said, monkey boy?' she asked, putting her arms around my neck and pulling me towards her, so I was staring straight into her enchanting pale green eyes.

'That you have to be careful in your condition.'

'And what condition do you think that might be?'

'You're not?'

'I am.'

'You're sure?'

'I've done five home tests. They all say the same thing.'

I felt my mouth stretch into a wide grin. 'Wow. That's amazing. But ... I thought you weren't ready yet. And what about your new dental practice? You said you wanted to get properly established first.'

'Stuff it.'

'But how? What about the pill?'

'Remember that night at the hotel in Birmingham. I forgot to take it until the next day. I didn't think it would matter.'

'Oh, right,' I said, smiling at the memory. 'It happened then?'

'I think so.'

'And you're happy.'

'Yep. You?'

'Me? You know I wanted this. I'm … I'm over the moon. We're having a baby. Wow. We're having a baby!'

Alice pulled away for a moment, quickly scanning the surrounding area. Then she pulled me into a passionate kiss, led me behind a large bush and started unbuttoning my jeans.

'Someone might come,' I said. 'Everyone knows me around here.'

'There's no one else around. We need to celebrate.'

'But, I mean, is it okay to do that now? Could it not, you know, do some damage?'

'Of course not. People have sex right the way through pregnancy.'

'You're sure?'

Her reply was to push me down on to the ground and straddle me. I didn't need any more convincing. God, I felt madly in love then. How had I ended up wrecking everything?

As my mind floated back to the wintry present, a wave of sadness and guilt washed over me. Alice and I had been so happy at that magical moment, blissfully unaware of the awful pain to come. It could have all turned out so differently.

But it didn't, I told myself, and there's nothing I can do about it. I need to concentrate on the present. There are important things here that are still within my control. So what do I do: stay or go?

On the one hand I had the evidence of Lizzie's vision of the future, which had shown me how staying with Ella had the potential to go badly wrong. On the other hand, now that I knew how things could turn out, didn't that enable me to act differently? Surely I didn't have to become the bitter version of myself that I'd witnessed. What if I stayed with Ella but gave her enough space to live her own life and not feel beholden to me? Was that really possible or was I deluding myself?

I knew I also had to consider the possibility of passing over to the other side, allowing myself to be engulfed in that alluring white light. But how could I ever explain that to Ella? She'd think I was abandoning her.

I'd really hoped that learning Arthur's story would help me move forward, but here I was, as confused as ever. His situation immediately after he'd died had been comparable to mine, but it had also been quite different. I wasn't sure what message to take from it. After wandering in circles around the meadow for several hours, the best I could come up with was to discuss the matter openly with Ella. And yet ... was this really something a six-year-old should have to consider? If so, I'd certainly have to choose my words carefully.

CHAPTER 21

It was nearly 5 p.m. when I returned to the house. All the doors were shut, which meant I was trapped outside for the time being. I peered through the lounge window, hoping to see Ella so I could signal for her to let me inside, but the room was empty. I walked around to the kitchen, where the window was ajar. There was still no sign of my daughter, but Mum and Lauren were sitting opposite each other at the table, locked in a heated debate. I could see Dad's black clamshell phone lying open between them.

Oh God, I thought. What's going on now?

'What the hell were you thinking, Lauren?' Mum snapped.

'I don't know. It just came out. Do you think he knew what I was talking about?'

'I hope not, but it was bloody obvious to me.'

Lauren flung her arms up in the air. 'I can't see past what he's done. It's all I think about every time I look at him. I don't know how you can feel any different. It should be even worse for you.'

Mum slapped her right palm on to the table with a loud thump. 'For goodness' sake, Lauren. We've been through this. We agreed to leave it for now. Remember what we discussed about pulling together in a crisis?'

'Yes, I know, but … I can't do it. It's not in me to go to the hospital every day and pretend everything's hunky dory between us when it's not. The fact is that Dad's been deceiving us. God knows how long it's been going on. This woman, whoever she is, may not even be the first. We're no better than him if we lie to his face every day. The truth has to come out.'

'Your father needs time to recover. That takes precedence over everything else.'

'What's wrong with you? It's like you're using Dad's illness as an excuse to bury your head in the sand. I'm starting to wonder whether you knew about the affair all along and chose to turn a blind eye.'

Mum gasped. Then her arm shot across the table as she gave Lauren a hard slap to the face. 'How dare you.'

Lauren's jaw dropped as she raised her hand to her reddening cheek. 'I can't believe you just did that.'

'You're not in Holland now.'

'What the hell is that supposed to mean?'

'You need to learn some tact; to be less blunt. Speaking your mind might be the Dutch way, but here we think first. You're supposed to be helping me.'

Lauren stood up, grabbed the mobile phone from the table and stuffed it into a pocket of her jeans. She picked up her coat, which was draped over an empty chair, and stormed out of the back door, walking straight past me on her way to the street.

'Hey! Where do you think you're going with that phone?' Mum shouted after her. 'Don't do anything stupid, Lauren. I'm warning you.'

I almost followed my sister, but the lure of the open door was too much, so I slipped past Mum into the house.

'Ella?' I shouted from the hallway. 'It's Daddy. Where are you, love?'

No answer.

That's odd, I thought. She wasn't downstairs, so I assumed she was up in her bedroom, perhaps plugged into the old mp3 player I'd filled with music for her. But there was no sign of her there either. 'Ella?' I called out again. 'Where are you, love?'

At that moment the front doorbell rang. I went to see who it was, arriving at the same time as Mum.

'Hello, Sylvia,' she said as she swung open the door to reveal her friend and neighbour. 'Are you coming in?'

'Yes, go on then, Ann. I will for a minute. How's Tom doing?'

'He's, um, still not great. It looks like his recovery's going to be a long process.'

'I'm sorry to hear that. He is on the mend, though?'

'Hopefully. They've got him on medication to stop him having another stroke. There'll be no more smoking and drinking, mind.'

'Oh dear. Tom won't like that. How is he in himself?'

'It's hard to say. He can hardly talk at the moment.'

'Poor thing. Larry and I would like to visit him, but we wondered if it might be too soon. What do you think?'

'It's a nice thought, but I'd probably leave it for now. He's not in much of a state to welcome visitors. Maybe in a few weeks.'

'Do you think he'll be there that long?'

Mum nodded. She led Sylvia through to the lounge, switching on the lights along the way. 'It's dark so early now, isn't it? Would you like a brew?'

'No. I'm fine, thanks,' Sylvia said, sitting down. 'Where's the little one?'

'Yes, good question,' I sniped.

'She's having tea at a friend's house. A little girl called Jada. They came out of school holding hands this afternoon and begged me, like I was going to say no. It was so sweet. It's the first time Ella's wanted to do anything like this since Will's death.'

That solved the mystery of where Ella was, anyway. Although I knew Jada and her parents, I couldn't help feeling concerned that she was out of sight and in someone else's care. I hope Mum gave them her car seat, I thought, before telling myself to chill out. It would be good for Ella to have some fun.

'Everything all right with Lauren?' Sylvia said.

'Why do you ask?'

'Oh, er, I just passed her walking down the street. She looked flustered.'

'She'll be fine,' Mum said with a confidence that surprised me. 'She's finding it difficult seeing her dad so helpless, that's all. You grow up thinking your parents are immortal;

it's always a shock when you first realize they're not.'

'I know what you mean. I remember when my mum fell ill with angina. She was suddenly so frail. Don't worry: Lauren will get used to it. At least she's here to help you. What an awful period you've been through.'

Mum nodded slowly, her eyes welling up.

'Sorry. I didn't mean to upset you, love,' Sylvia said, taking Mum's hand in hers. 'Are you coping?'

'Yes … I'll be fine, honestly.'

'Well, you know that Larry and I are here for you. Whatever you need.'

'Thanks, Sylvia.'

At that point Mum insisted on making a brew; when she returned with two mugs and a plate of chocolate digestives, she looked far more composed.

'I wanted to tell you something,' Sylvia said, holding a hand in front of her mouth as she finished chewing on a piece of biscuit.

'Oh,' Mum replied, taking a tiny sip from her mug before returning it to the coffee table. 'What's that?'

'Probably nothing, but I thought I'd better mention it, just in case.'

'Go on.'

'There was a man parked outside your house this morning in a black car. Usually I wouldn't have thought anything of it, but he was there for ages and kept the engine running.'

I'd only been half listening to their conversation by that stage, but Sylvia's words caught my attention.

'A black car? Who was it?' Mum asked.

Sylvia shrugged. 'I thought you might have some idea.'

'What type of car was it?'

'Um, I'm not great with cars, Ann. I did make a point of looking, though. It was one of those smart ones with the four circles badge.'

'Audi?'

'That sounds right. It was blocking your drive and the man behind the wheel was staring at the house, like he was scoping it out.'

'Like a burglar, you mean?'

'The thought crossed my mind. That's why I went out to speak to him.'

Now my ears really pricked up. 'And?' I said, as if she could hear me.

'What did he say?' Mum asked.

Sylvia shook her head. 'Nothing useful. I tapped on the window; he wound it down and I asked if I could help him with anything. He smiled and politely declined. Then he said what a nice dress I was wearing. That rather threw me.'

'What did you say?'

Sylvia's cheeks reddened. 'I, er, thanked him for the compliment and made my excuses. I couldn't think what else to say.'

'What did he look like?'

'Rather handsome, actually: early fifties, slim, well groomed. From the car and the suit he was wearing, I'd say he was wealthy. Does that ring any bells?'

'No,' Mum replied. 'But he doesn't sound like your typical burglar.'

'I suppose not. He drove off a few minutes later.' She rummaged through her pockets before pulling out and handing over a scrap of paper. 'Here, I made a note of his number plate for you, just in case.'

Written in black ink on the crumpled sheet was the same personalized registration I'd recently noted, D3 VLN.

'Do you recognize it?' Sylvia asked Mum.

'No. I'll keep hold of it, though. You never know. There haven't been any break-ins nearby, have there?'

'Not that I've heard.'

'Oh, well. It's a mystery. Probably nothing to get our knickers in a twist about, but thanks for telling me.'

'You're welcome. Any time.'

I wouldn't be so quick to dismiss it, Mum, I thought. That bloke's up to something. I don't know who or what he is, but I intend to find out.

Not long after Sylvia left, a beaming Ella returned full of envious stories of Jada's amazing house and huge toy collection. It had always wound me up when she'd acted like that in the past. It still smarted now, although it hardly seemed to register with Mum. 'That's nice, darling,' she said. 'I bet you're tired now. Let's get you in the bath and then bed.'

'Can I have a book?'

'Of course.'

'Can Auntie Lauren read it?'

'Um, she's had to pop out. I'm not sure if she'll be back in time.'

In fact when Lauren eventually returned, Ella had been in bed for an hour – and asleep almost as long. Having noticed how tired she was, I'd decided to delay our serious chat. I knew it couldn't wait much longer, but I was glad to have more time to decide what to say. I wasn't looking forward to it at all.

'Where have you been?' Mum asked Lauren.

'How about an apology for hitting me first?'

'Hitting you? It was a little slap – and you deserved it.'

'What, because I spoke the truth? You'd rather I was more British about it, would you? Sorry, Mum. That's not me. Sweeping things under the carpet isn't my style.'

'Where did you go?'

'None of your business.'

'Well you missed your niece going to bed. She wanted you to read to her.'

'You shouldn't have driven me out of the house, then. I'll go and give her a kiss in a minute.'

'Don't you wake her up. That's the last thing she needs.'

'And I suppose you'll hit me again if I do. Come on, Mum. Credit me with some intelligence.'

'Stop saying that,' Mum replied, bursting into tears. 'You know I didn't hit you.'

Lauren's face softened. 'Don't cry, Mum. I didn't mean it. I know it was only a slap.'

She pulled Mum into a hug and started crying too. 'I'm sorry,' she said. 'Why are we fighting? We should be supporting each other.'

'You're right. I'm sorry too. I never should have slapped you. You know I wouldn't hurt you for the world. I just got so frustrated.'

Once they'd both calmed down, Mum cautiously broached the subject that had sparked their row in the first place. 'Please drop this affair business for now, love.

211

I'd really appreciate it if you could stick to what we agreed and wait until your father's better.'

Lauren looked down at the floor and offered no reply.

'You're not exactly filling me with confidence here. Come on, Lauren. I really need you on my side. I can't do this without you.'

My sister stayed silent and a look of dawning horror spread across Mum's face. 'Oh no. You've done something, haven't you? Oh, Lauren, what is it? Have you been back to see your dad again? You have to tell me.'

Lauren shook her head and wearily raised her eyes to meet Mum's. 'Relax. I haven't been back to the hospital.'

'So where have you been all this time?'

'I popped in on a couple of old school friends: Sophie and Helena. That's all.'

'What about that phone? What did you do with it?'

Lauren looked sheepish. 'Um …'

'I knew it. What did you do? Just tell me. It can't be any worse than I'm imagining.'

'Promise you won't get mad?'

'Tell me, Lauren.'

She took a deep breath. 'Well, I was so angry when I left the house that I dialled that number again.'

'And?'

'The call was answered, but there was no one there. I could hear muffled noises in the background: music playing and an engine sound. It was like the phone was in a pocket or something. This woman must have answered it without realizing. She was probably driving.'

'What did you do?'

'I shouted "hello" a few times and then hung up.'

'That's it?'

'Not exactly. I mean, yes, I hung up. But … I tried again later.'

Mum glared at Lauren, arms folded across her chest, until she continued. 'It went straight to voicemail. Still no personal greeting or anything, but I, er, left a—'

'What did you say?'

'That I had an urgent message from Dad. That she should call me straight away or come round to the house.'

Mum froze. She said nothing but blinked several times, her face haemorrhaging colour with each movement of her eyelids.

'Mum?' Lauren asked eventually. 'Aren't you going to say anything?'

'Why … on earth … did you do that?'

'I had to do something. It was driving me crazy. At least we'll find out who she is now.'

'What if I don't want to know?'

'You have to, Mum. It's your right. There's no point burying your head in the sand.'

Mum stood up. 'Don't pretend you did this for me, Lauren. You've done nothing but ignore what I want. I'm going to bed.'

'Bed? It's not even nine thirty.'

Mum ignored her, banging the door shut on her way out.

So how do I put it? I asked myself for the umpteenth time. How do I tell my daughter that I'm entertaining the idea of leaving her for good? As much as I thought about it, sitting alone in the dark while everyone else slept, the right words wouldn't come to mind. Were there any right words? At one point I decided the best solution was to tell Ella everything – even detailing my own uncertainty. But then I came back to the fact that she was only six. How could I expect her to take all that on board? She needed certainty from her father, not indecision. Oh God, this was hard.

'Anything I can help with?' a familiar voice enquired from across the shadowy lounge.

'Jesus, Lizzie!' I said, holding my hand over my mouth as I acknowledged the poor word choice. 'Sorry. You shocked me. I didn't mean to, you know … I mean, I guess—'

'Relax,' she replied as all the lights switched on.

I winced at the sudden brightness.

'Sorry. Too much?' she added, dimming them with a flick of a finger.

'That's better. Thanks. Not a fan of calling ahead, are you?'

'I had a feeling you might need some advice.'

'How—'

'I'm a guide. A certain level of knowledge comes with the job. Now what are you struggling with? I'd love to help.'

'Yes, but it's not exactly independent advice you're offering, is it? We both know that you have a vested interest.'

'You're crotchety today.'

I argued with her for a little longer but soon gave in. What did I have to lose? It wasn't like I had to take her advice.

'Okay,' I said. 'My gut feeling is, as always, to stay here with my daughter, but I haven't completely ignored the advice you've been giving me. Obviously my priority is what's best for her. What I saw – in the future. Will that definitely happen?'

'It could do. It's one possible future, but it's not set in stone. You have the power to change it.'

'But do I really have to pass over and leave Ella behind in order to do that? Can't I stay and do things differently?'

'I don't think growing up in their dead father's shadow would be good for anyone. There's a natural order to things and diverting from that path rarely works out well. You also need to remember the paradise you'll be passing up if you remain here.'

'This is about my daughter, not me. My decision has to be based on what's right for her.'

'But the two things are intertwined, William. Don't forget that in the version of the future you saw, your unhappiness was one of the main problems between you and Ella.'

'I know, but that's what I meant before when I talked about doing things differently.'

Her nose twitched. 'I've given you my answer.'

I paused to think and a heavy silence fell on the room. I could feel Lizzie's eyes scanning me, calculating my next move. 'So what the hell do I tell Ella?' I blurted out.

'I can understand how that would be difficult. It's one reason why people can't usually see the spirits of their loved ones.'

'She thinks I'm back for good. Even if I decided that passing over was the right move, I'd need her blessing first. But I haven't got a clue what to say to her.'

'Asking Ella for her blessing would be like putting the decision in her hands. Do you find that fair? Imagine if she said she wanted you to stay. How would she feel about that when she was older: when she understood what she'd made you give up? How would that help her? You're the parent here. It's your choice and yours alone.'

'I'd not thought of it that way, but ... I guess you're right. It's an impossible decision, though. How do I make the right choice?'

'You will.'

'I wish I shared your confidence. I can't believe the deadline's so close now. It's December the twelfth, right?'

Lizzie nodded. 'Two weeks on Monday.'

'Just before Christmas.'

'You've already had longer than most people, William.'

I tried to ignore the anxiety that washed over me at the mere mention of it. 'I know. Any particular time?'

'Noon.'

'Really? Oh. I'd actually assumed I'd have the full day – until midnight.'

'Sorry, no.'

CHAPTER 22

FIFTEEN DAYS LEFT

Dad gave Ella a crooked smile and reached over his vast stomach with his left arm – the good one – to take her hand.

'How are you feeling?' she asked him.

He made a so-so gesture with his left hand. A few minutes earlier we'd witnessed him walk awkwardly across the hospital ward with a nurse. Now he was resting.

'Can't you talk any more, Grandad?'

'I told you, love,' Mum said. 'He's having a few problems with his speech because of the stroke. But look how well he was walking just now. He'll be back to normal in no time, won't you, Tom?'

Dad's face had become so gaunt that it looked out of place on top of his huge body. It was the first time Ella had seen her grandfather for a few days and it wasn't easy for her. Her eyes searched out mine, looking for support.

'You're doing great,' I whispered. 'Just keep talking to him like you normally would.'

He had a sudden coughing fit. Mum rushed to his aid, pouring him some water from a jug at his bedside. As she fussed around him, I reassured Ella it was nothing to worry about.

'You will get better soon, won't you?' Ella asked him once he was settled again. 'I miss you. We all do – even Sam. He told me this morning in doggie language. Auntie Lauren would have come as well, but she had to do food shopping.'

I could see Dad's eyes welling up, which in turn made me feel emotional. Although I'd visited him in hospital a few times now, I couldn't get used to seeing him in this state. It was so … not Dad. He'd always been such a strong, powerful presence in my life. The only chink in his armour had been his fondness for drinking and smoking – his two big crutches – and food too, I suppose. But he'd always appeared to have those things under control. I couldn't once remember him being drunk. And his size had never seemed to get in the way of him doing anything. He'd always been like an iceberg, slowly sliding through life, carrying along the people and things that mattered and pushing away those that didn't.

Was Dad's and my relationship a close one? Yes and no. He wasn't someone I'd ever felt comfortable telling my deepest secrets or greatest fears. We'd never done man-hugs or talked about our feelings together. However, Dad had always been there for me when I needed him. After Alice died, Mum had been amazing at helping me to deal with my grief and to care for Ella. But it was Dad who'd got me through all the practical stuff, like organizing the funeral, handling the will and informing all the necessary people. I'd always been able to depend on him for these kinds of things.

Dad might never have specifically told me that he loved me – not since I was a child, at least – but the unwavering support he'd given me over the years said plenty. He'd done even more for Lauren, so I couldn't understand why she was being so tough on him. Okay, this affair thing was shocking and painful, but it wasn't a deal breaker. He was still our father. He'd stuck by us through thick and thin and deserved the same in return, especially in his current fragile state of health.

Besides, how could I blame Dad for what he'd done? I was no better. I knew how easy it was to get sucked in. I also knew that Dad's actions, whatever they were, didn't necessarily mean that he no longer loved Mum.

The seed of that thought threw me into the past. It was a full-blown flashback: the vivid kind that appears of its own volition and takes you along for the ride, like it or not. I could smell the sweet allure of her perfume – a heady mix of vanilla and almonds. I could feel the excitement of her grinding against me with a promise of more.

Her.

The other woman.

My dirty little secret.

The guilt was just a seed back then: a fragment of what it would become, pushed into the background by booze and desire. If only I'd stopped myself. If only that was as far as it had gone. But I hadn't. It wasn't.

Like father, like son.

I snapped back to the present as Dad nodded and gave Ella's hand a squeeze. He looked like he was about to try to speak but then thought better of it. Instead, he twisted himself awkwardly towards the bedside cabinet and reached over to pick up a notepad and pen. Unfortunately, he knocked over the water jug in the process, sending Mum into a flap. She raced off to find some tissues.

'What a mess,' Mum puffed as she knelt on the floor, frantically mopping up the water. 'Why on earth did you try to reach over by yourself, Tom?'

'Come on, Mum,' I said. 'It was an accident. Give the man a break. Ella, keep talking to him. Let him know that it's all right. Nana doesn't mean to snap like that. She'll calm down again in a minute.'

Dad lay quietly on the bed, staring at the ceiling, his contorted face a mixture of frustration and embarrassment.

'Don't worry, Grandad,' Ella whispered into his ear after shuffling over to the dry side of the bed. 'At least it was only water.'

Dad turned and looked fondly at his granddaughter. He slowly raised his good hand and traced one finger down the side of her face.

'I love you, Grandad,' she whispered. 'I really hope you get better soon.'

He ruffled her hair and gave her a little wink.

Meanwhile, Mum stood up with a groan, rubbing her knees. 'These hard floors are not meant for kneeling on. Not at my age.' She lifted the sodden clump of wet tissue from the floor and dropped it into Dad's now-empty jug. 'I'm going to put this in the bin,' she told him. 'I'll fill

220

you up a fresh jug while I'm at it. No more knocking it over, please.'

Addressing Ella, she added: 'You'll be all right on your own with him for a couple of minutes, won't you?'

Ella nodded.

'Good girl. If there's any problem, you just have to press that button and one of the nurses will be over in a flash.'

'Okay.'

As soon as she'd gone, Dad picked up the pad and pen and started writing. When he passed Ella the note, I moved behind her so I could also see it. If I'd been a cartoon character, my eyes would have stretched out of their sockets as I read the words: *Can you see him too?*

'You can see Daddy?' Ella asked as I gaped at my father.

He nodded, frowning at me before reaching for the pad again. This time he simply wrote: *How?*

'How?' I repeated, still getting my bearings following this unexpected turn of events. 'How what? How can you see me? How come I'm here?'

He nodded again twice.

I looked to Ella for support. 'Just tell him, Dad,' she said.

'Well. I, um. I'm … a spirit. I found myself like this as soon as I died and I've been hanging around ever since. Ella was the only one who could see me until now. The only one I knew about, anyway. It took a lot of effort to get through to her. I never expected it to happen with anyone else. How long have you been able to see me?'

Dad turned back to the notepad and wrote two more words: *Since stroke*.

221

'Really? Wow. You hid that well. I guess the stroke must be something to do with it, then. Why didn't you say anything sooner?'

Thought gone mad, he wrote in reply.

I laughed. 'Yeah, I can understand that. He's not mad, though, is he, Ella?'

'No. Daddy really is here, Grandad. I'm so happy you can see him too. It's—'

'Shh,' I said as Mum approached with the fresh water. 'Not in front of Nana.'

It was hard to keep quiet after that, especially as Ella kept looking over at me and grinning, but I was determined to keep things normal in front of Mum. How had I not noticed Dad looking at me before? Had he hidden it that well? Or had I grown so used to being invisible that I'd stumbled blindly past obvious clues?

When it was time for us to go, Dad beckoned Mum over and whispered something into her ear. She didn't understand him at first and then, after he repeated himself, there was a look of horror on her face. No, Dad, what have you said? I thought, fearing the worst.

'You want your phone?'

Dad nodded.

'Your smartphone?'

He nodded again, seeming to miss the pertinence of Mum's second question.

'Why? What use will it be if you can't talk? I thought mobile phones weren't allowed in hospitals.'

Dad indicated that they were permitted on the ward. He wanted it as a way to communicate: a quicker version of the notepad. A little of the colour returned to Mum's cheeks once she understood his intention.

As we left I promised to return soon for a one-to-one chat. Dad looked troubled by this, actually recoiling when I approached him, but he gave a short nod of his head in reply.

Back at the car Ella asked Mum, who was still visibly shaken, if she was okay.

'I'm fine, darling. Don't worry about me. I should be the one asking how you are. I've been meaning to talk to you about your daddy. You seem to be managing so well, but you must be missing him terribly. I know I am. We can talk about it any time you like. It doesn't have to be now, if you don't want to, but I'm always here for you. And it doesn't matter if it makes you upset. That's normal. It's not something to be embarrassed about.'

Ella gave me a sideways glance before replying. 'Thanks, Nana. I'm fine at the moment.'

'Are you sure, darling?'

'Yes.'

'Well, I mean what I say. Whenever you do want to talk about it, just let me know. Any time you like. And if you don't want to talk to me, there's always Auntie Lauren instead. Or we could even arrange for you to talk to someone independent.'

'What do you mean?'

'A counsellor,' Mum replied. 'Do you know what that is?'

'Someone from the council?'

'No. That's different. The kind of counsellor I mean is someone who can help you discuss things you find it hard

223

to talk about. They can help you understand your feelings about difficult things, like losing your dad, so you can come to terms with them.'

'But I'm all right, Nana. Really.'

'I know, love. But I'm concerned that you're bottling things up. You almost seem to be managing too well. Just have a think about what I said, anyway.'

'Okay.'

Mum paused before adding: 'The other thing we need to talk about is, um, what to do with your daddy's ashes.'

Ella looked at me, next to her in the back of the car, and grimaced. The urn containing my remains had been on the sideboard in the dining room ever since Dad had collected it from the crematorium.

'I know the idea is a bit creepy,' I told her, 'but it's better to put them somewhere nice than to keep them in the house. That's what I did with your mummy's ashes. I scattered them into a lake at a park she loved in London.'

I remembered it well. It had been just before we moved back up north. Mum and Dad had come with me and they stayed with Ella on dry land as I hired a pedal boat and headed out alone into the middle of the lake. It was a warm afternoon in early autumn, the gold-tinged leaves just starting to accept their looming demise. This had been the place where I'd proposed to Alice, here in the middle of the lake on an almost identical boat. I was still in bits, although I'd been doing my best to hold it together in front of the others. As soon as I was alone, the tears started streaming. I pedalled ahead, on and on, averting my eyes whenever I passed another boat. Eventually I found a quiet spot, opened my rucksack and carefully lifted out the urn. I stood on my seat, doing my best to keep my balance, removed the lid and spun it around in the air.

Unfortunately, it wasn't quite the moving send-off I'd planned. It was windy that day and there was a gust just as I released my wife's ashes, meaning half of them ended up back in the boat and all over me. I had bits in my eyes, my mouth and stuck to my sodden cheeks. Frantically, I fought to remove them. Then I used my hands to scoop the rest out of the boat and into the water.

It was what I deserved, I told myself. What right did I have to play the devoted widower after cheating on my pregnant wife? It had only happened once and I'd felt absolute regret ever since. I'd sworn to myself that nothing like that would ever happen again. But why had I allowed it to take place, encouraged it even? A need to prove I still had it, perhaps, in the face of impending parenthood. I'd debated endlessly whether or not to come clean to Alice but concluded it was a bad idea to upset her while pregnant. I'd sworn to myself that I would tell her at a later date, but I never got the chance to see if I had the guts to do it.

Now I was receiving everyone's pity when all I deserved was their disdain. The truth of the matter was that Alice and I might no longer have been together if she'd known what I'd done.

When I'd finally finished clearing up the ashes, I vowed never to tell another soul what had just happened. 'Alice,' I said. 'I don't know where you are right now – if you're even anywhere any more – but I'm so incredibly sorry for what I did to you and for messing this up now. You deserved so much better. All I can promise you is that I'll spend the rest of my life doing everything I can to nurture and protect our daughter. I won't let you down again.'

Who knew the rest of my life would be so short?

I smiled at Ella, sitting next to me in the car, and thought how proud Alice would have been of her; how much she would have loved her daughter.

'Where do you think your daddy would have liked his ashes to be scattered?' Mum asked her.

Ella raised her eyebrows at me.

'You're asking me?' I said, to which she replied with a tiny nod. 'Gosh. I haven't given it any thought. Um … I don't know. I'm happy for you to choose. Is there somewhere special you can think of?'

'What about the beach near where we stayed at Cornwall?'

'Oh, right,' Mum said. 'Yes. I'd not thought of that. Wouldn't you prefer him to be somewhere closer?'

'That sounds like the perfect place to me, Ella,' I said, smiling at the memory of our reunion there in her dream. 'Just make sure it's a nice calm day.'

'I'd really like to do it there, Nana. I know Daddy would like it too.'

'Very well. We might have to wait a bit, though. It's a long journey.'

CHAPTER 23

FOURTEEN DAYS LEFT

'How are you, Dad?'

Not bad. Took myself to the loo today. He nodded towards a nearby walking frame before continuing to type. *Like a geriatric.*

I smiled, leaning forward. 'All progress is good.'

Dad shrank back into his pillow, eyeing me with caution.

'You don't have to be afraid of me,' I said, pulling away nonetheless. 'Sorry. Didn't mean to spook you.'

Dad didn't show any sign of amusement at my feeble attempt at an icebreaker. If anything, it had the opposite effect as he frowned and silently scrutinized me.

'You don't believe I'm real yet, do you?' I said. 'Even though Ella can see me too.'

I don't know what to believe.

I read his reply on the screen of his smartphone, which had turned out to be an effective means of communication. For a man of his age, he was pretty adept at using the virtual keyboard, although he avoided many of the

227

texting abbreviations favoured by his younger counterparts. It certainly helped that he was a leftie and had full use of his good hand. But I couldn't help wondering whether it was all the text messages to his mistress that had made him so speedy.

'I am really here, Dad,' I said, pushing that thought to one side. 'Listen, I had a word with a friend of mine, another spirit, to try to find out what's going on.'

I was talking about Arthur, of course. I'd managed to get hold of him again last night for a brief chat. I'd been keen to get his take on my father's sudden ability to see me.

'Getting through to Ella was really tough,' I explained to Dad. 'So you seeing me too – without any of that work – was fantastic, but quite a shock. Anyway, this friend, he reckoned it must be something to do with the way the stroke affected your brain: somehow opening it up to seeing me. He's no doctor, so he couldn't give any more detail than that, but he's been around a while and I trust his opinion. I guess it makes sense. What other explanation is there?'

I was sitting on a plastic chair at the left side of his bed. If I'd had the benefit of a full set of senses, the seat would have no doubt felt warm, having just been vacated by Mum. She'd insisted on cutting Dad's fingernails and toenails during her visit and I noticed that she'd left her nail scissors behind on his bedside cabinet. I'd accompanied her and Lauren to the hospital this morning with the sole intention of staying to chat with Dad after they left. Now, after waiting patiently for over an hour, I was finally getting my chance.

Dad stared at me for a moment, nodded, and then looked down at his phone. *Do you mean any harm to Ella?* he typed.

'Of course not,' I replied, forcing myself to stay calm despite the affront. 'She's my only daughter. I love her more than anything. I know this is a lot to take in, but you have to believe me. I'm here to help; to watch over her.'

So either ghosts are real, he typed. *Or I'm in one long, messed-up dream.*

'It's no dream, Dad. And yeah, this whole thing surprised me too. The first I knew of it was when I found myself staring down at my own battered body after the accident. The official term for us is spirits, though. The word "ghost" has too many negative connotations, apparently.'

Says who?

'Them up there,' I replied, gesturing towards the ceiling.

Heaven? he asked.

I nodded.

Why aren't you there?

'It's a long story.'

I'm going nowhere.

'No, I guess not. Where do I start?'

The crash. Tell me the lot.

'Very well. I ... what's wrong?'

Dad let the phone slip out of his left hand and on to the bed. He closed his eyes and started shaking his head.

'What's the matter, Dad?'

It was a couple of minutes before he finally opened his eyes again and fixed me with a glare. 'Whaaattheellsgoingon?'

he slurred, his face contorted from the effort of speaking. 'SSscan'tbereeeeal. Waasapeningtomeee?'

'Dad, calm down. You'll draw attention to yourself.'

But it was too late. The ward sister looked across from where she'd been talking to another patient and walked over. It was the same one who'd taken Mum and Lauren into her office the other day. 'Hello, Tom,' she said. 'Everything okay?'

He shook his head angrily and nodded in my direction. 'Look!'

The sister stared straight through me. 'Sorry. I don't understand. What am I supposed to be looking at? What's got you all worked up?'

'Dad. Don't do this,' I said. 'I really am here, but if you say anything, she'll think you've lost it. I know it's a lot to take in, but you need to get a handle on it. Calm down and let me tell you my story.'

I wasn't that surprised by Dad's reaction. His initial acceptance, or seeming acceptance, had been out of character. He'd always been a sceptical type, so this was actually more like what I would have expected of him.

He took a deep breath, blinked several times at me and then turned back to the sister, who was waiting expectantly for an answer. 'Sallright,' he said, his twisted lips barely moving. 'Ssnothing. Sorry.'

'Are you sure?'

He nodded.

'Right. You could do with some rest now that your wife and daughter have gone. It's good to see you talking. You mustn't shy away from it. The more you work at it, the easier it will get.'

As soon as she'd gone, I jumped straight in with my story, not wanting to give Dad another chance to over-think the situation. I decided not to go into Mum and Lauren's discovery of his affair, which didn't seem like a good idea at this stage. I also skipped the bit about my deadline and the dilemma I was facing about whether to stay or go, telling him only that I'd been allowed to remain here because of Ella. I hoped that by going into detail about the things I'd observed as a spirit, such as his mini-stroke and how awful I'd felt seeing him cry at the crema-torium, I would help him to believe. He kept quiet throughout, his phone lying untouched at his side.

'And that brings us up to the present,' I concluded, 'with you able to see me, presumably because of the stroke's effect on your brain.'

There was a long silence after I finished. 'Are you not going to say anything, Dad?' I asked eventually. 'I can leave if you like.'

He was staring into the distance, motionless, as if asleep with his eyes open.

I got up to leave. 'I get it. You need time. That's not a problem. I'll come back with Mum tomorrow.'

I made it as far as the foot of the bed before he finally spoke. 'Sidown,' he said just loudly enough for me to hear. I turned back to see him pick up his mobile and start tapping out a message with his thumb. *Where did we spend your fourteenth birthday?*

'You still don't believe me?' I said. 'No problem. In Florida. We were on holiday there: me, you, Mum and Lauren. It was the last family holiday we all went on together.

We had dinner at the Hard Rock Cafe in Orlando. I ate too much and felt sick afterwards. Anything else?'

What was my name for you as a boy?

'Scamp. You called me that until I asked you not to. I'd just turned seven and was in infant three at school at the time; I was worried that one of my friends might hear you and make fun of me. I actually missed it once you stopped, but I was too proud to admit it. What else do you want to know, Dad? I had a blue and white BMX for Christmas when I was eight; it had back-pedal brakes. I was so nervous before my first day at secondary school that I was sick all over the kitchen floor at breakfast. I did it again when I was seventeen and drank too much gin at a party. You were the first person I spoke to after Alice died. You were in the car, on speaker phone, going to pick Mum up from the station. You told me how sorry you were and to "hold it together" until you could get to me; you drove so fast that you picked up two speeding tickets along the way. It's me, Dad. Honestly.'

There were tears in his eyes as he slowly nodded his head and keyed three words into his phone: *I believe you.*

CHAPTER 24

We chatted for ages. Dad wanted to know more about my experiences since the accident and what it was like being a spirit. He told me how devastated he'd been by my death and how much he'd missed me. He even spoke a little about the anger and frustration he felt at the effects of his stroke, admitting he feared not making a full recovery. It was probably the longest conversation I'd ever had with him. Even though Dad had to tap his questions or answers into his phone, we made it work. Besides, if Dad had been talking out loud to me, he'd have probably got himself sectioned.

'Are you going to put that thing down for five minutes to have some food?' one of the nurses asked him when she brought his dinner over.

'You go ahead, Dad,' I said. 'Your hand could probably do with a rest and it's important that you eat something to get your strength up. We don't want you starving now.'

He made a sarcastic gesture towards his large stomach.

'You know what I mean,' I replied. I knew from my previous visits that Dad had become very self-conscious about eating and drinking in front of people since the stroke. On top of everything else, he had problems chewing and swallowing; he needed the kind of help I couldn't offer and tended to make a mess. Knowing how proud he was, I thought it best to leave. 'I'm going for a quick stroll. I'll be back in a few minutes.'

I'd decided to stay the night at the hospital since my ride home had long gone and I couldn't face finding my way back by public transport in the dark. For all I knew, I'd already missed the last bus anyway. Mum would be back in the morning. I only hoped that Ella didn't worry where I'd got to. I had told her before school of my plan to stay for a chat with Dad, so I kept my fingers crossed that she would put two and two together and work out where I was. I'd wondered about getting Dad to send a coded text message to Ella via Mum, but I couldn't come up with anything suitable.

I slipped out through the open door of the ward into the corridor, narrowly avoiding running into, and thus being repelled by, a young orderly pushing a trolley of linen. Having nothing better to do, and with him conveniently opening all the doors for me, I decided to follow. But after a few twists and turns through the sterile maze, he stopped at a lift. I decided against following him inside for fear of too many obstacles blocking my route back to Dad.

The dull silver doors slid shut. I peered down the empty corridor, its pale walls bare but for the black rubber stripe of a handrail running along them. Night or day, the light would always be the same here on this windowless stretch: bright and artificial, courtesy of fluorescent tubes hidden behind dusty ceiling diffusers. I couldn't help but think of the corridor or tunnel that people who'd had near-death experiences often described. This was close to how I'd always imagined it. But there was no alluring glow at the end – just a ninety-degree turn, beyond which was no doubt more of the same.

I was about to head back when I heard the faint sound of sobbing coming from beyond the corner. The investigative streak I'd honed as a journalist wouldn't let me ignore it, so I continued down the corridor and around the bend. There I spotted a waiflike young woman sitting in a closed doorway. She was dressed in only a thin nightdress and her bare arms, skinny and pale, were hugging her raised knees as she cried into them.

'Are you all right?' I asked instinctively. No sooner had the words left my mouth than her head snapped up, revealing bloodshot eyes. She threw me a deranged glare.

I took a step backwards. 'You can see me?'

The girl, who looked to be in her late teens, sprang to her feet with inhuman speed and snarled like a wild cat, her mad eyes beaming pure hatred at me. She was terrifying.

'Whoa there,' I said, holding my arms up defensively and backing up two more steps. 'Easy now. You're a spirit too, right? I didn't mean to startle you. I just heard you crying and—'

The girl snarled loudly again, baring a set of spiky yellow teeth that further intensified my fear. It looked like she'd

235

been human once, although that must have been some time ago. There was little evidence in her soulless eyes.

'Listen, I don't want any trouble,' I said, hoping she understood. 'What I'm going to do is keep walking slowly away from you, okay? Very slowly. Let's forget we ever ran into each other. Yes? No harm done.'

There was a banging noise further down the corridor, which caught her attention, and as she turned back to see what it was I saw my opportunity and raced for the corner, desperate to escape. I ran back the way I'd come, hoping and praying that she wouldn't follow me; not daring to look over my shoulder to check.

When I saw the closed door up ahead, barring my way, I felt panic land on my shoulders and start coiling itself around my throat. Convinced she was right behind me, but still not daring to look, I wondered what awful thing was about to happen.

I heard a pinging sound. Out of the lift walked the orderly I'd followed here, now apparently on his return journey.

'Thank you,' I whispered, shuffling into his slipstream and following him through the door. Only once I'd heard it swing shut behind me did I dare to look back through the glass panel. Nothing. She wasn't there. My panic eased as I kept up with the orderly and he led me back to Dad's ward.

Why had I been so scared of that girl? It was partly down to the shock of witnessing her transform from a fragile teen to something so animalistic. Arthur had warned me about how some spirits eventually lost their minds, but hearing about it and seeing it for myself were two altogether different things.

But what harm could she have done to me?

I was snapped out of my introspection by the sight of Dad waving his good hand at me from across the ward.

'Easy, Dad,' I said after reaching his bedside. 'People will start wondering about you if you carry on like that. To them it looks like you're waving at thin air.'

He shrugged in a way that said he couldn't care less; rather than arguing with him, I asked if he'd enjoyed his food.

Delicious! he typed on his phone screen, a wry smile confirming the intended irony.

'Oh well. Better than nothing, I suppose.'

Dad indicated that he wasn't too sure. *Where did you go?* he asked.

'Just down the corridor. Nowhere exciting.'

Glad you're back. Sorry about before, but had to be sure.

I could see tears in Dad's eyes as he paused, lowering his phone to the bed, before looking intently at me. 'Love … you … son,' he enunciated in a slow whisper, his face screwed up in intense concentration. It was the clearest I'd heard him speak since the stroke.

'I know, Dad,' I replied, my voice wavering. 'I love you too and I love being able to talk to you again.'

I decided on the spot to come clean about the big dilemma I was facing and to seek his advice, but he got in there first.

Need to ask you something, he keyed into the phone.

'Sure. What is it?'

What's up with Lauren and your mum?

'What do you mean?'

Just a feeling. Especially Lauren. She got angry the other day. Ann sent her away. Why?

'Um, have you asked Mum?' I said, dodging the question. I was very conscious that she thought the truth wouldn't be good for Dad's recovery.

He shook his head. *I'm asking you. Please.*

'Um, I'm not sure where you're coming from. Why do you think there's something wrong? What have they said to give you that impression?'

It was no good. Dad was on to me. He'd had years of experience sniffing out the truth in his professional life as a solicitor. He also knew how to read his son's body language. He looked at me like I was a child caught doing something naughty. There was no hiding from those probing eyes of his. I lasted about another minute before caving in and telling him what he wanted to know.

All I had to say was that they'd found his other mobile phone – the clamshell – and the colour drained from his face. *What do they know?* he asked.

'Only what they've read in the text messages they found.'

Have they used it?

'Um. What do you mean?' I wasn't sure how much to tell him.

Have they called the number?

'I, er—'

Dad's eyes widened with fear. His breathing quickened and his left hand started to shake. He had a wild air about him, like a man on the edge, which his twisted features exacerbated. I'd never seen him like this before. Mum had been right not to say anything.

'Calm down, Dad,' I said. 'Lauren tried it a couple of times but never got through to anyone. She has no idea who this X person is. None of us have.'

Does Ella know?

'No, of course not. This isn't something for a six-year-old, is it?'

His relief at that small piece of good news was barely visible through the mask of horror encasing his face.

'Come on, Dad,' I said. 'You must have seen this coming. You must have realized Mum would find that other phone.'

Thought was hidden, he tapped into his mobile.

I shook my head. 'You had it with you when you had your stroke. Mum found it when she was looking through your things that night. She was devastated, obviously, but decided not to say anything until you were better. She put your recovery first.'

Tears were pouring down Dad's face now. It was a hard sight to witness, but I held my gaze. He'd always been there to pour glue into the cracks in my life; now it was my turn to be strong for him.

'Whatever you've done and whoever you've done it with, Dad, it's not too late to sort things out. Mum's standing by you, despite what she knows. She loves you so much. We all do. We can get through this.'

He was looking away from me, but I could see that the tears were still flowing.

I sighed, knowing what I had to say to him. 'Look, I don't approve of what you've done, Dad. How could I when I know how much it's hurt Mum? But I don't judge you for it. I know ... how easy it is to be tempted. I've been there too. It was only the once – and I've regretted it every day since – but I thought it was important to tell you. I hoped it might help.'

Dad turned slowly back to face me. He fixed his red eyes on mine and stared into them, barely blinking, for an uncomfortably long time. An eerie calmness had descended on him. I tried to figure out what he might be thinking, but I hadn't got a clue. Finally he tapped a new message into his mobile. *You cheated on Alice?*

I nodded. 'When she was pregnant with Ella. It was a girl from work: Suzie, she was called. All very clichéd and pathetic. It's the biggest regret of my life. You're the only person I've ever told, apart from that grief counsellor Mum persuaded me to see.'

He gave me a sad look, took a deep breath and then typed: *I've done much worse.*

'What do you mean?'

At that moment a nurse walked up to the end of the bed.

'How are we doing?' she asked Dad. 'One of the other patients said you looked a bit upset.'

'Am ... fine,' Dad managed to say.

'You do look a bit worked up. You've had that mobile phone glued to your hand ever since my shift started. How about we put it away for a bit and you get some rest?'

Before Dad could argue otherwise, she snatched it from him. 'I'll turn it off, shall I? We don't want it ringing in the night and waking everyone up.'

She slipped the powered-down phone into one of the drawers in Dad's bedside cabinet and moved on to another patient.

'That's great,' I said. 'How are we supposed to talk now? You were about to say something, weren't you? Is that pad and pen still around?'

Dad shook his head and indicated that he'd had enough.

'Okay, I'll give you time to think. We can chat again tomorrow. I'm going to hang around, anyway, as there's no easy way for me to get home now.'

It wasn't long before Dad fell asleep. Once they dimmed the lights on the ward, I dropped off too, slumped in the chair next to his bed.

I was dreaming of being eight years old again and racing up and down the village on my new blue and white BMX when I was woken by the sound of a woman screaming. The first thing I noticed was that the lights on the ward were still dimmed; the digital wall clock facing me read 4.42 a.m. Then I turned to look at Dad and saw that the bed next to me was empty. His 'geriatric' walking frame was also missing.

The screaming hadn't stopped.

'Dad?' I shouted, springing to my feet and running for the open doorway of the ward, towards the brightly lit corridor and the awful sound of that never-ending shriek.

'Dad? Where are you?' I shouted again, a terrible sinking feeling in my stomach.

I ran into the corridor just as two night staff sprinted past and sent me careering along the polished vinyl floor.

That was when I saw the pool of blood.

CHAPTER 25

THIRTEEN DAYS LEFT

'What the hell have you done, Dad?' I bellowed over the other voices.

More and more hospital staff gathered outside the lavatory, their feet splashing in the blood, spreading it further across the corridor. Doing my best to stay out of their way, I watched as they banged on the locked door and called out to whoever was on the other side. I already knew it was my father. There was never any doubt in my mind, but it took them a few minutes to work it out from a sweep of the nearby wards.

'For God's sake, Dad. Let them in to help you.'

I called out to him again and again without getting any reply. I prayed that was a good thing: a sign he was unconscious but still alive. And yet I had visions of him standing in there as a spirit, staring at his dead body. If that was the case, though, why wasn't he answering me?

'Why haven't you idiots got the door open yet?' I shouted at the staff. They'd managed to unlock it, but something was blocking the way and they couldn't open it more than a few centimetres. It was enough to let yet more blood escape. The sheer amount of the stuff seeping out of there terrified me.

A doctor had appeared by this time. A tall nerdy chap, who looked barely old enough to be qualified, he seemed clueless about how to proceed. Fortunately, he'd called one of his superiors and, when she turned up, things finally got moving. A slight woman in her late thirties, she pulled out her mobile phone, squeezed her arm through the gap and took a photo of the scene on the other side of the door. I'd already prepared myself for the worst, but it wasn't enough. I cried out in horror as I caught sight of the image on her screen. It revealed the obstruction to be Dad's lifeless, blood-soaked body slumped on the floor, a gaping wound in his neck.

'We need to get in there,' she said. 'Right now.' She instructed some of the others to push the door as hard they could, widening the gap just enough for her to slip inside.

'You selfish bastard,' I said as his body was lifted on to a trolley and wheeled away.

I found myself bouncing between shock and anger as I fought to get my head around what Dad had done to himself. Once everyone on the ward was asleep and no nurses in sight, he'd used the walking frame to get to the lavatory. There, in a chilling act of vicious desperation, he'd used the pair of nail scissors Mum had left behind yesterday to stab himself in the neck, severing a carotid artery and painting the room crimson.

It didn't feel real, despite the horrendous image of his corpse seared into my mind. I couldn't comprehend how anyone, never mind my own father, could willingly do something so brutal to themselves. It must have required immense determination. There can't have been any doubt in his mind. He'd even stuffed paper towels under the door to slow his gushing blood's inevitable path on to the corridor, ensuring the alarm wasn't raised too soon. Blocking the door with the huge bulk of his body had sealed the deal. He was long gone by the time the doctor reached him.

What I didn't understand was where his spirit had gone. As soon as I was certain he was dead, I called out to him. 'Dad, where are you? What the hell have you done? At least have the guts to face me. Tell me why you did it. You owe me that.'

There was no answer. I tried various approaches – from angry to conciliatory – but it made no difference. No matter how many times I wandered up and down the corridor or how thoroughly I scoured the ward, he was nowhere to be seen. I didn't understand it.

Dad had blindsided me. I wouldn't have thought him capable of this in a million years. It was incomprehensible. Yes, he was upset about his affair being discovered, but surely not enough to want to take his own life. Why then? Because of the stroke? Because of seeing his dead son? It didn't add up.

I thought back to his words last night: 'I've done much worse.' What had he meant? What had he done more terrible than my cheating on Alice?

Then the guilt started. How could I have allowed this

244

to happen? How did I sleep through the whole thing? Why had I gone against Mum's wishes and told him that she and Lauren knew about the affair?

It was nearly 8 a.m. when Mum arrived at the hospital. She looked dreadful: her unmade-up face a sickly grey colour; her eyes wild with anxiety. I'd half expected Lauren to come with her, but that would have meant bringing Ella too, which they'd obviously decided against. I was glad. The earlier chaos might have abated, but this was still no place for a child. I hoped she was unaware of the latest tragedy.

Whoever had phoned had obviously not disclosed any details of what had happened. 'Where is he?' Mum asked immediately. 'What on earth's going on?'

The sister she'd spoken to the other day had come on duty. She ushered Mum into her office, steering well clear of the cordoned-off lavatory and the meeting room where police were interviewing the night staff. She offered her a chair, but Mum declined. 'I want to see my husband. What's going on? The man I spoke to on the phone wouldn't tell me anything; I'm worried to death. I need to know. Has he had another stroke?'

'Please take a seat, Mrs Curtis. I'm afraid I've got some bad news.'

Mum slapped her palms down on the desk. 'No! I'm not sitting down. What is it? Tell me.'

'I'm afraid your husband died overnight. I'm very sorry.'

Mum slumped back on to the chair. She sat there in stunned silence, staring blankly ahead, like she was unable to process the information.

'Can I get you something, Mrs Curtis?' the sister asked. 'A glass of water?'

'Dead?' Mum said. 'How?'

The sister fidgeted on the other side of the desk, her eyes searching the room as if the right thing to say next might be hidden somewhere in there. She cleared her throat. 'There will, um, obviously have to be a full investigation into what happened. However, at this stage all indications point towards your husband having taken his own life. I really am sorry.'

'What?' Mum snapped. 'What did you say?'

'Mr Curtis was found by one of our night staff. By the time we got to him, it was already too late.'

'This can't be real,' Mum said, shaking her head. 'I feel like I'm still dreaming.'

'I'm afraid it is real.'

'I don't understand. How could it happen? I mean, I thought you were supposed to be looking after him. How—'

'Of course I can give you more details, Mrs Curtis. But it will be distressing for you. What about I get you that glass of water first?'

Mum shook her head, her eyes brimming with steely resolve. 'No. Tell me now. How did my husband die?'

'He died from severe blood loss following a puncture wound to an artery.'

'What? I ... don't understand.'

The sister cleared her throat again. 'Um. There's no nice way to say this. Your husband. He, er, appears to have stabbed himself. In the neck.'

Eyes wide, Mum gasped, clamping both hands over her mouth. She shook her head.

'I really am terribly sorry, Mrs Curtis.'

Mum, still shaking her head, looked deathly white all of a sudden, the colour drained from her face. 'How?' she asked in a tiny voice.

'He locked himself in the toilet. He'd got his hands on a pair of, um, nail scissors.' The sister leaned forward, concerned. 'Mrs Curtis? Can I get you that water? You look—'

Mum keeled over to one side in a dead faint.

'Lizzie! Where is he?'

'Hello, William. I'm so sorry about your father. How are you holding up?'

'He did it right under my nose, Lizzie, as I was sleeping. Now I can't even find his spirit. Where is he?'

'I wish I could help, but I really don't know.'

'Come on, Lizzie. Is that the best excuse you can come up with?'

'It's the truth.'

'So a guy disappears after dying and you have no idea where he's gone? I don't believe it. Picking up souls is what you do. You must know.'

I was back at the old oak tree where, in much happier times, Alice had revealed she was pregnant. Ella had already gone to school when Mum, who luckily hadn't been hurt when she fainted, had got hold of Lauren. They'd decided to wait until she got home before breaking the news to her.

I'd stayed in the house with the two of them for as long as I could bear. I wanted to offer moral support, but the fact was that they had no idea I was there. The atmosphere was awful. Neither of them had a clue what to say to console the other. They were shell-shocked, taking it in turns to make tea that didn't get drunk and repeatedly questioning how and why this had happened.

Eventually I gave in to my craving for open space and slipped outside when Mum let the dog into the garden. It was wet and a fierce wind was rattling fence panels and blowing trees around like rag dolls. I must have cut an unusual figure out there in my jeans and T-shirt. I walked on autopilot to the isolated spot: the best place I knew of to get away from people and to think. Then I called Lizzie.

'Don't make the mistake of thinking I know everything,' Lizzie said. 'I don't. I'm just a cog in the wheel. I've not been assigned to deal with your father; I haven't got a clue where he is.'

'But you knew he was dead before you got here. If you're so unconnected, how come you were already aware of that?'

'I'm told what I need to know. That was relevant because of its effect on you.'

'Well, doesn't the same thing apply to Dad's whereabouts? Not being able to speak to him is definitely having an effect on me.'

Lizzie huddled into her mac, tightening the belt and flipping up the collar. 'How about we go somewhere more sheltered?'

'No, thanks. The weather's irrelevant to me. I wish I did feel cold and wet. I'd prefer that to feeling nothing at all. Besides, if you're not going to tell me where my father is, then we've nothing more to discuss.'

'Look, William, I honestly don't know.'

'What can you tell me, then? There must be something. Is there a chance that he's already passed over?'

'That's possible. But I can't give you a definite answer because I don't have one.'

I stared into her eyes, trying unsuccessfully to gauge whether or not she was telling the truth. 'Can you at least make some enquiries? Maybe you could find out who is dealing with him and ask them some questions. I have to speak to him, Lizzie. I have to find out why he did what he did. I can't understand how he could abandon his family like that.'

'I'll see what I can do, but I can't promise anything.'

'Thank you.'

'No questions about yourself? Don't forget you're in the last fortnight now before decision time.'

I shook my head.

As soon as she'd gone, I allowed myself to think the terrible thought that had been hiding in my mind from the beginning. What if the reason I couldn't find Dad was because he'd gone to Hell? Suicide was, after all, considered a mortal sin in some theologies. I swore loudly, wishing I'd thought to ask Lizzie. Surely if that was the case, she'd have said so. Wouldn't she?

I thought back to Arthur's explanation of how death worked. I definitely remembered him saying that only the

249

worst souls went to Hell. Mind you, he'd also said that those souls were snatched immediately. Could that account for Dad's disappearance? No, surely not. Apart from the suicide, he'd not done anything so awful, had he? He wasn't a bad person. And yet there was the affair. What had he meant when he'd said it was 'much worse' than my betrayal of Alice?

Stop it, I told myself. You're being ridiculous. There's no evidence to suggest that's the case. It's pure speculation. This voice of reason stopped me from calling Lizzie back. I decided to seek Arthur's counsel instead.

The school was closest by, so I tried there first without any luck. I carried on to the church, but a quick tour of the grounds was also unsuccessful. The front door of the building was shut; without anyone to open it for me, I had no way of checking inside. There did appear to be a light on, though, and with my ear to the door I was semi-convinced that I could hear the faint sound of voices within.

'Arthur?' I shouted. 'It's Will. Are you in there?'

There was no reply, so I walked over to one of the nearest stained-glass windows to see if I could catch a glimpse of something. But all that did was confirm the fact there was a light on inside. I couldn't see or hear anything else. Maybe I imagined the voices, I thought. If not, it was most likely the vicar in there with someone, or some cleaners perhaps. The car park was empty, but that didn't mean much in a small village where everything was within walking distance.

'Arthur!' I shouted again, figuring it was worth one more try. 'I need to talk to you. Please.'

250

There was a creak as the door swung open behind me. I spun around. 'Arth—'

'You again,' the tall man said. 'What do you want?'

I was dumbstruck. It was the fellow in the black trench coat with the slicked back, white-blond hair. Not a man at all, in fact, but a guide. I'd last seen him leading a spirit into a pure white light at his graveside. And how could I forget the way he'd silenced me?

He was holding his trilby in his right hand. 'Who is this elusive Arthur, anyway? I recall you were also looking for him the last time we met.'

He stared at me, his intense sea-grey eyes demanding a reply.

'I, er. He's … a friend.'

He raised one eyebrow. 'Really. Another spirit?'

I was in danger of landing Arthur in trouble; I evaded the question with one of my own. 'Who's asking?'

'That's not your concern.'

'Then don't expect me to answer your questions.'

'You're wasting my time. I'm in the middle of something and you're interrupting. Go home.'

'You can't make me,' I replied, surprised at my boldness. 'I've as much right to be here as you do.'

'Are you sure about that?'

He raised his right hand, as if ready to unleash some kind of power on me, and I saw I'd pushed him as far as I dared.

I was out of my depth, with no option other than to back off.

'Okay, okay,' I said. 'I'm going.'

CHAPTER 26

'Tell me again how Mummy died,' Ella said, her red cheeks glistening with tears.

I'd finally managed to coax her out of her princess castle. She'd been in the tent ever since learning of Dad's death. Both Mum and Lauren had tried getting her to talk about how she felt, but she'd asked repeatedly to be left alone and eventually they'd agreed. They'd implied that it was the stroke that had killed Dad, steering clear of any mention of suicide for now.

When Ella climbed out of the tent and came to sit alongside me on the bed, I'd expected questions about her grandfather's death, so it threw me when she brought up Alice instead.

'What happened to her?'

'Um, like I told you before, she got very sick when she was giving birth to you. She, er, she died a few hours after you were born.'

'So I killed her.'

'No. Of course not, Ella. You mustn't say that. It was just terribly bad luck. Tragedies happen sometimes. We all wish they didn't, but there's nothing we can do.'

'How exactly did it happen?'

Reliving Alice's death was the last thing I wanted to do at that particular moment, yet I couldn't decline. Ella had a right to know. I'd sketched out the details for her before, but this was the first time she'd asked for specifics.

'She had a thing called a brain haemorrhage. It's a type of stroke, like Grandad had, only a really bad one. Do you remember how I told you that in Grandad's case the blood supply to his brain got cut off for a while?'

Ella nodded.

'Okay. Well, what happened to Mummy was that one of the tubes carrying blood to her brain actually burst.'

'Because she was having me?'

'Having a baby puts a woman's body through all kinds of strain.'

I could still picture the look of horror on the midwife's face as if she was standing right in front of me. It was an image I'd never forget. 'Call nine nine nine!' she'd barked. 'We need to get her to hospital immediately.'

They'd advised us against Alice having a homebirth for her first baby, in case of complications, but she was determined. She'd always hated hospitals. And so she died in the back of an ambulance weaving through rush-hour traffic, never reaching the doctors who might have been able to save her. The doctors who would have been at her side in minutes had she already been at the hospital.

'So it was my fault,' Ella said, whisking me back to the present.

I knelt down in front of her. 'No, Ella. Not at all. You mustn't think that. Please, don't think that. It's not your fault in any way.'

I understood self-blame better than anyone and it was the last thing I wanted Ella to have to go through. It had taken me many counselling sessions to move beyond my own belief that I was responsible for Alice's death. At one point I'd been firmly convinced that if I'd not cheated on her, she'd still be alive. My logic was based on the fact that I would have preferred the safer option of a hospital birth, but I let Alice have her way because I was so racked with guilt about my one-night stand. I should have pushed harder against it, I told myself over and over in those terrible first days and weeks after her death. If I'd put my foot down instead of trying to ease my conscience, things could have been so different.

It took me a long time to accept that life was far greater and infinitely more complex than me and my decisions, good or bad; that I had no way of knowing how my actions might or might not have affected things. Only then did I appreciate how important it was to live in the present with my beautiful daughter, rather than waste away in a past I could do nothing to alter.

'How come Grandad died too, then?' Ella asked. 'If I'd told Nana straight away that he was sick, he might never have been stroked.'

'No, Ella. We've been through this before. It was me who told you not to say anything until the morning. You weren't responsible.'

She started sobbing again. 'Why does everyone keep dying? You were coming to get me from school when you got killed. So that's my fault too.'

'No. None of this is your fault. You have to stop thinking like that.'

I closed my eyes, hunting for the right words; hating not being able to take her into my arms and comfort her. 'I'm sorry, Ella. I wish I could give you a proper answer, but there isn't one. It's totally unfair. No one, never mind a child your age, should have to experience so much loss in such a short time. I wish I could wave a magic wand, like one of the wizards in your story books, and make it all better, but I can't. I am here for you, though, and I'll do everything I can to help. The same goes for Nana and Lauren. You know that, don't you? You're never alone.'

Later, once Ella had calmed down, she asked me about her grandad's spirit. 'Where is he, Daddy? Will I be able to see him?'

I sighed. 'I don't know where he is, love. I haven't seen him either. I'm trying to find out.'

'Might he be in Heaven already?'

'That's possible.'

'What's it like?'

'Heaven?'

Ella nodded.

I let out a wistful sigh. 'I don't know for sure, darling. I haven't been there, but I imagine it as somewhere incredible, full of happiness and warmth. I think it will somehow appear different to each person there, so it can be everyone's perfect place.'

'Do you think Mummy's there?'

'I do.'

'Wouldn't you like to go there too, so you can be with her again?'

Her question caught me off guard. I ought to have seen it coming, but I didn't. Perhaps now was the time to have the big discussion with her. I considered it for an instant, but I couldn't forget Lizzie's warning not to burden Ella with my impossible decision. Besides, how could now be a good time? She'd just lost her grandad. What could be crueller than talking about the possibility of losing me again as well?

'Um, I've not really thought about it,' I lied. 'Sounds like you're trying to get rid of me.'

I pulled a silly face, managing to coax a hint of a smile out of her, before asking how she was feeling about her grandad's death.

She looked down at her bare feet and rubbed them along the carpet. 'Sad. I thought he was getting better.'

'I know. We all did.'

'Um, Daddy ... I'm a bit worried about Nana now.'

'What do you mean, love?'

'What if she dies too?'

It was heart-breaking to hear my six-year-old daughter ask that question. It was no surprise she thought like that, after all the death she'd experienced, but it wasn't right. At her age, she shouldn't have to think about anything more pressing than which doll to play with or what TV programme to watch. It reminded me again of Lizzie's warning, pushing me further towards her way of thinking.

The last thing my daughter needed right now was to be concerned about my future.

'Your nana's as fit as a fiddle,' I said. 'She's going nowhere.'

I immediately regretted my choice of words, as I remembered an evening not so long ago when Dad had claimed to be 'as fit as a fiddle' to Mum. 'You know you've got your Auntie Lauren as well,' I added. 'And your Uncle Xander. All three of them love you so much.'

'I guess,' Ella replied, reaching across the bed for Kitten and squeezing the toy animal tight against her chest.

I thought back to the days when I could hug Ella like that; a sudden swell of emotion caught me unawares.

'What's wrong, Daddy?' Ella asked as I gulped down the pain and uncertainty.

'Nothing, darling,' I replied, forcing a smile. 'I'm fine.'

CHAPTER 27

TWELVE DAYS LEFT

I had a bad feeling as soon as I heard the doorbell. I'm not sure why, as there had been plenty of recent visitors calling to pass on their condolences. This time felt different. And as soon as Lauren swung open the door to see who was there, I knew my gut had been right.

Standing in the cold, his breath smoking out before him, was a man I'd last seen from behind the cover of the neighbours' large conifer. Carefully sculpted hair. Business attire. And yes – a glance over his shoulder confirmed it – that black Audi parked in the street. If I'd still been in possession of a heart, it would have been pounding like a double bass drum. What the hell was about to happen?

'Hello,' he said with the brief flicker of a pinched smile. 'You must be Lauren.'

My sister frowned. 'And you are?'

He extended his right arm through the doorway, spiky fingers emerging from a smart cuff. 'Devlin. Charles Devlin.'

Lauren stared at his hand like something not to be trusted, before granting him the briefest of shakes. 'Have we met before?'

'No. You usually live abroad, I believe. Holland, isn't it?'

She squinted at him, shivering as the cold outside air crept in through the open door. 'You seem to know a lot more about me than I do about you, Mr Devlin.'

He offered that pinched smile again, sustaining it for longer this time. 'I'm a good friend of your father's.'

His words hammered a crack into Lauren's icy exterior. 'Oh, I see,' she said. 'Sorry. I didn't realize.'

'Such awful news,' he added with what looked like genuine emotion. 'I can't believe he's really gone.'

'You'd better come in.'

I'd been standing at Lauren's shoulder the whole time and this man – Devlin – had given no indication whatsoever that he could see me. Perhaps he is human after all, I thought. Just to be sure, I shouted as loudly as I could into his ear while Lauren took his coat. He didn't flinch.

'Who on earth are you, then?' I said. 'Dad never mentioned you. You can't have been that close.'

'Mum, there's a friend of Dad's here,' Lauren said, leading Devlin through to the lounge.

My mother, red-eyed from a recent crying session, looked up from the newspaper she was reading on the couch. She'd been stuck on the same page for the past twenty minutes. 'Oh, hello,' she said, flashing a look of confusion at Lauren as she stood to greet the visitor. 'Sorry. I don't think we've met.'

259

'Charles Devlin,' he repeated. 'Please accept my condolences. Your husband was a wonderful man.'

'Thank you,' Mum replied, her eyes asking Lauren who on earth she'd let into the house.

My sister, who was standing behind Devlin, shrugged her shoulders, mouthing that she thought Mum must have known him.

Mum, ever the polite host, invited him to take a seat and sent Lauren off to the kitchen to make a pot of tea.

'I'm terribly sorry,' she said. 'I'm sure we must have met before, but I can't place you. My head's all over the place at the moment.'

'We've never met, although I feel like we have. I heard lots about you and your family from Tom.'

'Oh, I see. So how did you know each other?'

'Through work. I'm a barrister. We collaborated on several cases over the years.'

'That explains it. My husband was never one for talking about work at home. I was lucky to hear whether he'd had a good day or not. I suppose it must have been a while since you saw him, then.'

'We kept in good contact, actually.'

Mum kept talking in a bid to hide her confusion, but I'm sure it was as obvious to Devlin as it was to me.

By the time Lauren had returned with the tea and poured everyone a cup, she and Mum looked as perplexed as I was about this mysterious man. And they didn't even know about the fact he'd been following us – watching us – for weeks.

'There's something I need to tell you,' Devlin said, his voice taking on a sense of gravity that you could imagine silencing a court room. 'There's no easy way to say this, so forgive me if I shock or offend you, but you deserve to know the truth.'

'What truth?' Mum whispered.

Devlin took a deep breath. 'Tom and I were very much in love.'

It was a race to see whose jaw would hit the floor first.

'I beg your pardon!' Mum snapped as Lauren and I gaped at Devlin.

'We were lovers,' he said. 'We had been for some time. Tom was going to tell you, so that we could be together. But he had second thoughts after William was killed.'

'What in God's name are you talking about? How—'

'Tom was gay. I knew it the moment I met him. There was an immediate attraction between us, but it took him a while to accept after so long in the closet.'

'This is preposterous,' Mum said. 'Is this some kind of sick joke? Who the hell are you?'

'I've told you who I am. This is no joke, believe me. This is …'

Devlin paused, running a finger under each of his eyes and taking several deep breaths. 'I've lost the man I love,' he said with wavering voice.

'I think it's time you left,' Lauren said, standing up. 'The last thing my mother needs right now is more upset. She's just lost her husband; I've lost my father. Why would you come here and tell these lies?'

'I'm not lying. You say you don't know who I am. I'm the person you left those voicemails for. I'm the one you called "the scum of the earth". You asked me to call you

261

straight away or to come around to the house. Well, here I am.'

His words were like a slap in the face to Lauren, whose eyes clouded over as she fell backwards on to the couch in muted shock.

'That was … you?' was all Mum could manage before she too sank into a stupefied state.

I felt like my brain – or whatever it was that kept me thinking as a spirit – was in meltdown.

Dad was gay.

What? That couldn't be right. My father was the least likely closet homosexual I could think of: overweight and oblivious to fashion; stiff and unemotional; not remotely camp. And yet … some small part of me, somewhere I couldn't put my finger on, wasn't entirely surprised. The rest of me remained staggered, especially at the level of deception. How could he have kept a secret like this from his family? How long had he known in his heart that he was gay? My whole life? He'd never been the most open person, but I thought I knew him as well as anyone. How wrong could I have been? Apparently his family didn't know him at all. Not the real him. He must have saved that for this Devlin chap.

I shook my head, like I'd been having a daydream and needed a reality check. But it made no difference. Nothing changed.

So this was the 'much worse' thing he'd mentioned. And it was me telling him that Mum knew about the affair, meaning he'd have to come clean, which had pushed him over the edge.

'I'm sorry to have to break it to you like this,' Devlin said, shattering the silence that had descended on the room. 'I really am. But I had to tell you. It was the only fair thing.'

'Why?' Mum replied, stony-eyed.

'Because it's the truth.'

'How does that help us now he's gone?'

'Surely you'd rather know who your husband really was.'

'You think you can tell me that, do you? You knew him five minutes. I was married to him for forty years.'

'It was a little longer than five minutes.'

'Shut up. I don't care. I don't want to hear any more of your sordid stories. If you loved my Tom so much, where were you after he had his stroke? I was the one at his side; not you.'

'I didn't—'

The doorbell rang again.

'Who's that now?' Mum said, looking at Lauren.

'Oh, um, shall I go and see?' my sister replied hazily.

'Yes, please. Get rid of them if you can.'

I followed my sister to the door. She opened it to reveal the familiar face of a certain attractive newspaper reporter. She was wearing the same sympathetic smile as the last time I'd seen her, when my untimely demise was still breaking news. I'd been expecting her or one of her colleagues to get wind of Dad's death; what great timing she had.

'Hello there. Awfully sorry to bother you. My name's Kate Andrews, from the *Evening Journal*. We heard the terrible news about Tom Curtis. I wondered if a family member was available for a quick chat. We're very interested in running a tribute article.'

263

'You're from where?' Lauren asked, confused.

'The *Evening Journal*. Sorry, I don't think we've met before, but I spoke to Mrs Curtis just after William died. She was very keen to speak to me then. Is she available at all?'

'Could you wait there a minute, please?' Lauren said, shutting the door in her face before letting out an exasperated sigh. 'Why the hell now?' she muttered.

'Dammit,' I said. She almost certainly knew it was suicide. That was exactly the type of information reporters sought out when they rang up the coroner's office looking for news. The type of information that got them rushed out on death knocks by eager editors. The fact I'd been killed just weeks earlier made it a better story still. Probably a guaranteed front page.

As soon as Mum realized who it was, she flew into a panic. She did her best to hide it from Devlin, but I could see it in her eyes. Luckily, I don't think he'd heard what was said at the front door; Lauren had the good sense to mention Kate's name but not the fact she was a journalist.

'I'm afraid I'm going to have to ask you to leave now, Mr Devlin,' Mum said. 'I have important business to attend to. I wish I could say it had been a pleasure.'

'What? That's it? Surely there's a lot more we need to discuss.'

'I have your phone number,' she replied. And with that she swept him out of the front door, whisking Kate inside before either had the chance to properly register the other.

I was just thankful Ella was out of the house while all of this unfolded. On my advice she'd declined Mum's offer to take a few days off school. I was hoping the pre-Christmas activities there might take her mind off all the misery at home.

'Hello, Mrs Curtis,' Kate said, shaking her hand while flashing a well-rehearsed look of pity. 'I'm sorry to turn up unannounced, but we just heard the awful news about your husband. I couldn't believe it. Especially so soon after your son's death. You poor thing. They were going to send someone else to see you, but I insisted they let me do it. I thought it would be easier for you to talk to someone you knew. Please accept my condolences.'

'Oh, you're good,' I said. 'It's nothing to do with the fact you want to get your paws on a juicy story, is it? Of course not. You're just here out of the goodness of your heart. Watch out for this one, Mum. She's more cunning than she lets on.'

'Thanks, love,' Mum said, oblivious as usual to my advice. 'You'd better come through to the lounge. Can I take your coat?'

A little later, over a fresh cup of tea, Mum finished giving Kate the lowdown on Dad's stroke. It was like she felt that she had to talk to her because I used to be a journalist. In fact, I'd have rather she kept quiet; particularly considering the bombshell Devlin had just delivered.

I couldn't believe how composed she looked. My mind was all over the place, still reeling from the shock of what I'd learned about my father. I could only imagine that Mum was feeling the same, although she was doing a damn good job of hiding it. Lauren, on the other hand, had disappeared upstairs, unable to cope with the situation.

Kate, who had let Mum do most of the talking so far, took a long sip from her mug. A look of discomfort flitted across her disarmingly young, pretty face.

'Brace yourself, Mum,' I said. 'Here it comes.'

'This is a bit awkward,' Kate said. 'We, um, heard from the police and the coroner that your husband didn't die from natural causes. They said foul play had been ruled out, so …'

Mum took a sharp intake of breath. I feared she was about to lose it: either to start shouting at Kate to mind her own business or to break down in tears. But she didn't. Somehow she held it together. For years I'd thought of Dad as the strong one out of my parents, but it was clear now how wrong I'd been. He might have been the one with the big physical presence and the aura of confidence, but when his family needed him most, he'd cracked under the pressure; he'd taken the coward's way out. Mum's ability to keep on going no matter what – when things went from bad, to worse, to rock bottom – was incredible.

'I see,' she said. 'Do you know how he did it?'

Kate winced, as if imagining the gruesome scene of Dad's death. She nodded. 'I'm so sorry. I can't imagine what you and your family must be going through.'

'Will you be printing the details?'

The reporter shifted in her seat. 'I'm afraid we'll have to include what we've been told by the coroner, as it's a matter of public record, but we're not in the business of printing lurid details. We won't be giving it the red-top treatment.' She paused before adding: 'I'll happily include your side of the story. Anything you want to say. I mean, how would you describe your husband's state of mind the last time you saw him?'

'Don't fall for that old trick, Mum,' I blurted out. 'She's fishing.'

'I don't want to say anything about that,' Mum replied.

'You must be angry at the hospital, though,' Kate added. 'Where were all the doctors and nurses when it happened? They had a duty of care towards him. I'm sure you're considering legal action.'

'I don't want to say anything about that,' Mum repeated.

I thought for a moment that Kate was going to push her some more. If she had, I think that might have been the straw that broke the camel's back. But it didn't come to that. 'Very well, Mrs Curtis,' she said. 'I understand, but please let me know if you change your mind. Do you still have my contact details?'

Mum nodded, although I could tell she had no intention of ever calling her.

'Well played, Mum,' I said. 'You handled that just right.'

When Kate had gone, Lauren came back downstairs. Her face was red and puffy from crying. 'Are you okay?' Mum asked her.

'No. Not remotely. What have we done to deserve all this shit; all this misery? It's like our family is cursed.'

Mum didn't reply.

'How are you doing?' Lauren asked her after a few minutes of silence.

She shrugged, her eyes unfocused. 'I don't know. I'm so numb. If anything, I suppose I'm wondering what's next. I daren't think that things can't get any worse. I'm not making that mistake again.'

'What did you tell the reporter?'

'She already knew how he died, if that's what you're asking.'

'So that'll be spread all over the paper for everyone to gossip about?'

'Yes.'

'Hold on. Does that mean Ella will find out?'

Mum frowned. 'I'd not thought of that. Maybe. It's unlikely she'd read it herself, but suppose someone else did and then said something to her. We can't let that happen.'

'So we're going to explain to a six-year-old that her grandfather killed himself? There's no way we can tell her how he did it. She'd have nightmares for the rest of her life.'

'Oh God, I don't know.'

'What about the rest?'

'You mean what that man said? Of course I didn't tell Kate. Do you think I'm stupid?'

'Do you believe what he told us?'

'I don't want to believe it,' Mum sighed, her eyes somewhere else for a long moment. 'But why would he make it up?'

CHAPTER 28

NINE DAYS LEFT

'Nana and I need to talk to you for a minute,' Lauren said, gesturing for Ella to sit down beside her on the couch.

'Why? What's wrong?'

'Go on, darling,' I told her. She threw me a probing glance, but I said no more.

'It's about Grandad,' Mum said.

'I really miss him.'

'We all do. You know that Auntie Lauren and I are both here for you whenever you want to talk about things, don't you?'

'Yes,' Lauren added. 'It doesn't matter whether it's about Grandad, your father or even just how you're feeling. Whatever you need, we're always here. We've all been through a lot lately, but we realize it must be especially hard on you.'

Ella stared at the ground, on the verge of tears.

I watched in silence as Mum and Lauren told her about Dad's suicide, thankfully minus the gory details. Did I agree it was necessary? Just about, although I found myself questioning the likelihood of her finding out from someone else. What responsible adult would drop the fact that her grandfather had killed himself into a conversation? And yet there was a chance that another child might get wind of it, perhaps by overhearing their parents talking – and I wouldn't want Ella finding out that way. I remembered only too well the cruel playground taunts of that nasty girl Kaylee. It was unbearable to think of Ella learning the truth from her poisonous lips.

She took the news surprisingly well, bless her. It broke my heart to think it, but she was getting used to dealing with this kind of thing now. Poor child. What had she ever done to deserve such a bad lot in life?

After asking a couple of questions, nodding silently as Mum and Lauren replied, she said she'd like to be alone for a while in her bedroom.

'She was very quiet, Mum,' Lauren said once she'd gone upstairs.

'What did you expect?'

'I'm not sure. I guess I thought she might cry. Did she understand what we were saying?'

'I think so, as much as any child can grasp the idea of someone committing suicide.'

'We'll have to keep a close eye on her.'

'Definitely. She needs to know that we love her very much and that we're not going anywhere. It's important she feels wanted.'

'What about me flying home?'

A look of panic spread across Mum's face. 'What do you

mean? I thought you could stay for a while. You're not going to abandon me, are you?'

'No, Mum. Relax. I'm not leaving. I was just wondering whether it might be something preying on Ella's mind. I came and went before, remember, after Will died.'

I was glad to know that Lauren was staying for a while. It did worry me how Mum would cope without her husband and children around. She was strong, sure, but the sturdiest of buildings is only as stable as its foundations.

I left the two of them talking and headed for Ella's bedroom. There was no sign of her when I entered, but I knew where to look. 'Boo,' I said gently, peering in through the pink mesh window of her usual hideaway. 'How are you doing in there?'

'Not good.'

'Would you like to talk about it?'

'No.'

'Did you understand what Nana and Lauren told you?'

Avoiding my eye, she replied with an annoyed grunt. I decided to change tack. 'Is that Kitten I can see in there with you?'

Another grunt, but less annoyed this time.

'How's she doing?'

'Good.'

'Have you ever taken her to Cat Land?'

Ella picked the soft toy up and squashed it against her face while sucking her thumb. She shook her head.

'No? Oh, you should do. Hey, I saw one of the neighbour's cats in the garden today – a big ginger one. He looked really soft and cuddly.'

271

'Where?' Ella whispered in between sucks.

'Under one of the bushes in the back garden. He was huge, almost as big as Sam. I bet he eats ten bowls of cat food per day.'

Ella giggled.

'Have you ever seen him?'

'No,' she replied, still sucking her thumb and hugging Kitten, but looking in my direction now. 'Where's he from?'

'I don't know. He must live around here, though, because I've seen him a few times. You'll have to keep an eye out.'

'What's his name?'

'I call him Fat Cat.'

Another giggle.

'Do you know what Kitten did when you were at school today?'

She shook her head.

'She was so naughty, you wouldn't believe it. She kept sneaking out of your bedroom window and running across the roof. I had to shout at her to get her to stop. She might pretend to be good, but she's very cheeky when you're not here.'

Ella had always liked it when I talked to her about animals or made up stories about her toys. Eventually she came out of the tent and started chatting to me. We had to stop a couple of times when Mum and Lauren popped their heads in to check on her; she pretended to be playing a game with her toys. I didn't push her at all to talk about Dad, but eventually she did.

'Why did Grandad want to leave us?'

I hadn't seen the question coming, as a moment earlier we'd been discussing her latest wobbly tooth and whether there were any male tooth fairies.

'What was that, love?' I asked, buying myself a few seconds to come up with a decent answer.

'Why did Grandad want to leave us? That's why he died himself, isn't it? He didn't love us any more.'

'Of course he still loved us. You especially. He was crazy about you. He was always telling me how he couldn't have wished for a better granddaughter.'

'So why did he leave?'

'I don't know, darling. I suppose he was just really sad. I know he found it very hard to deal with the effects of his stroke.'

Thank goodness Mum and Lauren hadn't mentioned anything to Ella about the secret gay affair. Explaining this was hard enough.

'But he would have got better, wouldn't he?'

'Yes. In time I'm sure he would, but he might never have fully recovered.'

'You were with him at the hospital. Why couldn't you stop him?'

'I wish I could have, Ella. But he sneaked off when I was asleep.'

She fell silent, her eyes focused intently on Kitten as she slowly turned the toy around in her hands. 'Is he already in Heaven?'

'I don't know.'

'Well, I hope he's not. He doesn't deserve it. He died when he didn't have to and he didn't even say goodbye.'

'Ella! I don't want to hear you say that ever again. I know you're upset, but you shouldn't wish that on anyone; especially not your grandfather.'

I hadn't spoken particularly harshly, but my words made her cry. She crawled back into the tent and told me to leave her alone. I'd experienced this kind of thing plenty of times before, although this was the first occasion since I'd returned as a spirit. I guess that was the reason it hurt so much. I thought it best to give her some space.

'Sorry,' I whispered. 'I didn't mean to upset you. You know where I am if you want to talk some more.'

Her reply was another angry grunt as she zipped up the tent door.

CHAPTER 29

SEVEN DAYS LEFT

One week. That was all I had left. One measly week.

Seven days.

One hundred and sixty-eight hours.

Ten thousand and eighty minutes.

Well, that wasn't entirely accurate. It was slightly more than that, as I had until noon next Monday and it was currently only 6.25 a.m. No point splitting hairs, though. The hard truth was that in a week's time I had to make my final decision: stay here forever or take up my place in Heaven.

I felt the decision process ought to have been getting easier by now. In fact, the opposite was true. A large part of the problem was the deadline itself, its looming proximity trapping me like a rabbit in the headlights. Then there was Dad's death. That was totally unexpected and hadn't figured in any of my earlier mental wrangles.

How did it fit in with what Lizzie had shown me of the future? Had that already taken into account his impending death, without me being aware of it? Or – and this scared me most – had my actions brought it about? If I'd passed over straight away, would Dad still be alive? It was too confusing. I was a mess. How was I ever going to decide in time?

'Morning, Daddy,' Ella said, her face appearing above me. 'Sleep well?'

'Yes, thanks. You?'

'Uh-huh.'

I wondered for a moment why I'd started sleeping here, on the carpet next to Ella's bed. She'd often asked me to stay in her bedroom when I was alive, especially after a nightmare, but I'd always resisted. So was this doing her any good now? Probably not, although it wasn't like I had a room of my own any more. I felt most comfortable by Ella's side. But it wasn't about me, was it? If I was still here after next week, maybe I'd have to rethink the sleeping arrangements.

'How old is Auntie Lauren?'

'Sorry?'

'Auntie Lauren: what age is she?'

'Um, thirty-eight. Why?'

'Really? Oh, that's good news. I thought she might already be forty.'

'No. She's definitely thirty-eight. Why does it matter?'

'Oh, nothing,' she replied, her face reddening before she hid it under the duvet.

'Come on, Ella. You've got to tell me now. I'll be wondering all day if you don't.'

Her head reappeared. 'Promise you won't laugh?'

'I promise.'

276

Her right hand appeared above me, little finger held out from the rest. 'Pinky promise?'

I held one of my little fingers up to hers, so they were almost touching. It was close enough to feel a hint of the invisible force itching to repel me, like Ella and I were two opposing magnets. 'Pinky promise.'

'Okay, then. I was just thinking that it might be nice if … she had a baby.'

I hadn't seen that coming. 'Right. Why's that?'

'I'd like to have a cousin. And it would help make our family bigger. Jada says mums can have babies until they're forty. After that, they're not allowed any more. Her mum's forty-two, so she can't. But Auntie Lauren's still young enough, isn't she?'

I felt a swell of emotion at her words, which made me want to laugh and cry all at once.

'Do you think she might want one, Daddy? A baby girl would be nice. Then I could teach her stuff and style her hair for her.'

I wasn't sure what to say. I had no idea whether Lauren wanted kids or not. Since she and Xander had been together for so long without having any, I had speculated that they probably didn't – or couldn't. But I'd never talked about it with either of them, not wanting to pry. There was a time when people used to ask, especially when Ella was a baby, but Lauren's standard reply was that they were too busy with the business. Eventually the questions stopped.

'Um, maybe,' I said. 'Now might not be the best time to ask her, though, so soon after Grandad's death.'

'Why not? A baby would make everyone happy again.'

A child's logic, perhaps, but I could understand where she was coming from. Ella's own birth, despite being intrinsically linked to Alice's death, had been a huge help when it came to getting through my grief.

'You might be right, but I'd still be careful what you say. Whether or not to have a baby is a matter for Auntie Lauren and Uncle Xander to decide for themselves. And I imagine she's far too busy arranging Grandad's funeral to even think about things like that.'

The funeral, like my own, had been delayed by the need for a post-mortem. But a date had now been set for next Monday: my deadline day. The church service would be at 10 a.m., two hours before I had to make my final decision. It almost seemed like fate had planned it.

As for Dad, I was none the wiser about what had happened to him. Lizzie had yet to get back to me and Arthur was nowhere to be found. If Dad was still hanging around as a spirit, he clearly didn't want me to find him. It seemed that his funeral might be the only chance I'd get to catch up with him.

There was the further worry that the funeral could turn into a spectacle. It wouldn't be difficult for Charles Devlin to find out the details, so it was conceivable that he might turn up and make a scene. Would he announce Dad's secret to the entire congregation? Mum and Lauren were discussing the possibility at the kitchen table that afternoon.

'Do you think we ought to invite him?' Mum said, sitting back down after letting Sam into the garden.

'What? Are you mad? Why on earth would we do that?'

'I just thought it might be a way to get him onside, Lauren, to stop him causing a scene.'

'But then he'll definitely be there. If we don't invite him, there's always the chance he won't.'

'Not likely. He's going to be looking out for it; that's why inviting him might work. He won't be expecting that. It'll disarm him.'

Lauren thumped the table. 'Bloody man! As if we haven't got enough to think about already. How about I just phone and tell him we don't want him there? That works for me.'

'Don't you dare. That would be the worst thing. I'm sure that would make him all the more determined to go – and it's not like we can ban him from the church.'

'Why not?'

'It's a public place.'

'But he's got no right to be there.'

'Hasn't he? He'd argue otherwise. And if they really did love each other, maybe he'd have a point.'

'Mum, how can you say that? He was your husband. I can't believe how blasé you're being about this whole thing. Why aren't you shouting and screaming? Honestly, some-times I wonder if you knew what Dad was up to all along.'

I couldn't believe what I was hearing from my sister's lips. Mum burst into tears, upon which a look of regret spread across Lauren's face. She got up and rushed over to put her arms around Mum. 'I'm so sorry. I didn't mean that. I take it back. I don't know what I'm saying. It's all so much to take in.'

Mum buried her head in her folded arms and let out a flood of emotion. Eventually, still sniffling, she sat up, took a deep breath from way down in the pit of her stomach and started to speak. 'No. You're right, at least partly. I am reacting strangely – and there's a reason. I think I blame myself.'

'Oh, Mum,' Lauren said. 'You mustn't—'

'Listen. I need to say this now. I have to get it off my chest. I had no idea your father was having an affair. Not until I found that secret mobile phone of his. But when Charles Devlin came here and told us what he did, it wasn't quite as much of a surprise to me as it was to you.'

'What?'

'Just listen, Lauren,' Mum snapped. There was no stopping her now. A part of me wondered whether I really wanted to hear what she had to say, but the rest of me knew I had no choice.

'Not long after your father and I got married, we went through a rough patch. He was working all the time and I was lonely at home. We'd been trying for a baby for a while, but nothing was happening. One night we had a huge row. Tom slept on the settee and when I got up the next morning, he'd already left for work. I moped around the house all day, hoping he'd call, but when he finally did it was only to say that he'd be working late again.'

Mum ran her fingers through her hair and let out a sigh. She went on: 'I shouted down the phone at him and called him all sorts of things. I immediately regretted it after hanging up; a couple of hours later, I decided to drive over to the office with some supper, hoping to sort things out between us.

'The building was all shut up when I arrived, but I could see a light on in Tom's room on the first floor, so I knew he was still busy in there. Just then the cleaner turned up, recognized me and let me inside. I sneaked up the stairs and tiptoed to his office door, which was ajar, keen to surprise him. Only it was me that got the surprise.'

Mum took several more deep breaths and fanned her reddening eyes with her right hand. 'Sorry. I've never told anyone about this before.'

'It's okay, Mum,' Lauren said. 'Take your time.'

'He wasn't alone. There was another man in there with him. A young chap: must have been all of nineteen. He was perched on your father's desk, right in front of where Tom was sitting, and whispering something into his ear while running one finger along his neck. I must have gasped or something, because a second later Tom saw me and jumped to his feet. He hurriedly introduced me to the man: a work placement student called Nicholas, who was supposedly helping him with a case. Tom pretended nothing had happened, but I knew what I'd seen. I suppose I could have walked in on something worse, but it was bad enough, believe me. It was just so … intimate. Seeing my husband like that with another man, ugh, it made my skin crawl. And then there was the look that boy gave me. He was all piercing eyes and cheekbones, with a swagger to match. He turned and threw me this cold, superior smile as he walked out of the office, like he couldn't care less; like I was a piece of dirt.'

'What did you do?'

281

'Nothing at first. I was too shocked. I didn't know what to say to your father, so I played along with his pretence. He paid me lots of attention. Tried to convince me that nothing was wrong – even in the bedroom, if you know what I mean – but I couldn't get what I'd witnessed out of my head. Eventually I tried to talk to him about it, but he refused. He got angry every time I tried and things quickly grew frosty between us. I started to fear for the future of our marriage. Then I discovered I was pregnant.'

'With me?'

'Yes. And that changed things. It forced us to talk to each other; to face up to what was happening to our relationship. Your father finally came clean about that night in his office.'

'And?'

'He admitted there had been something between him and Nicholas but said it had never gone any further than what I'd seen. I asked him if he was gay and he said not. He said he'd got a bit confused – gone through "a stupid phase" – but my pregnancy had clarified things. It had made him realize that he wanted to be with me and to raise a family together.'

'And you believed him?' Lauren asked, taking the words out of my mouth.

'I was sceptical, but at the same time I wanted to believe him. I still loved him and I didn't want to be a single mother. He swore nothing like that would ever happen again.'

'And did it?'

'Not that I'm aware of. Apart from this thing with Charles Devlin, obviously. Mind you, it's not like I saw that coming, so who knows? When I found his secret mobile and discovered he was having an affair, the idea that it might be a man went through my head. But I buried it, preferring to think of him with another woman. Of course it was naive of me to believe him all those years ago. You can't just turn feelings like that on and off.'

'He never did anything to make you suspect?'

Mum shook her head. 'I took him at his word. I didn't want to think of my husband like that, which is why I never told anyone until now. The physical side of our marriage cooled some time ago, but I convinced myself that was normal in a long-term relationship. Maybe I should have questioned it more, but he was such a good husband in every other way. And he was a fantastic father.'

I'd heard enough. Mum had stopped talking for now and I felt a sudden urge to get outside. Sam was still in the garden. I shouted at him through the door until he barked enough to get let back inside, allowing me to do the opposite. I was looking for an escape: a moment's peace and quiet to regroup my thoughts. But it didn't work out like that.

'Hello, Will,' a voice said from behind me as I stepped out on to the grass, still white from the previous night's heavy frost. It was a voice I hadn't heard in more than six years, but I recognized it immediately.

'Alice?' I gasped, spinning around. 'Is that really you?'

She smiled that wonderful smile of hers, looking incredible in a swirling red dress. 'What do you think, Will?'

'But how? I mean …'

She swept back a long curl, tucking it behind one ear. 'You mean what? That you've missed me?'

'That's the understatement of the century. I've longed for you every second of every day since I lost you.'

I held my arms out to embrace her, but she took a step back, shaking her head. 'No. You mustn't.'

My heart sank. 'Oh. Sorry.'

'It's not that I don't want you to. That can't happen here.'

'Why not? I don't understand. We're both spirits.'

'That's just how it is. You'll have to take my word for it. I shouldn't even be able to visit you like this.'

'How are you here, then?'

'Lizzie.'

'Really? How did she—'

'Never mind that. I can't stay long.'

She gestured for me to join her as she walked to the middle of the frozen lawn and sat down, cross-legged.

'Aren't you cold in that dress?'

'Not at all. Don't you like it? I wore it for you.'

'I love it,' I said, sitting opposite her, oblivious to the white frost beneath me. 'I love you. I can't believe you're really here and we're talking after all these years. I thought I'd never see you again.'

She beamed those huge eyes at me, flooding me with their pale green intensity. 'That's why I'm here. To let you know that we can be together on the other side.'

Time halted. I'd dreamed of this possibility and yet I'd never truly allowed myself to believe it. How could I deserve that when I'd betrayed her like I had? Was it possible she still didn't know about my infidelity?

'Alice. There's something I have to tell you. It's awful, but you have to—'

284

'Stop. There's no need. I already know.'

'But—'

'I saw what the guilt did to you, Will. How it ate you up inside. When you thought you were alone, begging your dead wife for forgiveness and believing yourself crazy, I was there. I followed you and our baby daughter as a spirit, just as you follow her now.'

She paused for a moment, her composure slipping as emotion crept into her voice. 'I'm not saying I'll ever forget what you did. I thought ... you were better than that. I thought what we had was stronger—'

I tried to respond, but she held her hand up to stop me. 'The point is, despite all of that, I have forgiven you. You've done a wonderful job of bringing up Ella. You're my husband. I still love you and I want to be with you again.'

I was choked. I couldn't believe what I was hearing; what I was seeing.

'Isn't that what you want too, Will?'

'Of course it is,' I replied, fighting to keep my voice steady. 'But I'm so ashamed of what I did. I feel like ... I don't deserve your forgiveness.'

Her eyes met mine in an intense gaze. 'That's not for you to decide.'

Then something caught her attention. She turned her head to one side, a puzzled look crossing her face.

'What is it?' I asked, looking around but not seeing or hearing anything.

'I don't have long. Listen, I know you don't want to leave Ella. Believe me, I've been there. Letting go of a child is the hardest thing imaginable, but sometimes it's the right thing to do. We're not meant to stay here as spirits. That's not the natural order of things. As difficult as it might be for you to believe, she will be better off without you.'

'But … I … after everything that's happened. How could I … leave her? I promised her I wouldn't.'

'You've seen what will happen if you stay.'

'She'll think I'm no better than Dad.'

'You have to let go. There's a wonderful place waiting for you: everything you've ever dreamed of and more. We can be together again and one day, when it's her time, Ella can join us.'

'But. I'm not sure I can.'

Alice leaned forward, stretching her right arm out towards me. She raised her hand so it was almost cradling my cheek. She moved her face directly in front of mine, tilted to one side, as close as she could get without contact. I didn't dare move for fear of touching her.

'You have to find a way, my love,' she whispered. 'I'm sorry. There's no more time.'

She darted forward to kiss me and, as our lips touched, I felt a jolt – like a static electric shock – and then she was gone.

'Alice, wait,' I called after her, although my experience with Arthur and Lizzie told me it was futile.

I started pacing up and down the garden. I had to work out what to do: who to listen to; who to believe. Mind you, no one was advising me to stay. Not even Arthur, who'd chosen to do so himself. That was all me. It was a voice inside my head that kept telling me I couldn't leave her. It was always there, banging on at me, no matter what advice I received to the contrary. 'She's your little girl, your baby. You're the only parent she's got left. You promised you'd never leave her. How could you go back on that?'

'Because that is what's best for HER,' I imagined Lizzie replying. 'Stop thinking about yourself and focus on your daughter. You staying will do her far more harm than good. I've shown you that.'

I felt like my head was about to burst.

'Well, Lizzie? Why don't you come and tell me so?'

I'd been expecting her all day. I thought she'd be only too keen to remind me how little time I had left; to nudge me further in the 'right direction'. That was why she arranged for Alice to visit, wasn't it? So where was she?

'Lizzie?' I called. 'Can I speak to you, please?'

I stood in the garden, expecting her to arrive any second. Why not? She always had when I'd called her previously. But after a few minutes had passed, I knew she wasn't coming. I waited nonetheless, staring at a Christmas tree twinkling at me from a neighbour's conservatory. December the twenty-fifth was fast approaching, although that fact had hardly registered in the minds of my family yet. How could it after everything that had happened and with the huge hurdle of Dad's funeral standing in the way?

'Are you coming or not, Lizzie?' I bellowed one last time.

CHAPTER 30

SIX DAYS LEFT

By lunchtime the next day, despite several more attempts to contact her, Lizzie still hadn't shown up. It was driving me mad now – like she'd abandoned me when I needed her most – so, to distract myself, I went with Mum and Lauren to see the funeral director. They had an appointment to discuss the arrangements for next week. I was in the back seat of Dad's BMW, which Mum had just pulled up outside the funeral parlour. It was the first time I'd seen her drive his car, rather than her Corsa. She usually claimed to find it hard to park, but today she'd grabbed the keys and muttered something about it needing a run. As Lauren undid her seat belt, I braced myself to slip out of the door behind her. But before I had a chance to grab my window of opportunity, I felt a tap on my shoulder. The shock of being touched, when I was so unused to feeling anything, caused me to lurch forward into Lauren's arm. That in turn catapulted me back on to the rear seat. There, with my head squashed against the fabric, I found myself staring into Lizzie's eyes.

'Hello, William. Sorry about that. How are you?'

'How am I? Where on earth did you get to? I've been trying to reach you since yesterday. I thought you'd abandoned me.'

'I know. I can only apologize for that. I've been ... well, let's just say things have been hectic.'

I shook my head. 'Hectic?'

'Yes. But I'm here for you now. Shall we go somewhere more comfortable?'

I pulled away from her before she had a chance to touch me. 'No. Here's fine.'

'Okay. No problem. What did you want to discuss?'

'How about we start with Alice coming to visit me? That was a surprise. I believe you had something to do with it.'

'Yes. And? Did it help?'

'Was it really her?'

'Of course.'

'She said that Ella would be better off without me here and asked me to join her on the other side. She said she was waiting for me. Now that I've had time to think, it all seems a bit convenient. Like she was saying what you wanted me to hear.'

Lizzie nodded. 'I see why you might think that, but I can assure you there's no conspiracy going on. Alice spoke for herself. I sent her because I'm trying to present you with all the facts before you make your decision. I think you know that I'm also the one who brought Arthur to you. It's thanks to his advice that you made contact with Ella. Why would I do that if I wanted to push you towards passing over? My goal is for you to make that choice

289

yourself because you believe it to be the right one. Anything less and I've failed.'

'So you're admitting your link to Arthur now, are you? Last time I mentioned him to you, you played dumb.'

'There was a good reason for that,' Lizzie sighed. 'He and I both stepped outside the rules. He shouldn't have—'

'I know, I know. Arthur already explained. So why did you ask for his help?'

'For you. I don't want his fate to be yours.'

She explained that Arthur had been one of her early assignments as a guide. The sacrifice he'd made by staying with his wife and then letting her pass over without him, forsaking his own chance at happiness, had always weighed on Lizzie's mind. She still blamed herself for it. Then I came along: someone acquainted with Arthur, facing a comparable dilemma to his own. Plus there was the fact that Lizzie and I had both been killed in cycling accidents. Collectively, it felt like more than coincidence. So she interpreted it as a sign – and decided to act on it.

'I had to do something different,' she said. 'I knew as soon as I met you that there was a chance of history repeating itself. Because of that, I chose to bend the rules, hoping it would lead you to the right decision. Bringing Alice here yesterday was part of that.'

'But Arthur's all right,' I said. 'He might have given up his chance of passing over, but he seems to be managing.'

'He puts a brave face on it,' Lizzie replied. 'But he'll never see his wife again. He could be with her in paradise now. Instead he's trapped here. Alone. I do my best to stay in touch – to keep him sane – but I fear that one day it will get too much for him and he'll lose what's left of his humanity. I wouldn't wish that fate on anyone.'

I thought back to the ferocious spirit I'd encountered in the hospital corridor and shuddered at the idea of Arthur ending up like that.

'So he made a mistake?'

She shrugged. 'Arthur did what he felt he had to. What he thought was right. It was a selfless act of love. But I doubt he'd advise anyone to do the same.'

'Where is Arthur, by the way? I can't get hold of him. I know he's had to be careful since the pavilion incident. He said that was under control, but … he is all right, isn't he?'

'Yes. Don't worry. He's having to keep an extra low profile for now, that's all. Unfortunately, another guide has got wind of him helping you: Hardy, he's called. Bit of a stickler for the rules. I think you ran into him a couple of times at the church. I've managed to contain the situation so far, but – well – as I said before, it's been hectic.'

'Oh no. You're joking. I know exactly who you mean. Shit. Sorry. Um, I, er, think that might be my fault. I was calling Arthur's name, trying to find him. The last thing I meant to do was land him in trouble. I didn't tell this Hardy who he was when he asked me, but he must have worked it out. Damn.'

Lizzie screwed up her face. 'It gets better. Hardy's also your father's guide.'

'What? I don't believe it. He never said a word to me. I … oh, don't tell me Dad was with him in the church that last time.'

She nodded. 'I'm afraid so. I've asked Hardy repeatedly if you can meet with him, but he won't allow it. He says your father doesn't want to and, considering the circumstances, I daren't push him any further.'

'Fantastic. Just brilliant. What's that guy's problem?'

'He's very single-minded. Uncompromising. It's all about results with Hardy: getting the spirits from A to B, like a cowboy driving a herd. It's ironic, as he was reluctant to pass over himself when he died, apparently.'

'Really? How come?'

'I don't know the specifics. I wasn't directly involved and it was some time ago. But I have heard he took some convincing to leave his family.'

'So it's a poacher turned gamekeeper situation.'

'Exactly.'

'Any good news?'

'Um, no. Sorry. Not yet. I am working on something, though.'

'Such as?'

'It's just a proposal at the moment. I don't want to say too much in case it doesn't come together. But put it this way: if it does, I think it might help with your decision.'

Lizzie refused to reveal anything else about this mysterious plan. I was intrigued. However, the rules of the afterlife were clear. As much as I wanted to believe her, I failed to see how any last-ditch intervention could truly ease my dilemma.

CHAPTER 31

THREE DAYS LEFT

Mum was at the kitchen table staring at a letter she'd opened. She looked upset.

I stepped around the table to read it as Lauren entered the room behind me. 'What's that?'

Mum didn't reply. She kept staring at the letter, which I could now see came from the Crown Prosecution Service. It listed a date next June for the crown court trial of the woman charged with causing my death by dangerous driving.

'What's the matter?' Lauren asked. 'What are you reading?'

Mum handed her the letter.

'Oh,' Lauren said after staring at it for a minute. 'Well, that's good. She needs to be punished. If it wasn't for her, Ella would still have a father. June's sooner than they told us, isn't it?'

'Yes. It is good news, I suppose. It's just …' Mum's eyes welled up with tears. 'I miss him so much. The letter made me feel bad. I felt guilty that after everything with your father, I've not been thinking about Will enough. Also—'

293

'Don't be ridiculous, Mum,' Lauren and I said in sync, like she was channelling my voice. I stared at my sister in shock as she continued: 'You're doing your best to lead this family through a series of impossible situations. I think you're doing an unbelievable job, honestly.'

She stood behind Mum and hugged her.

'No one's forgetting Will. How could we? We're just coping as best as we can with all the crap being hurled at us. That crash was the start. Let's hope it ends with the right verdict in court.'

What is the right verdict? I wondered. Do I actually want the driver to go to prison for what she did? With everything else that had been going on, I hadn't thought about her for a while. And now my anger had faded, I accepted that I didn't need her to be jailed. How would it help? I'd still be dead and the lives of another family would be ruined. It wasn't like she'd killed me on purpose. I remembered seeing her at the scene, deathly pale and shaking, vomit on her shoes and hair. She'd have to live with what she'd done for the rest of her life. Perhaps that was punishment enough.

'She tried to contact me,' Mum said, grabbing my attention.

'Who did?' Lauren asked.

'The one on trial; the driver. I can't bring myself to say her name.'

Lauren looked as shocked as I felt. It was the first either of us had heard of this. 'What? When?'

'A few days after it happened. She approached me outside Will's house. God knows how she knew where he lived. I'd been out doing some shopping; when I got back she was there at the front door. I didn't realize who she was at first. She told me she was sorry about my son's death, so I assumed she was a friend or a neighbour. But when I asked how she knew him, she broke down and told me everything.'

'What did you do?'

'I lost it. I shouted at her to get the hell away from me and my family. I called her a killer and said I'd never forgive her for taking my son away and orphaning my granddaughter. She asked about the funeral; I told her if she dared to come, I'd throw her out myself. I called her every awful name you can think of.'

'Shit, Mum.'

'She looked so wretched, so pathetic. I'm supposed to be a Christian. I'm supposed to forgive. But I couldn't. It was too raw. Was it awful of me to behave like that?'

'No, Mum. It's only human. I'd have done the same. Hell, I'd have probably thumped her.'

'At least she was trying to make amends. Do you think I should contact her now?'

'No. Definitely not. It might affect the case. Seriously, you're not going to do that, are you?'

'No. You're right. I hadn't thought of that. I'll stay away.'

'Good. And don't you go feeling guilty about anything. You're the best person I know.'

Mum's confession explained a few things. I had wondered whether the driver had considered coming to my funeral. I'd also been surprised not to hear of her contacting my family in some way, although I'd put that down to legal advice. Armed with this extra information, I was even more certain of my feelings about her punishment. It was something that stayed in my head for the rest of the day. That and the fact that this might be the last Friday I'd ever spend on earth.

'You know the woman who was driving the car that I, um, had the accident with?' I asked Ella as I sat at the side of her bed that night.

'Yes.'

'How do you feel about her?'

'I hate her.'

I was taken aback by the speed and ferocity of her answer. Unsure how best to counter it, I simply replied: 'I don't.'

Confused, Ella asked me why not.

'Hate is so negative,' I said. 'It only makes us feel worse. She didn't do it on purpose. It was an accident and I know she's really sorry.'

'But it's all her fault. If she hadn't died you with her car, everything would be like it used to be.'

'She made one stupid mistake. That's all. I don't think she's a bad person. I don't think we should hate her.'

'Well, Auntie Lauren says she's going to be on a court soon and after that she'll have to go in a prison. That's where bad people go.'

I looked towards the bedroom door, which was open as usual to let light in from the landing. 'The thing is, Ella, I don't think she should go to prison. I'd rather she didn't.'

I probably shouldn't have been discussing this with my daughter, but I felt I had to say something and there was no other family member I could tell.

'There are other ways of punishing her for what she did,' I added.

'Like what?'

'Well, she definitely won't be allowed to drive any more. And sometimes they get people to do unpaid work in the community instead of prison: picking up litter, sweeping the streets, that kind of thing. I've even heard of drivers who've caused accidents having to go into schools to teach children about road safety.'

Ella gasped. 'She won't come to my school will she?'

I cursed myself for giving such a stupid example. 'No, of course not. Don't worry. That would never happen.'

The reporter in me couldn't help imagining the fallout if it did. The papers would be all over it. I could picture the headline: ORPHAN MEETS DAD'S KILLER IN ASSEMBLY.

'Why are you talking about this now, Daddy? Auntie Lauren said she wouldn't be at court until summer – and that's ages away.'

'It is a long way off, love. I, er, just wanted you to know how I feel … in case.'

'In case what?'

I did my best to sound calm as the unthinkable left my lips. 'In case I'm not around any more.'

Ella jolted up in bed. 'What do you mean? You said you'd never leave me. You promised.'

Despite everything I'd been told to the contrary, I was still struggling to accept the idea of leaving my daughter. My mind was far from made up. But with such little time left and no word from Lizzie about her mysterious proposal, I felt I had to at least prepare Ella for that

297

possibility. God, it was tough, though. I could barely look her in the eye. 'I did say that, darling. And I meant it. But I didn't know then what I do now.'

Tears welled up in her eyes. 'What do you mean? Are you leaving or not?'

I forced the words out of my mouth before I had a chance to change my mind. 'I might have to, darling.'

'Why?' she wailed. 'I need you.'

'Shh, Ella. Calm down, please.'

But it was already too late. I heard the sound of feet on the stairs. Lauren appeared at the bedroom door. 'What's the matter?' she asked, racing over to her niece. I had to duck and roll out of the way to avoid her. She perched on the edge of the bed and Ella threw her arms around her, sobbing into her jumper.

'What's up, Ella? You were all smiles when I said goodnight. Did you have a nightmare?'

Ella shook her head and continued to bawl her eyes out. I felt awful. And I'd not even told her the worst part yet: that I could be gone by Monday lunchtime.

Then I looked at the way she was hugging her auntie, squeezing her with all her might and getting the same back. The sight reminded me of all the things I could no longer offer her and how important it was to have someone physically there for her. Someone who could give her hugs, who could tie her hair up in a ponytail, cook for her and protect her from harm. That wasn't me – not now – and it never would be again.

But Lauren would be back in the Netherlands soon. Mum would do her best for her granddaughter, but would she be able to cope all alone while grieving for her husband and son? As well-behaved as Ella was now, what about when she became a teenager? She'd be a prime candidate to rebel after everything she'd been through. Would Mum be able to handle it alone?

Ella's tears had abated, so Lauren asked again what was wrong.

'It's Daddy,' she said, making me fear for a moment that she was going to tell Lauren the truth. 'I miss him so much.'

'Of course you do, my love. I know how much you and your daddy meant to each other. It's not fair that he's gone. None of what we've been through is fair, but we have to stick together and help each other through it. I miss my dad too. That's what Grandad was to me.'

'I know,' Ella sniffed. 'And my daddy's your brother.'

'That's right. And I loved him very much. It's only normal to miss people when they're not around. I've missed Xander terribly over the last few days, even though I know I'm going to see him again when he flies in tomorrow night. And I always miss you, my favourite niece, when we're not together.'

A tiny smile appeared on Ella's face. 'I'm your only niece.'

Lauren tickled her under the chin. 'There's no getting anything past you these days, is there? Well, guess what.'

'What?'

She pulled her into another tight hug, whispering: 'Even if I did have other nieces, you'd still be my favourite.'

'Are you all right?' I asked Ella once Lauren had gone and Mum had also popped in to give her a kiss. She was

299

sucking her thumb and her eyes were heavy. She didn't reply. Not even a nod or a shake of the head.

'I didn't mean to upset you,' I whispered. 'That's the last thing I want. You're more important to me than anyone or anything else. You're my everything.'

She turned her head away from me on the pillow, facing the wall.

'Okay,' I whispered. 'I get the hint. You don't want to talk to me now. I'll let you sleep. Goodnight.'

Still no reply.

That went well, I thought, as I trudged down the stairs, wondering whether or not I'd done the right thing. Then I heard a familiar voice.

'Lizzie,' I said in surprise.

Early the next morning Ella ran up to me in the kitchen with her arms wide open, like she was going to hug me. I think it was only when I took a nervous step backwards that she remembered to stop. 'Sorry. I forgot.'

'Don't be sorry, love. I wish we could hug. There's nothing I'd like better.'

'Me too.'

It was just after 5.30 a.m. I'd been standing there, staring out of the window, for ages. A light covering of snow had fallen during the night, which created a magical floodlight effect across the garden despite the fact it was still dark outside.

'What is it, darling?' I asked, noticing that Ella had been crying.

She looked away. I knew better than to push, but I guessed

300

that she'd woken up and, not seeing me in her room, had panicked. Who could blame her for fearing that I'd gone after the conversation we'd had last night?

'I couldn't sleep,' I explained, 'so I decided to give Sam some company.'

I glanced over at the chestnut and white lump of fur sprawled before the radiator. He'd raised his head and opened one eye when Ella had entered but was zonked out again now.

'Sorry for upsetting you last night, love. Are we friends again?'

She nodded, still not looking at me.

This wasn't the moment for more serious discussions. Ella was too emotional and I was exhausted. All I wanted right now was to spend some quality time with my girl.

I'd been thinking non-stop for hours following Lizzie's visit last night. Her plan to help with my decision had come to fruition. She'd confounded me with a new option – a third way forward. It was a possibility only offered in extraordinary circumstances, she'd explained, and it demanded to be considered. Little wonder I'd not been able to sleep.

'Come on, darling,' I said, leading Ella out of the kitchen, glad of a break. 'Let's go to the lounge so we don't wake up the others. Shut the door behind us, there's a good girl.'

I suggested playing a game, but Ella didn't want to. 'What would you like to do, love?'

'Read story,' she said in the baby voice she sometimes adopted when tired or wanting attention.

'Sure. Would you like to read to me?'

She pulled a sad face and shook her head. 'Daddy read to Ella.'

I'd usually have told her to speak properly and to say please, but in the circumstances I didn't have the heart. 'Very well then, but you'll have to turn the pages for me.'

She ran upstairs to her bedroom, returning with an armful of colourful books about fairies, kittens, princesses and puppies. An hour later, just after 6.30 a.m., we'd got through the lot. I couldn't remember ever reading quite so many books to Ella in one go before, although I was happy to do it. When it comes to escapism, there's little better than a good children's story and a wide-eyed youngster to enjoy it.

'That's the lot,' I said. 'We can read another one if you like, but you'll have to run upstairs and get it.'

'That's okay,' she said, removing her thumb from her mouth and twirling one of her longest curls into a corkscrew. 'I've had enough now.'

She scrutinized me with those big green eyes of hers before adding: 'I thought you'd gone when I woke up.'

I nodded. 'I know you did, darling. I could tell when I saw how upset you were. Sorry I made you think that.'

'Are you going to leave me?'

I fought to keep my voice steady. 'I don't want to.'

Her bottom lip quivered as tears began to flow. 'You promised you'd stay.'

I looked at the heartbreak on my beautiful little girl's face – a face I loved more than any other – and in that awful moment I made my final decision. I found a pinprick of light in the darkness and finally knew what I had to do in two days' time.

302

CHAPTER 32

TEN HOURS LEFT

'Wake up,' a voice whispered in my ear.

'What?' I muttered, one foot still in the land of nod.

'Wake up. I need to talk to you.'

I kept my eyes shut. 'No. Not yet. It's too early.'

'Shh. Keep it down, son, or you'll wake Ella.'

Then it clicked. 'Dad?' I said, jerking awake. And there was my father. His huge frame was draped in the same pyjamas and dressing gown he'd worn in hospital, but there was no sign of his fatal neck wound or the effects of his stroke. He placed a hand on my right shoulder and squeezed it, looking relieved when I didn't pull away. Then he did something he'd not done since I was a lad and pulled me into a hug, adding a couple of slaps on the back to keep it manly.

'It's so good to see you,' I said. 'Where on earth have you been?' But before he had a chance to answer my question, the anger came rushing to the surface. 'How could you?' I snapped.

He turned towards the bedroom door. 'Let's not do this here.'

It was 2 a.m., according to Ella's watch. That meant it was already here: Monday, the morning of the funeral. My deadline was just hours away. I followed Dad down the stairs and was surprised to find Hardy standing in the hallway. 'You,' I snarled. 'You've got a nerve coming here.'

'Have you two already met?' Dad asked.

'You could say that,' I replied, eyeballing Hardy. He responded by grabbing hold of the two of us and transporting us to a familiar spot: the oak tree by the stream.

'I'll leave you to talk,' he said, vanishing.

'Where are we?' Dad asked, looking around the snowy field, which glowed in the moonlight.

'You must know where this is,' I replied. 'It's only a short walk from the house. The primary school's just up there. I used to come here all the time as a kid.'

'Really? Oh, right. I didn't recognize it. Never been much of a walker, have I?'

I pulled him towards me, so we were standing toe to toe, but he turned his head away. 'Don't give me that. Look at me. It's time to face up to what you've done.'

'I'm sorry, son. I'm so ashamed.'

I could feel the pent-up fury swelling inside me, clawing its way to freedom. And then I unleashed it. 'You're sorry? It's a bit late for that, Dad. What the hell were you thinking? Why did you do it? How could you be such a selfish prick? I was dragged kicking and screaming away from my life. It was stolen from me; I'd give anything to have it back. You threw yours away, like it was nothing. You turned your back on your wife, your daughter, your granddaughter when they needed you most. What kind of a man does that?'

Dad stared at his slippers, which I couldn't help think looked out of place in the snow. He kept shaking his head, over and over, moving his lips without any words coming out.

'Dad!' I shouted, trying to shock him back into the moment. 'Get it together. Stop feeling sorry for yourself and talk to me. Why did you kill yourself?'

'I was backed into a corner. I was desperate. The stroke, the secrets and lies: it felt like everything was going to shit, especially so soon after your death. I was terrified of never fully recovering; of the skeletons in my closet. Then I started seeing you, my dead son. And when you told me that Lauren and your mother knew about the affair, it was more than I could handle. I was facing being alone, losing my family, everything – my home, my friends. Suicide felt like the only way out.'

I had a flashback to the awful sight of his body being lifted out of the lavatory – and all that blood. 'But ... you must have been so resolute, so definite, to do it the way you did. I can't even begin to imagine—'

'I was. I wanted to die and was determined not to be stopped. But the minute I found myself like this – a spirit – staring at the sight of my own dead body swimming in my blood, the enormity of what I'd done hit me. I knew I'd made a terrible mistake. If I could go back and change it, I would. You have to believe me, son.'

'Where have you been, if you're so sorry? Why didn't you come to me straight away?'

Dad shook his head. 'I'm a coward. That's why. It was only tonight that I finally got up the courage. I had to see you before the funeral. I'm so sorry, son. For everything. I won't ask you to forgive me. How could I? But I need you to know how much I regret what I've done.'

I was too choked up to reply. We stared at each other in silence until Dad went on: 'Hardy, um. He said that you already know about, er—'

'About what?'

'My secret.'

'You mean that you're gay?'

My directness threw him. 'Well, I don't know if I'd, er—'

'Come on, Dad. It's time we called a spade a spade. You're gay. You must be. Okay, it feels weird to think of you like that, but it doesn't seem very significant in the light of everything else that's happened.'

'Wow. I thought you'd be disgusted.'

'You are who you are, Dad. Life's too short to think otherwise. But you need to accept yourself. If you'd done that, things would never have got out of hand like they did. How long have you got?'

'What do you mean?'

'How long until you have to make up your mind?'

'About what?'

It turned out that Hardy hadn't given Dad the choice of staying or going. He'd simply told him he would pass over after his funeral. So much for free will. Apparently the option of remaining on earth wasn't offered to you unless you specifically asked for it.

I raised an eyebrow. 'You never questioned what he told you?'

'Should I have? I mean, he originally wanted me to go straight away, but I refused. I said I needed time. I knew I had to speak to you first. That's when he told me I could have until the funeral, like he was doing me a big favour; there was no mention of any other choice. To be honest, I was counting my blessings that I hadn't been sent to Hell. I still am.'

I considered explaining to Dad about how he could choose to remain here forever. But I feared if I did, it would look as if I expected that of him, like some kind of penance for what he'd done, which was the last thing I wanted. Besides, if today went as planned, it wouldn't matter anyway.

At that moment Hardy materialized next to Dad. 'How are we doing?'

'Interesting timing,' I said. 'Almost like you were listening in on our conversation. And how do you know about this place? I bet you've followed me here before, haven't you?'

Hardy scowled at me then turned to Dad. 'We'd better get going.'

'I need a bit longer,' Dad replied.

'It's okay,' I said. 'You go. We can talk more at the funeral.'

'You're coming?'

'Of course. I'm your son.'

I turned to Hardy. 'And don't worry. I'm not planning to rock the boat. I just want to be there for my father.'

Fixing me with a cold stare, he placed a hand on Dad's shoulder and they disappeared.

'You look beautiful, darling,' I told Ella as she stood in front of the mirror in her black dress.

She sighed. 'I hate funerals.'

'Me too. You still look beautiful, though.'

'Don't you think my hair looks a bit ... weird?'

Lauren had styled it in a French plait for her before disappearing to get ready.

'No, it looks really nice. You're just not used to it.'

'I might take it out and put a hairband in instead.'

'Don't do that, Ella. Not after Auntie Lauren spent so long on it. It's lovely, honestly.'

'Can you really see yourself in the mirror, Daddy?'

'Yes,' I said, waving my hands at my reflection behind hers. 'Here I am.'

'How come I can't see you there?'

I stuck my tongue out. 'Beats me, but at least it means I can pull faces at you without you noticing.'

'Don't be cheeky,' she replied, turning and frowning at me with mock anger. 'What face did you pull?'

'Oh, nothing,' I said, sticking my tongue out again.

She stuck hers out too before becoming serious all of a sudden. 'Where did you go last night?'

It was Ella who had let me in earlier that morning, after a lengthy wait outside, but Xander had appeared in the kitchen to make coffee and we'd not been alone until now.

'Yes, I wanted to talk to you about that,' I said. 'I was with Grandad.'

'What? How? Where did you go?'

I recounted what had happened, emphasizing Dad's profound regret and reminding Ella how much he loved and missed her.

She asked if he'd be at the funeral.

I nodded.

'Will I be able to see him?'

I'd been wondering the same thing. 'I honestly don't know, Ella. I'm not sure how it works. We'll soon find out. If you do see him, you'll have to be careful, like with me. You can't speak to him in front of other people and you mustn't let on to anyone about it.'

'I know, Daddy,' she replied, her bottom lip quivering. 'You don't have to tell me that.'

I held up my hands. 'Sorry, love. I was just saying. I wasn't criticizing you.'

A single tear ran down her left cheek as she turned back to the mirror.

'I love you so much and I'm so proud of you,' I said, although as soon as the words had left my mouth, it occurred to me that they were only likely to make her more emotional. Sure enough, she turned and ran into her princess castle.

'Are you all right?' I asked, but the sound of her quiet sobbing was her only response.

A long shadow was cast across the bedroom carpet as Xander appeared at the door in his black suit and tie. His recent return had been good for everyone. Lauren had hardly left his side and regularly dragged him off for long conversations; Mum and Ella brightened up in his presence. The only shame was that it couldn't last. We all knew that he'd be heading back to his home country soon, with Lauren not far behind.

'Where's my favourite niece?' he said in his Dutch-accented but perfect English.

Ella didn't reply, so he peered through the door of the tent. Then, to my surprise, he squeezed inside too. I could see the shape of his crouching head stretching the fabric roof.

'What's up, *kleintje*?' he said. 'You look like you need a *dikke knuffel*.'

'What's that?' Ella sniffed.

'It's what I always give Auntie Lauren when she's sad. It means a big hug.'

I saw him lean over and take Ella in his huge arms through the tent window. I was glad that he was there for her, but I couldn't help feeling a pang of jealousy.

'What's the other thing you said?' Ella asked, sounding brighter.

'What thing?'

'You called me something in Dutch. It sounded like clean-shh.'

Xander gave a booming laugh. 'Oh, you mean *kleintje*. It roughly translates as "little one". Come on, you can say it too: *kl-ein-tje*.'

'*Kl-ein-tje*,' she repeated. '*Kleintje*.'

'Perfect. You're a natural. I think you could learn to speak Dutch very well.'

'You're not a *kleintje*, are you, Uncle Xander?' she giggled. 'You're too big for this tent. And you're not a princess. So you shouldn't be in here.'

'You want me to get out? What a meanie. What about if I tell you a secret instead?'

'What kind of secret? Is it a good one?'

'It's a very good one. I know you'll like it.'

'Um … okay, then. Tell me.'

'Are you sure?'

'Yes. Please tell me. Pleeease.'

'Right then. Here goes …'

CHAPTER 33

THREE HOURS LEFT

I thought Xander was going to tell Ella that Lauren was pregnant. Goodness knows why. It must have been because of what Ella had said the other day about wanting them to have a baby. Anyway, that wasn't it at all. What he actually said to her came as a total shock.

'You know how your auntie and I live in Holland, which means we don't see you that much?'

'Yes.'

'Well, we're actually going to move here.'

Ella's voice leaped in pitch. 'Here? In this house?'

'To start with. After a while we plan to buy our own place, but it will be somewhere nearby. Probably in the village. So it won't just be you and Nana. You'll have us too.'

'Really? You're coming here for good?'

'That's the idea. We've worked out a way that we can run our business over there while living here. The internet makes these things much easier than they used to be.

Meanwhile, we want to expand what we do into this country. The beauty of weddings is that people get married all over the world.'

'You don't mind? Won't you miss Holland?'

'Of course, but a change will be nice and I'll still be flying back on the odd occasion. Plus I'll have my favourite niece close by to play games with. What could be better?'

'Have you told Nana?'

'Yes. She seems to like the idea. What do you think of it?'

'Really good,' Ella replied, leaning over to give Xander another big hug.

'Well, you think about that today when you're feeling sad about your grandad. Hopefully it will make you feel a bit happier. Anyway, I'd better go and see what your auntie's up to. Otherwise we'll never get out of here in time.'

With a lot of bending and squeezing, Xander manoeuvred his way out of the tent and back on to his feet.

'Did you hear all that, Daddy?' Ella asked once her uncle was out of earshot.

'I certainly did, darling. It's great news.'

'I thought he was going to say they were having a baby,' she added. 'This is better, though, because if they had a baby in Holland, I'd never see it. Maybe they'll have one here. That would be brilliant.'

'Sure,' I replied, not wanting to dampen her spirits with any suggestion that might not happen. 'Will you be all right today?'

'I think so. But I'll be glad when it's over. Is Grandad getting crematoriumed like you did?'

'Cremated, you mean. No. He and Nana have a plot in the churchyard where they can be buried together.'

Ella's eyes stretched wide with panic. 'Together? But Nana's not dead.'

'No, darling,' I said, kicking myself for putting that idea in her head. 'It just means that when she does eventually die, which I'm sure won't be for a very long time, she'll be buried in the same place. Their coffins will be together.'

'Under the ground ... with their bodies still inside?'

'That's right.'

'Yuk. Won't creepy-crawlies get in there?'

'I think coffins are well sealed. But what would it matter? Bodies are empty shells, like clothes that aren't needed any more. Look at me: I'm still here without mine. And I've seen Grandad without his. He can walk and talk like he used to before the stroke.'

'Really?'

'Yep. Just like the old Grandad we know and love.'

'That's good. I don't think I'd like my body buried in the ground, though. I'd rather be crematoriumed.'

'Ella?' Mum's voice called from downstairs. 'Are you ready, love? We need to leave.'

'Coming, Nana.'

'I'll meet you at the church,' I told Ella.

A look of alarm flashed across her face. 'You are coming, aren't you?'

'Yes, honestly. I'll be there. I fancy a walk, that's all.'

'Promise?'

'Promise.'

314

'Pinky promise?'

I held my little finger close to hers. 'Pinky promise.'

Ella let me out of the front door. The garden was still coated in white. It hadn't snowed again, but what was left on the ground wasn't going anywhere. 'Nine twenty,' I said after peering through the window at the carriage clock in the lounge. Just forty minutes until the funeral service was due to start and two hours on top of that until midday. Here I was entering the final straight.

Although it wasn't the first time I'd walked in the snow as a spirit, I still hadn't got used to it. There was no crunch of it being crushed under my weight. And the fact I left no footprints felt weird, like I didn't exist.

'Lizzie?' I called after walking a little way along the street.

She appeared alongside me. 'Hello, William. Good to see you. How are things?'

I shrugged. 'Okay, I guess, considering what's about to happen. I assume you know Dad and I have spoken.'

She nodded.

'I've said I'll attend the funeral. I'm on my way there now.'

'Would you like me to come with you?'

'No, thanks. You can walk with me, but I'll handle it by myself when I get there.'

'Fine.'

'When it was my funeral, you offered to smarten me up. Any chance you could do that now?'

'Sure. Any preference?'

'Just a simple black suit and tie will be fine.'

She tapped my shoulder and it was done. No more frayed jeans and T-shirt.

'How's that?'

'Perfect. Thanks.' I paused before adding: 'All very neat the way it's fallen: Dad's funeral just before my deadline. Did you have a hand in that?'

A flicker of a smile darted across her lips. 'Why ever would you think such a thing?'

We walked a few more steps in silence before she asked me if I'd made my decision.

'I think so. Yes.'

'And?'

I stopped walking and turned to look her in the eye. I knew the words I wanted to say but they were so big – so final – they stuck in my throat. 'I, um. I—'

'William?'

She dragged it out of me. Made me say it. And then she nodded her acceptance.

I walked the last part of the route to the church alone. I got there a few minutes before Mum, Lauren, Ella and Xander. When they arrived Ella, who was arm in arm with her auntie, gave me a discreet wave.

'Come on,' Xander said to the others. 'We need to get inside before everyone starts arriving.'

At that moment the hearse turned into the driveway of the church. Mum, whose skin looked deathly pale against the black of her outfit, let out an involuntary yelp at the sight of the coffin in the back as it pulled up alongside them. It was the first thing I'd heard come out

316

of her mouth that morning and it was heart-breaking to witness. Her recent strength seemed to have left her and, standing there next to her giant son-in-law, she looked terribly small and vulnerable. At least Xander was there for her, unlike me and Dad. He put a strong arm around her, whispering something supportive, before having a brief word with the funeral director and then leading the others inside.

'I'll be there in a minute,' I called to Ella as she glanced back at me before entering the church. 'I'm going to see if I can find Grandad.'

A quick circuit of the building didn't turn up any clues. Perhaps he's already inside, I thought. But then it occurred to me that he might be at the grave. I remembered him showing me the plot once, several years ago when Alice and I had been up from London for a visit. They were expensive and hard to come by these days. I recalled him being proud to have got it, even though it was quite a way from the church.

'I'd have booked a spot for you too, son,' he'd said at the time, a sunny Easter Sunday. 'But I reckoned you and Alice would want to make your own arrangements. Not that you need to worry about things like that at your age.'

'You're not that old yourself, Dad,' I remembered replying. 'I don't think either of us has much to worry about yet.'

How wrong I'd been.

I followed the path that led to the plot, in a field behind a tall wall of snow-topped conifers. The graves here were more modern and less ostentatious than those in the main churchyard. Then I saw him, his bulky spirit form standing in sombre silence at the foot of the hole soon to contain his coffin. The dark brown of the freshly dug soil stood in stark contrast to the wintry blanket covering the rest of the plots. There was no sign of Hardy, although his handiwork was evident in the fact that Dad was dressed in a three-piece black suit and overcoat. It was much better than his pyjamas and dressing gown. He almost looked like his old self again.

He must have already spotted me, as he didn't seem surprised by my arrival.

'Hello, son,' he said, continuing to stare into the open grave. 'Do you think the ground was hard to dig with it being so cold? I mean, I guess it's cold. It looks freezing, but I can't feel anything any more. Can you?'

'No. Takes a bit of getting used to, doesn't it?'

'I'm really glad that you're here. All smartened up to boot. You look good, son.'

'You too, Dad.'

'Well, I didn't think my pyjamas would be suitable. Did you expect something more flamboyant?'

'What, because you're gay? Don't be ridiculous. The thought never occurred to me.'

'I know that's how they always portray, um … us. You know, in the media.'

'Camp, you mean?'

'Exactly. But I'm not like that. I never have been. It's not that I was hiding my true nature from you and the rest of the family. Well, I suppose I was, but … what I mean is … I'm the same person you know, apart from the obvious. I'm not some screaming queen in hot pink Spandex.'

'I never thought you were. Give me some credit. Being gay is pretty normal to someone of my generation, you know.'

'Right. Sorry, Will. I, um, just wanted you to know that it wasn't all lies.'

'Okay, Dad.'

'Are you coming in for the service?'

'Yes, of course. I told Ella I'd sit with her.'

'Oh, right. Good.

'There's something I don't understand,' Dad said. 'How come you're still here? You've been like this a lot longer than I have. Why haven't you passed over yet? Is it something to do with Ella? Is that why she can see you?'

'It is because of Ella. I said I needed some time and they gave it to me. The reason she can see me is more complicated. But now isn't the time for an explanation. We ought to be getting to the church.'

He looked back down at his grave. 'How was it at your funeral?'

'You were there.'

'Of course, but I mean … how did it feel for you to be there?'

'Um, weird, I guess. Heart-breaking. I don't know. It was all a bit of a blur. I suppose I felt I shouldn't have been there. Like I was intruding on something not meant for my eyes. But with hindsight, I'm glad I went. It helped.'

'Part of me wishes I wasn't here. I'm terrified of seeing your mum and sister; Ella too. How are they all holding up?'

His question sparked a surge of anger within me that took me by surprise. I almost snapped and started accusing him again of being a selfish coward. But I held still and let the feeling wash over me, waiting for the fury to pass before answering. 'As well as you'd expect. Mum's been really strong so far, but she was struggling when I saw her a few minutes ago. Lauren and Ella were doing better, but that probably won't last. Xander's trying to hold things together.'

Dad stared into the distance. Every pore of his spirit form oozed guilt and regret. My job now was to be his son, I told myself; not his tormentor.

'Do you think Ella will be able to see me?' he whispered.

I shrugged. 'She asked me the same thing, although she looked a lot keener on the idea than you do. I honestly don't know. Why don't we go and find out?'

'Yes, let's do that,' Hardy snapped, appearing next to us.

'Been eavesdropping again?' I said.

He glared at me before grabbing Dad's hand. The two of them disappeared, leaving me to walk back to the church alone.

It was a couple of minutes before 10 a.m. by the time I reached the front entrance. Fortunately it was still open as the last few arrivals made their way inside. One in particular caught my attention: Charles Devlin. As smart as ever, dressed in a black version of his usual business attire, he was standing alone a few paces from the door, taking long drags on the stub of a cigarette.

What are you doing here? I thought. I wasn't sure whether Mum had invited him in the end or not, but I hoped for everyone's sake that he was going to behave. He stubbed out his cigarette in the snow before flicking it into a bush and heading inside. He looked ill at ease; rattled. I followed him through the door into a sea of black jackets, ties, dresses, skirts, shoes and coats. Scanning the crowd, half of whom I didn't recognize, drew my attention away from Devlin for a moment. But when my eyes landed on Dad, standing at the back with Hardy, the look of shock on his face led me back to his lover. He took an order of service and hymn book and scuttled to an empty spot on a pew a couple of metres away from my father.

Ella beamed at me from the front row. 'Come on, face forward now,' Lauren whispered as I slid into place beside her.

'Is he here?' Ella asked in a tiny voice meant only for me.

A moment earlier she'd been looking directly at where Dad was standing.

'Yes. He's at the back.'

She whipped her head around again and then threw me a confused look.

'I don't think you're going to be able to see him, darling. But if there's anything you'd like to say, I can pass it on.'

Ella gave me a tiny nod and turned to face the coffin in front of us. It was strange to think of Dad's body being in there, especially when I knew his spirit was present too. At least it wasn't an open coffin.

Mum looked a mess. After holding it together for so long – being strong for everyone else – she'd finally crumbled. She was hunched up on the pew, her face ice white apart from the dark bags under her eyes, staring blankly ahead. Lauren and Xander were on either side of her, but she barely acknowledged them when they tried to speak to her.

Lauren had noticed Devlin and kept looking back at him, as if to check he wasn't causing a scene. I'd also spotted Kate Andrews, the *Evening Journal* reporter, who thankfully was several rows away from him. I wasn't surprised to see her, having been sent to plenty of funerals myself as a local reporter. As promised, her article about Dad's death hadn't been sensationalized, so I was fairly confident she would be discreet now and do nothing to intrude on my family's grief. I just hoped that Devlin wouldn't give her anything scandalous to report on. Little did she know the potential he had to upset the proceedings.

It wasn't long before the vicar appeared from the vestry and the service got underway. He'd known my father pretty well, as my parents had been members of the congregation for years, and he spoke fondly of Dad as a kind and popular man. He commented on how the tragedy of Dad's death was all the worse because of how soon it came after mine. And he called on everyone present to do their utmost to help Mum and the rest of the family to get through this difficult time.

It fell once again to Lauren to speak at the service. Mum had planned to say something too but wasn't in any state to do so.

'I never thought I'd be standing here again so soon,' Lauren said from the pulpit, her voice emotional but steady. 'Last time it was to talk about my brother, Will. Now it's Dad's turn. This family's been through the mill in the last couple of months. It's no secret how my father died. There's no way of sugar-coating it, so I'm not going to. But who are we to judge? Only he knows what was going through his mind on that night. I've tried being angry at him, but it won't stick. Instead I wish I'd been there for him when he needed me. And, more than anything, I miss my dad. We all go through dark times; some worse than others.'

Lauren paused to take a deep breath and to wipe away a tear. Then she continued, her voice increasingly fragile. 'I had my dark time several years ago. Some of you will remember. I hit rock bottom and it took a long time to get back on track. My dad was there for me without question or hesitation, despite everything I'd done to drive him away. All I had to do was turn to him and ask for his forgiveness, his help, and there it was. His love for me was unconditional, no matter what, and so is my love for him. That's what it means to be family. Dad, if you can hear me, know this: I love you; I miss you; I forgive you. I pray that you find peace.'

As Lauren climbed down from the pulpit, fighting back a flood of tears, I looked back to see how Dad had reacted. It was only then that I noticed he was standing next to me, eyes fixed on Mum's hunched figure. She looked frozen rigid with grief. I'd been so transfixed by Lauren's words that I'd not seen Dad's approach. His head was bowed. I reached my arm around the huge expanse of his back, but he jerked away.

'Dad, are you okay?' I asked. He shook his head, unable to meet my eye.

'Come on. Let's get you outside.'

I looked over at Ella, who'd heard my side of the conversation and nodded her understanding. As the congregation stood to sing a hymn, I led Dad back to where Hardy remained at the rear of the church.

'Can you zap us outside, please?' I asked, gesturing towards the closed front door. 'Dad needs some air.'

Hardy raised one eyebrow. 'Really? How so?'

Maybe it wasn't the best choice of words, seeing as air was pretty useless to me and Dad these days. We couldn't breathe it and we couldn't feel it. Nonetheless, Hardy knew what I meant; he was being obstructive.

'Look at him – he's breaking up. Please let me take him outside for a few minutes.'

'How do I know you're not up to something?'

'Like what? I don't know why you're so suspicious of me. It should be the other way round. All I want is to have a word with my father outside. I'm just trying to help him.'

'That's my job, not yours.'

Dad had slumped against the side of one of the pews. His chin was against his cavernous chest and he'd started sobbing. 'Come on,' I said to Hardy. 'We need to work together. You were human once, right? You've been through this. You know how hard it is. Can't you ease off on us for a minute and show a little compassion?'

324

He frowned at me before letting out a long, exaggerated sigh. 'Fine, but I've got my eye on you.'

Leaning over, he touched both of us on our shoulders and the scene around us changed.

CHAPTER 34

NINETY MINUTES LEFT

We found ourselves on the bench behind the church where I'd chatted with Arthur several times. I looked down at the ice-covered wooden slats beneath us and was glad to be immune to their frosty bite.

Dad was still in his slumped position. The combination of Lauren's words and Mum's silent devastation had broken him.

'Dad, look at me.'

His face was overrun with sorrow and shame.

'Come on, Dad. You need to talk to me. I know it must have been hard for you in there, but at least Lauren was able to forgive you. That's good, isn't it? It'll help you to move on.'

'I don't deserve it. She should hate me. You should too. And your mother. She ought to hate me most of all.'

'She doesn't. She loves you.'

'I couldn't bear to see her like that. She looked so helpless, so lost. And it's all my fault. I took the coward's

326

way out, instead of standing up and facing the music. I abandoned them all, even Ella. You must despise me for that. I'm not a real man. That's the problem. That's how all of this began. If I'd only fought the urges. Suppressed them.'

'Or you could have just told us. You can't bury your true nature, Dad. Lies breed more lies; especially the ones you tell yourself.'

'I couldn't. I was so ashamed and I feared it would rip our family apart. That was the last thing I wanted. I love you all so much.'

'Even Mum?'

'Yes, of course. She's my wife. You must find this hard to believe, but I love her dearly. I always have. It's an emotional love, though: a partnership, a friendship. Physically, well … you know the rest. Today obviously wasn't the first time you've seen Charlie.'

'Charlie?'

'Yes, I saw you follow him into the church. I hadn't expected him to be here. It was a shock.'

'Oh, right,' I said. 'He, um, came to see Mum and Lauren after you died. He told them about his relationship with you. He even suggested you were going to leave Mum to be with him.'

Dad put his head in his hands and groaned. 'Did they believe him – about the leaving bit, I mean?'

'I don't know. Maybe. Why? Was it true?'

'No. I'd never have left your mother. Not in a million years.'

'He seemed to believe you would.'

'That's what he wanted to believe and, well, I suppose I let him think that. It made it easier, although after you died I told him it was over. I wanted to put an end to all the lies, but it was too late. Did your mum know he was going to be at the funeral?'

'I think she may have invited him. She and Lauren certainly talked about it. They were keen to avoid him turning up aggrieved and making a scene.'

'Oh, he'd never do that,' Dad replied. 'It's not his style. Poor Ann, though, having to worry about that on top of everything else. The woman's a saint. I never deserved her. No wonder she's struggling so much now. What have I done?'

'Mum will be all right in the end; Ella and Lauren too. They'll stick together and get through it. Lauren and Xander are going to move here. I heard Xander tell Ella this morning.'

'Really? Wow. I never saw that coming.'

'What's done is done, Dad. It's almost your time to pass over.'

'What if I refuse to go? I could stay here, like you, and watch over them. It could be my penance. Why do I deserve to go to Heaven after everything I've done?'

'No, Dad. That's not an option.'

'Why not? It seems to be working for you. We could keep each other company. Or I could relieve you. You could pass over and I could stay. How about that?'

I shook my head. 'You staying here is more likely to cause harm than do good, trust me. You need to get your head together ready to pass over. It's the only way.'

'Are you sure?'

'I'm definite. It's your choice at the end of the day, but everything I've learned since my death tells me to advise you to go.'

'No doubts?'

'None whatsoever,' I lied.

'So why are you still here?'

'Like I told you: because of Ella. I'm a special case. Don't worry about me. That's under control.'

He shook his head as if trying to jolt his mind into focus. 'Right. I guess I need to stop feeling sorry for myself and get on with it.'

'Sounds like a plan.'

We sat together in silence for several minutes. I wasn't sure what else to say. And then, as the sound of the organ kicking in for another hymn leaked through the nearest stained-glass window, Hardy materialized.

'How are we doing?' he asked, although I had little doubt that he knew exactly what had been said.

Dad stood up. 'I'm fine. I'm ready. Will set me straight.'

Hardy eyed me quizzically before turning back to Dad. 'Good. Things are wrapping up in there. They'll be out in a minute. Shall we head over to the graveside?'

'Okay. Are you coming, Will?'

'No, I can't. Sorry. I have to take care of a couple of things.'

Dad's face fell. 'Oh. I guess this is goodbye, then. See you on the other side?'

He offered me his hand. I took it in a firm grip and then, wondering why we'd shied away from it when he was alive, pulled him into a hug. 'I love you, Dad.'

'I love you too, son,' he replied, his voice cracking with emotion. Gripping my shoulders tightly with both hands, he added: 'Tell Ella I love her too, will you?'

I nodded and he broke free. He walked a couple of strides, turned to hold up his right hand in a kind of farewell salute and then continued towards the grave, Hardy at his side.

It wasn't long before the funeral procession spilled out of the church. The vicar and an altar boy with a large cross led the way, followed by the coffin. It took eight pallbearers, including Xander and Larry, to manage the weight of Dad's body. Next came Mum, Lauren and Ella, who were supporting each other in a tight huddle.

Ella glanced up at me as I drew parallel and walked alongside them. 'Hello, darling,' I said. 'I know you can't answer me now, but blink once if you're okay.'

She blinked.

'Good girl. Sorry I had to pop out. Grandad was upset and I had to have a word with him. He's better now. He's waiting by the grave. If you want to say anything to him, just whisper it and he'll hear. He asked me to tell you how much he loves you.'

A tear raced down Ella's left cheek. I wished I could wipe it away for her. 'I have to do something now, sweetheart. I need you to be strong without me.'

Her face jerked towards me, eyes wide with panic and confusion. I feared for a moment that she was about to blurt something out in front of everyone.

'Don't worry. I won't be long,' I forced myself to say. I blew her a kiss and stopped walking, so the procession

– and my daughter – carried on without me. 'I'll see you later, yes?' I called after her.

Seeing the look of relief on her face as she nodded in agreement – believing my lie – was agony. I faked a smile, but inside I was going to pieces. It was horrendous. How could that be it? How could I slip off without a goodbye?

No, it's wrong, I told myself. I know it's what Lizzie and I agreed, but I can't do it. I have to tell her.

As I started back towards my daughter, I felt an arm grab me by the waist. 'Don't,' Lizzie said into my ear. 'You can't.'

The next thing I knew, the two of us were in the school cricket pavilion.

'No!' I shouted. 'You have to take me back. I can't leave Ella with a lie.'

'We talked about this before,' Lizzie said. 'I know it's hard, but it's the only way. The truth would be too much for her to comprehend. You'd never be able to go ahead with it. Trust me. You'll see her again. You'll get your goodbye.'

'But what will happen to her now? How exactly does this third option work? It's driving me crazy trying to understand.'

'Imagine how hard it would be for Ella to grasp. You have to trust me, William.'

'She'll definitely be all right?'

'Yes. She won't remember any of this.'

'Are you sure this reality won't continue after I've gone? I'm struggling with the notion of the whole of existence winding backwards because of me. I couldn't bear Ella thinking I abandoned her without saying goodbye.'

'There is only one reality. This is it. I'm going to open a window a little way back in your timeline and pop you through. It's exactly the same reality as the one we're in now, just earlier; before any of this took place. You're the only one making the jump. Once you get there, it's up to you.'

'What about the future you showed me before?'

'That was what would have happened if you'd carried on as you were doing. I simply took you further along the timeline as it was playing out at that moment. It's kind of the reverse of what I'm about to do now, although then we were only observers. Actually merging your current and past selves is considerably more complicated. There's only one window – the exact moment that you die – and I have to time it perfectly.'

'Nothing can go wrong?'

Her nose gave a telltale twitch.

'You have done this before, haven't you?'

'Listen, this isn't something that happens often, William. It's a lifeline very few spirits get offered. I had to argue a good case to get it approved. But don't worry, I can do it. It's under control.'

'Sorry, Lizzie. I know I've not been very appreciative of everything you've done for me. It's been ... so hard letting go. I realize you've gone the extra mile – far more than that – and, well, thank you. I mean it.'

'You're welcome.'

'You said I'm the only one going back, but you're coming too, right?'

She shook her head. 'It's not possible. It's your window; it will only work for you. I will be there, but not as I am now. I'll be as I was when we first met.'

'And Arthur? I haven't had a chance to say goodbye to him.'

'I'm right here, lad,' Arthur said, appearing next to me.

I embraced my friend. 'It's great to see you. I've missed you. I'm so sorry I got you into trouble.'

'Nonsense,' he replied. 'You've nothing to apologize for. It was my choice to help you and I'd do it again in a flash.'

'Are you going to be all right?'

'Don't you worry about me, lad. It'll be like none of this ever happened, remember.'

'But …' I thought back to what Lizzie had told me about him putting a brave face on his situation. How he was trapped here forever and she feared for his sanity in the long term. 'What will you do with yourself?'

'I'll get by. Keep busy. I'm sure Lizzie will find the odd thing for me to do. She knows where I am.'

'I certainly do,' she replied.

'But. It's not fair that—'

'What's not fair?' Arthur said. 'I made my choice. No regrets, remember. And don't fret about me going cuckoo anytime soon. I've lasted this long. Haunting the church-yard is not my style.'

Lizzie placed a hand on each of our shoulders. 'It's time.'

Arthur smiled. 'Goodbye, lad. Good luck.'

'Goodbye, Arthur. Thanks for everything.'

He winked and was gone.

'Ready?' Lizzie asked me.

'I guess so. When I get back, it'll be the same as last time, right? I just have to make different decisions.'

'Exactly. The key is not to hang around. The less you influence things, the better.'

'What about Dad? Is there anything I can do to stop what happened to him?'

She shrugged. 'I honestly don't know. The changes you make might be enough to alter your father's fate. But some things will happen however much you try to stop them – like they're written in stone.'

'And there's no way to send me back before my death, so I could stop it from happening?'

'I wish I could, but your death is the window. You can't beat that.'

What now? I asked myself, last-minute nerves kicking in. Perhaps I should stay after all. Was going back definitely the right move?

This was a conversation I'd had with myself countless times since Lizzie had first mentioned the third way. Its chief appeal was the idea of a return to the natural order of things. I'd come to accept that my being here as a spirit and Ella's ability to interact with me wasn't healthy. It was a situation I'd created with the best of intentions, but which ultimately wouldn't be good for either of us. I couldn't be a proper father to Ella as a spirit. All I'd achieve would be to hold her back in life, making myself bitter and twisted in the process.

On the other hand, if I passed over here, rather than going back, it would be impossible for Ella to understand.

She'd know I'd chosen to abandon her, just like her grandad had. What would that knowledge do to her?

No, going back was the only solution. I had to seize this opportunity to stop, rewind and let things happen as they should have done in the first place. It still felt terribly unjust for me to die in my mid-thirties; for my little girl to lose her only parent. But who was I to play God and interfere with that? I had to let go. I had to let Ella grieve properly, so she could move on and have a life without me.

'I'll definitely get to say goodbye to her this way?'

'Yes.'

'Okay. Let's do it.'

Without hesitation, Lizzie moved to stand directly in front of me. She placed her palms on my shoulders and fixed me with a hypnotic gaze. 'I know it's been tough, but you've made a good choice. All the very best, William.'

Before I could reply, I felt her hands tighten into a vice-like grip, exerting a sudden intense pressure that pinned me to the spot. She blinked and a blazing beam of white light burst from each of her eyes and into my own, searing through my very essence.

Then everything as I knew it was no more.

CHAPTER 35

I'm standing on the pavement watching two paramedics fight to revive my battered, bloody body. I desperately will them to succeed, even moving closer in the hope I can jump back into my skin at the right moment, but it's futile. I'm pronounced dead minutes later.

But I'm still here, I tell myself. What does that make me? And then my thoughts turn to Ella. What will happen to her if I'm dead? She'll be all alone, abandoned by both of her parents: the very thing I swore she'd never face.

'Wait! Don't give up,' I shout at the paramedics. 'Don't stop! I'm still here. You've got to keep trying. You don't know what you're doing. Don't fucking give up on me! I'm not dead.'

I scream my lungs out, begging and pleading with them to try to revive me again, but they can't hear me. I'm invisible to them and, ironically, to the onlookers gathered at the police cordon – several waving camera phones – keen to catch a glimpse of the dead guy.

In desperation, I almost try to grab one of the para-medics, but something holds me back. Some part of me knows that a spirit can't share space with a living person. But how am I so sure?

'Why am I still here?' I yell at the sky.

And someone answers me. A voice in my head. Like my own but different. 'Think. Dig deep. You know why.'

But I don't know why and the voice won't say any more.

I see the driver who killed me. She's chain-smoking menthol cigarettes under the watchful eye of a young bobby. She's telling him what happened. My immediate reaction is to shout at her; to vent my anger and frustration. But then I note the despair in her face. She's deathly pale and shaking. She knows what she's done. She has to live with it. That's punishment enough.

'Have you got the time?' one police officer asks another.

'Three o'clock.'

Shit. Home time. Ella. Instinct kicks in and I start to run towards her school.

The last few stragglers are leaving the school gates by the time I arrive. I rush to the back of the building, where Ella will be waiting, and see her standing there alone, a forlorn look on her face. I feel a strong sense of déjà vu but push it to the back of my mind as I run across the empty yard, waving. 'Over here, darling! It's okay. I'm here now.'

I don't know what I'm thinking. Why would she see me when no one else has? Watching my six-year-old daughter stare straight through me is quite the reality check.

337

'I'll tell you what's ridiculous,' the voice from earlier says. 'Ignoring your gut. That's denial. You need to think. Dig deep.'

'Ella, Daddy's here,' I say for the umpteenth time, kneeling in front of her so we are face to face. Her lips are chapped and her right hand, which is clenching her Hello Kitty lunchbox, is covered in red felt-tip ink. It reminds me of something, but I can't put my finger on what.

I gasp as I realize I won't be able to remind her to use her lip balm or to help her 'scrub those mucky paws'. Oblivious to my presence, she stares expectantly towards the far end of the playground.

I look at the open door behind Ella, knowing somehow that her teacher, Mrs Afzal, is about to emerge. She does. And she says what I know she's going to say. 'Is he still not here, love? You'd better get inside now.'

'He'll be here in a minute,' Ella insists.

'His watch might need a new battery again,' I say in sync with my daughter.

How did I know she was going to say that?

'Why do you think?' the voice asks me. 'Dig deep. She'll be here in a minute.'

Who'll be here?

Mrs Afzal mentions getting the school office to give me a call. I picture my mobile ringing in the back of the ambulance while they drive away my dead body. I imagine one of the paramedics, my blood still splattered across his green shirt, rooting through my pockets to find it. The panic I feel is strangely familiar. How long before Ella discovers what has happened?

338

I'm about to follow them inside when I feel a tap on my shoulder. It should surprise me, but it doesn't. I know that when I turn around, she'll be there.

'Who'll be there?' the voice asks me.

I don't know.

I turn, and then I do know.

Seeing her face is the key that opens up my mind, flooding it with memories of now and the future. Memories I shouldn't have. But I do, because I've been here before.

'Hello, William. Sorry to sneak up on you like that. I, um, I'm—'

'Lizzie.'

She looks puzzled. 'Yes … that's right. How did you know?'

'You already said.'

Her nose twitches. 'I did? Oh, right. Anyhow, you've probably got a few questions.'

Not as many as you might expect, I think.

I hang around for a short while, watching everyone. The clock's ticking but I still have a few hours to go. It's strange being back in my old house again, watching them all grieving for me afresh. It's my world – and yet it's not. This time I have to stay detached, an observer. I have no place here.

Everything happens pretty much the same as I remember it, although I'm able to observe more now that I'm not so confused and frustrated. Watching Mum break the news of my death to Ella is even more distressing than the first time I saw it. I was in a haze then, like everyone else is now, which must have cushioned the blow. There's

339

also the fact that I don't have long left with her. I'm harshly aware of that. She might not be able to see me now, but I savour every moment I spend with her. If only she didn't look so sad, so lost.

It breaks my heart all over again, even though I know it's coming, when she's sitting in her princess castle and says: 'I know you're not dead, Daddy. Please come home soon, so Nana can see that she's wrong. You promised you'd never leave me and I know you meant it. Please come home, Daddy. I miss you.'

Seeing my father alive again is hard as well. I wish I could talk to him and tell him what he needs to know. He's in shock, like Mum and Ella. Lauren and Xander too, I suppose, but they've not flown over yet. I wonder if they'll still end up moving here. I hope so. It'll be good for Ella to have the two of them around.

Everyone knows what's happened but can't fully comprehend it. That will last for a while, at least until the funeral. So too will that terrible feeling they'll have every morning when they slip free from the warm blanket of deep sleep and it dawns on them that the nightmare is real.

I wish I could spare them all of this, but I can't. It's part of a process they have to go through. At least they're not aware of having to go through it for a second time. That's my burden.

As this awful day draws to a close, I watch Ella go to bed and then I stay with Mum and Dad until they turn in too. I whisper my goodbyes at the foot of their bed before returning to Ella's room.

So, here we are, I think. This is it: my chance to say goodbye.

Once I'm satisfied that Ella's in a deep sleep, I kneel at the side of her bed and repeat the procedure as I carried it out before.

I place the open palm of one of my hands on top of the other. I hold them just above Ella's head, close my eyes and focus on my daughter. I try to blank my mind of everything apart from Ella. I picture her standing there in front of me, eyes twinkling above her gappy smile. I imagine myself ruffling her beautiful blond curls before picking her up for a hug. I think back to some of the best times we've spent together, some in a future that no longer exists.

It takes a couple of tries, but I'm not worried. I know it will work eventually. I continue to focus on my daughter, calmly battening down the hatches of my mind until there's no way anything else can get in there. Then comes that sudden lurching feeling of the world folding in and swallowing me whole. I'm falling.

Down.

Down.

Down.

When it ends and I breathe the cool, damp air into my lungs, I let out a scream of joy. I scrabble to my feet in the dark, breathing the same overpowering fishy smell as last time, and rush out through the tunnel.

I hoped this was where I'd find her again. Sure enough, as I spill out of the darkness on to the toasty, sun-drenched Cornish beach of Ella's imagination, I see the pink blur of her princess castle in the distance. Looking down at

341

my new outfit – the same chinos and checked shirt as on my last visit to this place – I ditch my trainers and socks and roll up my trouser legs. Then I race towards my destination as fast as my bare feet will carry me.

I'm the happiest I've felt in a long, long time. There's a tough conversation ahead. I know that. But it doesn't dent my elation, this incredible sense of liberation, because I'm finally sure that I'm doing the right thing. It won't be easy for Ella to come to terms with my death, but she'll get there eventually.

I can already picture us embracing outside the tent: me and my precious daughter. As I sprint towards her, I wonder what magic will unfold in this fertile playground of her sleeping mind. I know my stay here will be limited. Before long Ella's brain will recognize that I don't belong and I'll be ejected, like on my last visit. But I plan to make the most of my time here. I'll use it to prepare her as best as I can for life without me; to make sure she knows how much I love her. I also hope to plant a seed about Dad having a stroke, which might help to change his fate this time around. I don't know what Ella will remember when she wakes up, but I have to believe that my words will wedge themselves somewhere in her subconscious.

Not that I'll be staying to find out. My time as an observer is over. As soon as I leave this dreamland, I'll call Lizzie, take her hand and surrender myself to the pure white light that leads to the other side. I try to imagine what it will be like as I keep running and the pink tent draws closer. How can it be any more perfect than this place?

I hope Alice is waiting for me, like she said she would be; like she has been in my dreams. I hope we can get past what I did to her and love each other again as we did at the start. And I hope Ella will join us there one day – but not until she's old and grey with a happy life behind her. I hope …

I'm close enough. I can't hold out any longer. 'Ella,' I call. 'Ella? Are you there?'

Nothing happens for a second and my heart skips a beat. Then I see the door being slowly unzipped from the inside by a little hand. My incredible daughter's head pops out and she beams a huge grin at me. 'Daddy!' she yells, racing out on to the sand in her favourite red and white polka dot swimsuit; jumping into my arms. 'Oh, Daddy. I knew you'd come.'